J. K. MAYO ha...
new archetype of ...
seeming at one moment cynical, at the next
showing glimpses of integrity, but always
ambiguous, self-mocking, ironic and scornful
of the accepted hypocrisies of society. After
featuring in *The Hunting Season*, Harry Seddall
went on to take the leading role in *Wolf's Head*, a
thriller described by Martin Cruz Smith as
"an absolutely terrific book. The most fun I've
had since my first James Bond", and by the
Sunday Times as "an adventure thriller done with
intent savagery and brilliant, teasing verbal
sophistication".

J. K. Mayo's third Harry Seddall novel,
Cry Havoc, is just published by Collins Harvill.

J. K. MAYO

The Hunting Season

FONTANA/Collins Harvill

Lyrics from *I Get Along Without You Very Well* by Hoagy Carmichael
reproduced by permission of Chappell Music Ltd., London,
© Famous Music Corporation 1939.

First published by Collins Harvill, 1985
First issued in Fontana Paperbacks 1990
8 Grafton Street, London W1X 3LA

© J. K. Mayo 1985

Printed and bound in Great Britain by
William Collins Sons & Co. Ltd, Glasgow

Chapter 1

I opened my cabin door and saw a man kill a man.

The ships that carry you on the Le Havre-Southampton crossing from France to England take about seven hours. Though the English Channel can be rough, it is a short sea crossing and nothing ever happens; it is what they used to call a milk run.

This time for me, though, it was no milk run. The dead man in the cabin was only the start of it, and I was glad to get off that ship when she made port.

Now, thirty-six hours later and back in London, I was facing the certainty that my troubles had not ended. I was having a difficult lunch.

'What do you mean, *lost* it?' Joanna demanded. 'Nobody loses a play they've just written!'

Joanna Lee was young, stunningly pretty and confusingly wise. She was also my agent. She watched her long-nailed forefinger making an ever deeper groove in the checked tablecloth, tilted her tousled black curls on one side and glanced up from the busy fingernail and back again like a snooker player calculating the angle of a shot off the cushion.

But she was not calculating anything. She was losing her temper. Joanna had genuine violet eyes, and when she was in a good mood they shone far down in their beautiful depths like rare orchids waiting to be discovered. Now, when she looked up at me again from the tablecloth, they were bright with surface glitter.

'I wish you'd told me on the phone,' she said crossly. 'I'm not handling this well. I wasn't ready. You spend six months in France writing the bloody play and phone me from Montpellier – '

'Montelimar,' I said.

' – Montelimar to make a lunch date so that you can pass it over and we can celebrate and have a giggle, and I call Hector Clouston and he says send it over first thing, he has a theatre coming free in ten weeks . . . Oh, damn!' she said, and grabbed my hand and pressed it. Her eyes became orchidaceous again. They were sultry orchids, glowing in the deep dark rain forest, but at least they were orchids. 'Anthony,' she said. 'I am so *sorry*. It is rotten for you. How did you lose it?'

'I crossed on the car ferry from Le Havre to Southampton,' I said grimly. 'I was on deck. The play was in my father's old attaché case. A small man knocked me over and threw the case into the sea.'

Joanna stared at me and let go of my hand. 'That's not sensible, Anthony,' she said.

'It was more than sensible,' I said. 'It was exceedingly clever.'

Joanna gazed wildly about the room as if she were looking for a sane playwright lunching alone, who might want company.

The waiter came with veal and a green salad. Joanna was still refusing to meet my eye, and she focused her attention on the veal. She cut into it and laid down her knife and fork, and called back the waiter. 'Please take this away,' she said. 'I don't want it.'

'It is not what Madame ordered?' he asked politely, knowing quite well that it was.

The restaurateur drifted up, his professional radar homing in on atmospheric disturbance. 'Something is wrong, Miss Lee?'

'I asked for veal, Roberto,' Joanna said. 'Veal is milk-fed. This is not milk-fed; the meat is too pink.'

This was coming it strong. Milk-fed veal is as rare in London nowadays as a taxi in the rush-hour rain. Roberto gracefully avoided a debate on modern methods of rearing calves for the table by asking if Miss Lee would choose something else from the menu.

Joanna began to behave. 'I don't think I'm hungry,' she said, and patted his arm nicely. 'I had a late breakfast. I'll have coffee and some cognac, please.'

When we were alone again, Joanna said: 'Anthony, we're both a little edgy. I think it would help if you could make things more clear. Why was it *clever* of the man to throw your play overboard? I mean,' she asked carefully, 'did he tell you why he did that?'

'He couldn't,' I said. 'I was doing my best to throttle the little bastard.'

'God, you look angry,' she said.

'I am angry. I was angry then, I was more angry when I'd worked out why he did it, and I've been growing angrier ever since.'

Joanna swallowed some coffee and most of her cognac, and lit a cigarette with meticulously controlled movements. 'You're making this a little hard for me, Anthony, don't you think? A man throws away your play and you tell me it was a clever thing to do. I'm your agent, I would very much like to know *why* he threw it away.'

I gave up on the veal and decided it was coffee and brandy time for me as well. 'Joanna,' I said, 'you're going to find this hard to believe. There was a man in my cabin. I saw a man being – '

Roberto came up and asked if everything was satisfactory.

'What?' I said. 'Yes, yes. Everything's fine.'

Joanna stubbed out her cigarette. She went on killing it long after it was dead. 'I wish to goodness you'd had a copy made and mailed it to me.'

'So do I,' I said. 'It was a damned good play, but I really don't want to listen to you telling me what I might have done.'

'That's being edgy, all right,' she said, 'but I'll take it out of your hide some other time. Perhaps we shouldn't discuss this any more right now. Perhaps we should ask ourselves what you're going to do about it. How soon can you re-write the play?'

'I can't do it just now. I put too much into it from too far inside me; that energy's used up for now. If I tried it now it would be a pale copy of the real thing.'

'I know,' Joanna said. 'I expected you to say that. It's what makes your plays so good. But, damn!'

'Yes,' I said. 'Damn!'

We brooded. Joanna had been my agent for six years, since my first play was put on at a repertory theatre. My first West End success had been running for almost a year, and this would have been the perfect time to have another play ready. So, we brooded.

Joanna stopped brooding first. 'Look, come to dinner tomorrow night. You can tell me then about this bizarre event on the boat. Meanwhile,' she said briskly, 'when *do* you think you'll be ready to write the play again?'

'I think I could start on it again in about three weeks,' I said. 'Three or four, maybe. I don't know how long it will take. I've never had to do this before. Perhaps two weeks, perhaps two months.'

'Let's hope it takes two weeks. Say six weeks altogether, from now, I mean. That takes us up to Christmas, or early January. *Two for Joy* will be taken off before Christmas. You do realize that?'

'I knew that, yes.'

'I expect Hector will get the new one in by the spring, if he likes it. And I know he does want to like it. I'll try to speak to him today.'

Hector Clouston was the impresario who had backed *Two for Joy*, God bless him. I cheered up a bit. 'He does, does he? That's good.'

'Yes, of course he does. You're not a hot property yet, Anthony, but you're warm. Now then, since you're not going to start on it at once, what do you want to do in the meantime?'

'Work,' I said. 'Something different to get my head clear. Something not madly creative.'

'I've got two offers you might like,' Joanna said. 'One is to write a libretto for *Remembrance of Things Past*.'

'From Proust?' I exclaimed. 'They're crazy. Maybe they're not. It's seven books. Which book? I suppose it wouldn't have to be one particular book. Who is it? You know, visually and atmospherically it would be quite something. Then you have the hardness against the sweetness, and the style of mind, and that precise surgical violence of insight. And character, for God's sake, the characters. They *are* for the theatre, for opera. Who wants to do it?'

'It rather sounds as if you do, anyway,' Joanna said drily. 'That's a ·nice immediate response, Anthony. Glyndebourne want it and the composer is Marcus Nye. He's a very nice man. I think you should meet him anyway, but the thing is that it's much longer than your three or four weeks, it could take a year, don't you think?'

'Yes, it could. Still, I'd quite like to do it. I simply don't know if it's possible. I'd like to meet him and see how we get on. What's the other?'

'The other is rather more simple, except that it's in Canada. The theatre at Stratford, Ontario wants to do a big eight-hour adaptation like the National's *Nicholas Nickleby*, of another Dickens novel.'

I rolled my eyes. 'Lordy!' I said. 'Do they so? That's more than four weeks work.'

'Yes it is, but it's a thing you could start off on, and then leave while you wrote your own play, and then go back to. It's a straightforward adaptation. They're thinking of *Bleak House*; quite fun, I would think, and it won't take *that* long. It wouldn't stop you doing the opera afterwards.'

'That's true.' I thought about these things. 'I've never been to Canada. What do you know about Stratford? A show like that will cost a lot of money. How are they funded?'

The eyes were bright and businesslike now, if you can say that about orchids. 'It's one of *the* theatres in North America. Half their audience comes up from the States. They're funded part box office and part Canada Council, but they've got extra backing for *Bleak House*. They had a bad patch a few years ago but they're doing well now – a two-thousand seat theatre, Anthony, and if you do a good job between you they'll play to full houses. Stratford's a bit sleepy; rather like Stratford in England, swans and willow trees on the river. You might be best to get an apartment in Toronto and work from there, once you've made contact and sorted out how you're going to do it. You might like to be in a city after all this rusticating you've been doing in France. Toronto's quite a lot of fun, they tell me. They have intellectuals there too, Anthony. You'd like it.'

'I'm not an intellectual,' I said. 'Anyway, I don't know anyone in Toronto.'

'You'll soon pick someone up,' said Joanna prettily.

'What's that supposed to mean?'

'You want me to believe you didn't leave a broken-hearted girl behind you in France?'

'No, I did not. I was *working*, Joanna! None of your business, anyway.' I looked into those eyes. 'Who's the love of your life just now?'

'That's none of yours,' she retorted. 'I must run. Why don't you tell me what you think tomorrow?'

When I got upstairs into the flat the phone began to ring. I picked it up and said: 'Anthony Moore.'

'Mr Moore,' this voice said, 'my name is Kenna, Chief Inspector Kenna. I believe you crossed on the car ferry from Le Havre to Southampton two nights ago.'

'So I did,' I said. 'Yes.'

'I wonder if you might help us identify a body, Mr Moore. We hear from the purser, Mr Sutton, that you thought you saw a dead man on the ship. Do you confirm that, Mr Moore?'

'Yes, by God I do! I did see a dead man, in my cabin. I saw his murderer too. Nobody believed me.'

'Good,' Chief Inspector Kenna said. 'A body has come ashore on the Isle of Wight and it may be the man you saw. Do you

12

think you would recognize him again?'

'I'm sure of it, unless he's been nibbled by the fishes,' I said, with unseemly jocularity, doubtless attributable to mixing all that cognac with my new-found euphoria. 'But what makes you think it's the man I saw on the ship?'

The chief inspector allowed himself a little jocularity of his own. 'He didn't stay in the water long enough to make dinner for the fishes, Mr Moore, but when they opened his stomach they found his own dinner there, and it was all off the ship's menu. The same dinner you had yourself, Mr Moore.'

For a moment I thought I was going to be sick. It never pays to joke with the police.

Chapter 2

———◆———

I sat on the back seat of the three-and-a-half litre police Rover, scudding down the fast lane towards Southampton, in some confusion of mind. There was an atmosphere in the car you could have cut with a knife. It had something to do with the man beside me, whose presence was plainly a cause of great annoyance to Chief Inspector Kenna.

When the car arrived to collect me, Kenna had asked if he could come inside to use the phone, saying he had received a garbled message over the car radio he wanted to clear up. He came in and looked around the room, chewing his thumb and with a fearful frown on his face.

He made no move towards the phone but after a bit he looked at it and said, 'That was a neat idea of yours, to ring me back at the Yard.'

'I wanted to be sure you were the police,' I said. 'Once bitten twice shy. Do you have a warrant card – that's a plain car outside, no police markings?'

'Sure,' he said absent-mindedly, still thinking furiously. I had the impression he was playing for time while he made up his mind about whatever was exercising him.

He took the thumb out of his mouth and gave me a good look at the card, and then sat down on the couch, rubbed his face with both hands and glowered at the carpet. I found all this rather endearing, perhaps because with a name like Kenna he was obviously an Irishman like myself, and right now was behaving like one. He looked it too. He was a big man with black springy hair and one of those dark, high-blooded faces they breed in the

14

West. He had burly shoulders, full of energy, only partly disguised by the cut of his loose raglan overcoat.

'Donegal,' I remarked, for something to say.

He came up with a dour smile. 'Me or the coat?' he said.

'Both o' yezz,' I said.

'Aye.' He smiled, a shamefaced smile but done on purpose. 'Ah, to hell with it!' he said. 'Let's go.'

He stood up and wrapped the coat round him and we went down to the car. Once we were in he introduced me to the driver. 'Sergeant Gatenby, Mr Moore,' and the sergeant took the car up the end of the mews and whipped into the traffic with bewildering skill. There had been no space that I could have put a car into but none of the oncoming drivers had to give us an inch. To travel down to the coast we should have been heading west, but Gatenby turned the car back into London.

'Where's the body?' I asked.

'Isle of Wight,' Kenna said, and began chewing his thumb again. Then he stopped that, took a pipe out of his pocket and began filling it. 'We've a call to make at the Home Office,' he said, 'for our sins.'

Every light turned green for Sergeant Gatenby, and when we turned into the Parliament Street end of Whitehall I was almost certain his foot had not touched the brake all the way from Kensington.

'Back in a minute,' Kenna said, got out of the car, and disappeared through the gloomy portals of the Home Office.

I sat in the black Rover watching other black Rovers coming, going and waiting in Whitehall – the Government seem to use nothing else, just as the French use their black Citroens and the Germans their black Mercedes – and waited for the susurrations of power to whisper in my ear, quicken my pulse and lift the hair on the back of my neck. Nothing happened. Whitehall cannot do that any more. The over-scaled buildings have a fraudulent air now, like a row of ponderous faces pretending to wield the destinies of man when all they are able to do is handle the laundry once a week, and come up with odd socks like everybody else.

15

The chief inspector was taking more than a minute, in his particular launderette. A major- or minor-domo came out of the ministry and touched the passenger window with a knuckle. Gatenby moved a switch and the glass slid down.

'Shift her along a bit, son. The Permanent Secretary's sent for 'is car.'

Gatenby looked at him. His face was like the nine-tenths of the iceberg underneath the sea. 'That's all right,' he said.

The man thought about this and went away.

'What was that for?' I asked.

Gatenby put an arm along the back of the seat and turned, giving me the police look. It told him how many crimes I had committed, how tough I was or wasn't, my credit-rating, whether my position in life would allow for my being hassled without repercussions, and whether the Peugeot back in the garage was taxed, insured and in a safe condition to drive.

'He was just playing flunkeys,' he said. 'Traffic-wardens keep an eye on the parking, and the police run security.'

'But the Permanent Secretary runs the police,' I said.

Deep behind the pale blue eyes, a long way inside the iceberg, a glint glinted. He tipped his head a fraction to acknowledge that he had heard what I said, and the police look withdrew to the three-quarter line. He was a long, lanky man in his twenties, with pale brown hair cut very short and a milk and roses complexion laid close on the long bones of his face. There was a peculiar alertness about him, which if it had ever gone on holiday would have left him looking like God's gift to old ladies wanting to cross the street. I did not believe it ever left him. I had a thought about Sergeant Gatenby and Chief Inspector Kenna, but I kept it to myself for the time being.

'According to the purser's report,' he said, 'you may have seen this man murdered.'

'Yes, but the purser didn't believe me,' I said. 'So why did he make a report? Who did he report to?'

'He'd always make a report. You were an incident. He'd put it in the ship's log, and he reported to the police at Southampton.

You saw it happen?'

'If it's the same man, yes, I saw it happen.'

He gave that minimal nod again, made a casual survey of the scene outside the car, all round, just to make sure the IRA weren't trying to get away with anything while he wasn't looking, and turned the pale eyes back to me.

'You went straight up and told the purser?'

'Yes,' I said. 'What would you have done?'

He had answered enough questions. The police look came up to the half-way line. 'You did exactly what you should have done,' he said. 'We don't want citizens trying to perform the police function.'

I listened to this for a moment after he had said it. It sounded like a reassurance; it also sounded like a warning.

Gatenby leaned over to open the passenger door and Kenna got into the car. The back door opened too, and a man climbed in and sat beside me.

'Hallo,' he said.

If Kenna had been exercised before he went into the Home Office, he was in a rare taking now. He was red behind the ears and had his teeth clamped down far too hard on his nice Peterson pipe: he was nevertheless more punctilious than ever about introductions.

'Mr Harry Seddall,' he said, as if he were presenting us to his worst enemy. 'Mr Anthony Moore, Sergeant Patrick Gatenby. Go,' he said to the sergeant, 'and make noise if you have to.'

I saw a ripple of expression cross Gatenby's eyes in the mirror. He flicked the car round and ran through the traffic like wind in the grass.

'Mr Seddall,' Kenna said with the unnecessary vigour of a man trying hard against all the odds to think positively, 'is with the Home Office.'

'And you write plays, Mr Moore,' Seddall said.

'Yes,' I said.

That monosyllable of mine was involuntarily curt. Seddall's question had held that weight of courteous demand, confidently expecting to be fulfilled, that comes from the chairman of interview committees who knows that the subject of conversation is going to be *you*. But when I turned to take a good look at him I had the strange impression that it must have been someone else who had spoken. I had never seen a man who looked less likely to be the chairman of any committee – or less likely to work in the Home Office.

He was slouched in the corner of the car, a man in a crushed raincoat with brown unpolished shoes, a woollen shirt with half the collar on my side turned up, and an inappropriate peacock silk tie that had been tied too often, the knot of which was two inches below his neck. He had a loose-lipped, indulgent mouth with a cynical lift to it, which was well matched with the eyes, yellowish, hooded eyes that showed a blend of watchful candour and secretive, half-sleeping mockery. He had mousey, thinning hair on a round head, a stubborn jaw that had pulled a lot of lines to it in the flesh of his face, and faintly browned skin, as if once he lived in the sun but had thought better of it. He was a young-old man, either side of forty. He seemed slovenly, idle and disreputable; and he looked clever. The French word *louche* might have been coined for Harry Seddall.

To my surprise he did not follow up his first question; it was as if our severely limited exchange had told him all he wanted to know. Instead he fetched up, from that dilapidated human apparatus, a suprisingly pleasant smile, and then spoke to Kenna.

'I'm a bit short of sleep, Chief Inspector. Shall we tell Mr Moore the worst, and get it over with? Then he can digest it and you can catch up with your paper-work while I have a little kip.'

Kenna had, indeed, made quite a production of pulling a briefcase onto his lap and diving into the middle of a pile of papers, with every apparent intention of cutting himself off from the rest of us. Now, like an irritable father, he gave a sigh, took off his thick-framed glasses, and directed his speech straight ahead through the windscreen.

'Very well, Mr Seddall. Will you tell him or shall I?'

'You, I think, Chief Inspector. It may turn out not to be any of

18

my business, after all.'

Kenna eased round to look at me for a moment and then turned eyes-front again. 'Mr Moore, the man you thought had been committing murder in the cabin – can you give me a description of him?'

This was a startling question. 'Have you found him, then?'

'We don't know, Mr Moore. Can you describe him, please?'

'All right. Just under six foot, black hair, brushed flat and a bit shiny, as if there was oil on it, small head, neat-featured face – '

'Neat-featured, Mr Moore? What does that mean?'

'To me it means he had a small, sharp nose, chin coming to a point – it was a very triangular face. Also he had a thin moustache, you hardly ever see them now, just a line of hair it was.'

'Colour of eyes?'

'He had brown eyes. I remember them because they had rather a gentle expression, which was surprising in the circumstances.'

'And you told the purser you recognized his clothes?'

'Right – I'd seen him earlier when he drove onto the ship. Brown greatcoat, heavy grey knitted scarf, and a soft hat, brown with a slightly wider brim than usual.'

'Lastly, Mr Moore, the car. You said he drove on with a black Mercedes, bearing a Paris registration. What made it Paris?'

'The figure 75, but I'm sure you know that, Mr Kenna.'

'Now why should you think so?' he said. 'I'm a London copper.'

This seemed to me as good a time as any to test the thought that was in my mind about Kenna and Gatenby. 'But you're not ordinary policemen are you? You're Special Branch, yourself and Sergeant Gatenby?'

I was leaning into the corner of the car and saw reactions in both Seddall and Kenna. Seddall made no change of expression but gave a curious silent laugh – a jerk of the head accompanied by an outward sniff of air down his nose. Kenna, however, turned to me with a great arching of black eyebrows. 'Why do you say that?'

'Sergeant Gatenby, for a start. He looks like crack troops to me; what the SAS is to the army.'

'Explain that.' This was from Harry Seddall.

'Always alert, tuned in to his environment. Even in a parked car he watches the road all round him. But not looking for trouble; nothing shows up front.'

Kenna joined in again. 'That's not a compliment, bucko,' he said to Gatenby, and I saw the slightest pink blush come up the back of the sergeant's neck. 'We'll need to get you a disguise. What else?' he said to me.

'The Home Office,' I said, 'and you.' Gatenby's concentration must have slipped for an instant. We stopped at a red light.

'Well?' Kenna asked. 'What about me?'

'I'm not sure,' I said slowly, 'but it's there. The nature of the questions you deal with.'

'How can you tell what questions I deal with?'

'From the way you are,' I said simply.

Kenna gave me a wry look. 'And Mr Seddall,' he said, 'what kind of questions do you think he deals with?'

I looked across at Seddall and he looked blandly back at me; the yellow eyes seemed to veil not so much the man behind them, as the history inside him. 'I think I would be wiser not to find out,' I said.

Seddall moved his eyes off me, and smiled contemptuously at the factories of outer London. Kenna laughed. 'Now that,' he said, 'is what I call a canny insight.'

It was as if, though most of the questions had come from Kenna, it was Seddall who had been assessing the answers. I felt his eyes drift back to me, but I did not meet them. Instead I asked Kenna why he had wanted me to describe the murderer in the cabin.

'Yes,' he said, 'well, Mr Moore, this may come as a wee bit of a shock to you. We have two bodies to look at now, and he's the other one, by the sound of it.'

This took me by surprise, all right, but none of the larger implications came home to me until a good deal later. 'Why?'

was the first thing I said, and then, 'How did he die?'

'They tell me he was shot. We'll hear the story when we get there.'

With that he went back to the papers on his knees. Seddall had put the side of his head against the back of the seat ready to go to sleep. There was no expression on his face and while I watched him he closed his eyes. Gatenby was wiring even faster through the traffic now. I debated with myself whether I should go to Canada or stay in London and start reading Proust to see how his books might be made into an opera: perhaps a cycle of operas, I thought, idly, and fell into a doze.

When I woke it was to find myself asking the unpleasant question 'I wonder if they think I killed him?' – the man who had been found shot. They were not treating me like a suspect, so far as I could tell, but how did the police treat a suspect? How would I behave, if I had shot this man? Much as I was behaving now, if I had the nerve, though I did not see how a guilty man could fail to give himself away – especially one positioned as I was, who had not been accused of anything and therefore had no real excuse to show agitation. Doubtless an experienced criminal could put on an act, but they knew I was not an experienced criminal. I relaxed again.

Dusk was closing in and we were running on our headlights down the fast lane of the M3, into the red glow left by the setting sun. In a macabre and disturbing way I began to find the whole expedition stimulating. Events had moved fast since Joanna left me in the Italian restaurant, only three hours ago. I looked over Gatenby's shoulder at the speedometer. It was just over the 100 mark.

'You're awake then, Mr Moore.' This was from Chief Inspector Kenna, whose papers were back in his briefcase. 'We'll be there soon – our first stop, that is,' he added, and I realized I would soon be examining at close quarters a body that had been shot to death. My brief spurt of enthusiasm faded quickly away.

Our speed dropped and Gatenby took the car over to the inside lane. The motorway ended and we turned south towards

Winchester. 'We want one motorcycle patrol with his light flashing – there he is,' Kenna said, and Gatenby pulled the Rover onto the verge in front of the parked motorcycle.

The patrolman came to the chief inspector's window. 'It's six and a half miles, sir,' he said in a soothing Hampshire voice, 'and most of it's little winding roads. Shall I guide you?'

'Yes, please,' Kenna said. 'Little winding roads,' he said to himself.

We followed the flashing blue light up, down and around, but mostly up, until it turned off on a track down into a beechwood. The ground was hard from the November frost and we drove right in, about a quarter of a mile, until we came to a police car parked on the track – this one was painted white with the blue and red stripes round it. Beyond that was a Land Rover, and beyond that, turned off the track into the woods, was a black Mercedes – *the* black Mercedes. We got out of the car. Seddall, apparently only now waking up, trailed behind.

There was a group of uniformed and plain-clothes policemen. They had slung an inspection lamp over a low-hanging branch. There was a French 'F' sticker on the back of the Mercedes, and there were the numerals 75 on the number-plate. Kenna introduced himself briefly to the uniformed superintendent, and was introduced in turn to one of the plain-clothes men, but he was not making this a social occasion.

'Do your stuff, Mr Moore,' he said.

'Watch your footing, sir,' a uniformed sergeant said to me, and came with me to the driver's window of the Mercedes. Someone shone a very bright light onto the dead man's face.

'Jesus!' I said. 'What's happened to his eyes?'

'Rooks I'm afraid, sir,' the sergeant said. 'They do it to the living lambs in the spring, if they can get them away from their mothers. Nasty buggers. This was an out of season treat, you might say. At least he was dead first.'

His head was next to the window, leaning against the doorframe, and the small neat hole in the middle of the forehead seemed much less lethal than the bloody mess the birds had made

22

of his eye sockets. The window was half open. If it had been left like that, all the rooks had had to do for their breakfast was perch on the edge of the glass. Suddenly I remembered the joke I had made to Kenna about the fish nibbling at the corpse I had still to see, and nausea came up in my throat.

'Are you all right?' the sergeant asked me.

'Give me a moment,' I said, and looked into the dark shapes of the great beech trees. It was only then that I became conscious of the rooks cawing overhead, dozens of them, settling in for the night. I wanted to get away from there, and I turned back to the dead man in the car.

It was him all right, the man from the cabin, who had come at me with that hypodermic syringe in his hand and slammed the door in my face.

'Your name, sir?'

'My name?' I saw that the sergeant had a notebook in his hand. 'Oh. Anthony Moore,' I said, and gave my address.

'Do you recognize this man, sir?'

'Yes, I recognize him.'

So I told him where and how I had met in life the man who was now a corpse.

Chapter 3

---◆---

I had turned onto the dockside at Le Havre an hour before sailing and booked myself on the ferry with no trouble. It was the middle of November, outside the strike and holiday season, and the car-deck was only half full. As I switched off the engine the seaman who had guided me to my parking berth put his head to the window.

'Handbrake to the last notch, please, and make sure she's in low gear.'

'We in for a dirty crossing?' I asked.

'A bit choppy,' he said, and went off to bring up the next car.

At this time of year they were ferrying more heavy transport across the English Channel than private cars. The drivers of the extra long vehicles with the TIR plates were banging chocks under the wheels of their trucks and trailers, so I pulled the handbrake on hard and collected what I wanted for the crossing: a small attaché case, a thick fisherman's jersey and a rainproof jacket. I was ready to walk the decks during the night, wrapped up against the weather, for I was full of exhilaration to be going home to England after months of hard work in self-imposed exile.

The last car was a black Mercedes with a Paris registration. They berthed it against the port side and as I went over to the companionway that led to the upper decks I saw the driver, huddled inside the collar of his greatcoat, with his chin burrowed deep into a knitted scarf and a soft hat pulled low on his head. He looked every inch a victim of the virulent influenza that was sweeping France that autumn; the papers were full of it.

I made my way to the restaurant, which was almost empty. I reserved a table half an hour ahead, went to the bar for a quick swallow of Scotch, and then went out on deck to watch our passage through the harbour.

I dumped the attaché case on a seat while I pulled on the jersey and the stormproof jacket and went over to the rail. Even though I was on the lee side it was wet and cold enough. The rain eddied in the gusts of wind and blew into my face. I clutched the precious case to me as if it held a new-born babe that might be snatched away by the storm. Which it did, so far as I was concerned.

It held the fruits of my six months' isolation in south-eastern France, a two-act play that was a good deal better than my last one. For all that time I had worked in a mixed state of inspired concentration and exhaustion; I had kept the whole play alive to me, kept aware of all its essentials of movement, meaning and character and brought it up to its resolution with a completeness I had not achieved before. So I clutched that old case to me and took pleasure in watching other men at their work of getting the ship to sea.

As the car ferry left her berth stern first I looked down at the pilot boats and tugs lying in the inner harbour. Sheltered though they were, they were heaving up and down with a restlessness that presaged an awe-inspiring crossing. We passed an American container ship with *Galveston* painted across her stern and, still in reverse, turned into the outer harbour. The ship came to a stop, and as she began to move slowly ahead towards the harbour mouth the wind took her and leaned her gently over like a double-decker bus on a cambered road, and that's how she stayed for most of the crossing.

I was no longer on the lee side and the rain was pelting out of the storm with a vigour that only oilskins would have repelled. I had had my fun, anyway, and was feeling the cold, so I left the rail and went back into the warmth and light of A Deck.

The night before I had dined on partridge at a hotel in Gien, on the Loire, but tonight I played safe and went for steak and Stilton with a half-bottle of Burgundy. I had never been at sea in such weather. If I was ever going to be seasick this would be the night for it. An elderly man helped his wife, with the aid of a solicitous steward, out of the restaurant. She was as pale as parchment.

When the food came I ate heartily. I had eaten out only a few times while I was in France. And not at all in that last month of concentrated work. I was like a hermit let loose from his cell upon the fleshpots of the world, a little giddy with the first release from weeks of introspection and solitariness, and ,the sudden alteration to the flush of achievement that never came until I wrote the word 'Curtain' at the end of the play.

At last this elation got the better of me, and when the steward had cleared away the remains of dinner and brought my coffee, I put the attaché case on the table and took the typescript out to gloat over it.

'Are you Anthony Moore the playwright, sir?' The voice was American. Now, one West End success does not make you famous. It was true that the man had been helped to this recognition by the full name 'Anthony J. Moore' stamped on the case, which had been my father's, an Irish country lawyer too ebullient to content himself with mere initials, or to christen me with names different from those that had been good enough for him. But I was still agreeably surprised.

'Well, yes,' I said. 'But the name's not that well known.'

'My wife and I are on vacation, we saw your play in London before we went to Paris, Mr Moore. Congratulations, it's a good play.'

'Thank you,' I said. 'Thanks very much.'

'No, Mr Moore, I thank you. It was one of the most interesting evenings I've had in the theatre.' He looked down at the script on the table in front of me. 'Is that the new one?'

'Yes, it is. I've just finished it. Two days ago.'

'I wish you luck with it,' he said. 'It must be a great feeling.' He was a small dark man with a pleasant warmth in his voice. He went on his way and sat at a table with a group of other people. They had nice manners, and none of them turned to stare, but one way or another each of them contrived to glance at me.

If this was fame I liked it. It was altogether different from the sensations that are raised in one by reading favourable notices in the press. The humanity of this different style of approval warmed me.

At the same time, however, I felt suddenly exposed. Sitting there with the text of my own new play out in front of me on the table, I was now stuck with acting the part of a playwright in front of an audience. What I wanted now was a cabin to myself, where I could put my feet up, read the typescript in peace, and then let the rolling motion of the ship rock me to sleep.

The steward had left my check on the coffee tray, so I covered it generously with the last of my French francs, put the play back in its case, gathered up my coat and jersey and walked uphill to the door, where the ship reached the top of its roll, and down to the Purser's Office.

I reached the glassed-in office at something of a run, and the woman behind the glass looked up at me, frowned, and shook her head. She put her head down and went on with some paper-work. I supposed this meant the office was closed for the night, but I wanted a cabin, so I knocked on the glass and when she looked up again I smiled cheerfully at her. She slid back the glass panel and gave me that inquiring look that concedes nothing. She was a good-looking woman, French by her grooming, and tough with it.

'I should very much like a cabin,' I said.

'We closed the cabin list over half an hour ago,' she said, with only the faintest accent, and reached for the panel.

'I do realize that,' I said. 'But if there is a cabin unsold, I'd like to have one.'

'Did you not hear the call? It was broadcast all over the ship.'

'I was in the dining room.'

'It was broadcast in there too.'

'I was in the dining room to eat,' I said.

She lifted an eyebrow. 'C'est entendu,' she said.

'Look,' I said. 'I do need a cabin. What can we do about it?' I took out my cheque book and laid it on the shelf in front of me, as if it was about to be arranged.

Five minutes later I had bought my cabin and received the key, and was walking carefully down a narrow corridor, anxious not to let the movement of the ship throw me against some sleeping innocent's door. I came to the cabin that matched the number on the key-tag and quietly unlocked it. I was immensely pleased with myself, and I remember that I was smiling as I opened the door.

Chapter 4

———◆———

The dying man lay stark naked on a bunk. He had grey eyes and they were wide open, staring straight at me with absolute terror. Then the eyes went up in his head and his body tightened in a single spasmodic jerk and fell back, easing into death with a few last settling movements of the limbs. It seemed to grow smaller while I watched. His face turned slowly to the wall with a little blood leaking from the mouth.

The next moment a blanket was flung over the body, covering it to the neck, and as my wits began to function again I took in the other man in the cabin. I recognized first the brown greatcoat, the grey knitted scarf, and the soft hat with the rather wide brim that had been thrown onto the other bunk of the two-berth cabin: it was the man from the Mercedes, who had made the boat by the skin of his teeth. Beside his hat lay a black bag like an old-fashioned doctor's bag, and beside that a small case was open, elegantly lined with purple velvet and gleaming with the steel and glass of hypodermics.

He stood looking at me with no expression on his face, a man just under six feet tall with a small elegant black-haired head and precise, rather pointed features, and the ghost of a moustache drawn thinly over a thin mouth.

'Who are you?' he said.

'This is my cabin,' I said absurdly, and then: 'What have you done to him?'

'Nonsense, it is his cabin,' he said. His voice had the peculiarly perfect intonation which Austrians can bring to English, stroking the vowels with a caress that suggests a level of breeding

29

beyond the most aristocratic of Englishmen. 'He has been dreadfully seasick,' the beautiful voice went on. 'I have put him to sleep. He will be well again when he wakes.'

He held up his right hand and took a step towards me. The syringe in his hand showed two or three centimetres of a pale yellow solution, and the needle pointed at my eyes. I took a step back, hypnotized by the needle like a rabbit fascinated by a weasel. It was an extraordinary confrontation. The ship was not rolling so much now, and for the most part she lay tilted to port, leaning away from the wind, so that he stood a little above me. It had the effect of a surrealist shot in a film, but the effect was broken by the glittering realism of that hypodermic needle poised eighteen inches from my face. I forced my gaze away from the syringe and looked at him. He was smiling gently now, and his soft brown eyes were mild and tolerant. He spoke again.

'This is not your cabin. You have made a mistake. As for my patient, in some people seasickness can take a very dangerous form. He is one of them. Please go now and leave us alone.'

'I think he's dead,' I said. 'I think you killed him. In my cabin.'

He dropped his persuasive manner. 'You are being quite foolish,' he said. He sounded cross and impatient, no more, exactly like an irritated medical man being forced to deal with a deluded stranger. I would have welcomed loss of temper, some sign of the anxiety of a murderer caught in the act. I wondered if I was going to be convinced despite myself, and his next words almost completed the confusion in my mind.

'If you think this is your cabin,' he said curtly, 'go and take it up with the management, or whatever they are called aboard ship.'

'All right.' I said. 'I will. Just let me see him first.'

And suddenly those mild brown eyes were full of rage. 'Go to the devil!' he hissed at me, and shut the door in my face.

I was left staring at the numerals on the cabin door. Twenty-three, they said. I looked at the key-tag again and it answered, twenty-three. I found that I was shaking. I had not, after all, come near to being convinced by him. My body knew it, even if my mind had begun to doubt. I knew that behind that door there was one live man, and one dead.

I went as fast as I could along the canted passageway and up the stairs towards the Purser's Office. This part of the ship was deserted, occupied by sensible passengers sleeping the sleep of the just, or having a shower before turning in.

I was an unwelcome sight to the woman in the office. She shook her head at me, three pronounced, negative movements, and stayed incommunicado behind her glass wall.

I thumped the glass immediately in front of her, hard, with a clenched fist. Her mouth became a taut line across her face and she glared out at me, stood up, and vanished into the rear of the office. I thumped again.

'Please stop that, sir,' a man's voice said, and here she was, right out from behind the glass of her cubbyhole with a great deal of muscular ship's officer standing beside her – and beside me. 'What's this about?' he said. 'You're making a scene, you know.' He moved his chin the merest fraction, making me aware that there were still people around, coming out of the restaurant and saying their good nights to each other.

'Listen!' I said. 'First of all, there's someone in my cabin.' I held up the key, as if it were evidence, which it was in a way.

He took it from me. 'Right,' he said. 'That's first of all. What's second of all?'

I put down the attaché case and dropped the clothes I'd been carting around all night and managed to find my cigarettes. I was shaking again and had a difficult time lighting one. He waited with the patience and scepticism of a policeman. 'There's someone in your cabin,' he said, 'and you were going to tell me something else.'

I'd been trying not to smoke since I'd finished the play. I had gone without for two days, carrying a supply of cigarettes so that I would not get too nervous at being without them. I was suddenly furious at having started up again. I took a deep lungful of smoke into me. 'Yes,' I said angrily, 'there is something else. There's a dead man in my cabin. I saw him die. The murderer's in

31

there with him.'

I was round that corner and hidden away in the Purser's Office in three seconds flat. So far as I could tell, he had carried me there with one hand gripping my arm and my feet barely skimming the floor. Madame slipped in after us with my attaché case and the inevitable coat and fisherman's jersey.

'Let me see your passport,' he said, and sat me in a chair.

'Damn it – !' I began.

'Passport!' he said.

He looked at it closely, at the photograph and at me.

'I let him have the cabin after the list was closed,' Madame said.

He turned to me. 'This key opened the door?' I nodded. 'Tell it,' he said.

I was on my way to being institutionalized already, in the safe, efficient environment of the office with this man's competence taking command of the situation. I was calm and in control of myself again, and the shaking had stopped. I even stubbed out the cigarette. I told my dramatic story with speed and concision, and as little drama as possible. By the time I had finished Madame was looking at me speculatively, as if she was halfway to revising her first opinion of me as an idiot and a nuisance.

The purser spoke six words into a phone. 'Bos'n,' he said. 'Two men, my office, pronto.' He hung up.

'Stephanie,' he said. 'When the bos'n's heavies get here send them them to twenty-three. I want them there soonest, but they're to walk, not run. Now,' he said to me, 'we'll go and have a look.'

With his back to me he unlocked a drawer and transferred something from it to the pocket of his uniform jacket. Whatever it was, it was heavy.

'Is that a pistol?' I asked.

'Certainly not,' he said. 'Come on.'

Pistol or not, he was obviously confident of handling any assassin who might be lurking in one of his cabins. He had a massive head, completely bald, a calm face with a big rounded jaw and a pair of tough blue eyes. He was the right man in the right job, no doubt of that. He could have run a high-security jail or a five-star hotel with equal aplomb, and I was glad he had made his career at sea.

We went down the companionway and along the passage, he walking and not running, while I kept up as best I could with my landsmen's legs on the unsteady footing of the heaving ship. Either the wind or our course had changed, because the big ferry was pitching now more than rolling. Quite inconsequentially it came into my head to worry about my car, and whether with this new motion of the ship one of those long-distance trucks, homeward bound from Turkey or some equally outlandish place, would break loose and crush the Peugeot into scrap. I hoped it would crush the Mercedes instead.

The purser's iron grip on my arm brought me up short outside Cabin 23. He thrust the key into my hand and signalled me to stand to one side and unlock the door. He kept his right hand in that over-weighted pocket and put the flat of his toe to the door and nodded. I turned the key and the door flew open. The purser stood in the doorway a moment and then went into the cabin.

'Come in, Mr Moore,' he said. 'Come on in.'

The cabin was empty. The door of the shower stall was open, and that was empty too. Two large seamen turned up and peered in at us, a look of hopeful inquiry on each face.

'Sorry, boys,' the purser said. 'Problem's over. We had a riotous party complaint but they've settled down now.'

'No punch-up, then!' This came in a disappointed Glasgow voice from under a thatch of curly red hair.

'Nothing I can't handle, McElroy,' the purser said firmly. The two seamen looked at me and agreed with him, and went regretfully away.

The purser shut the door after them and sat on the dead man's bunk, and gestured to me to sit opposite him. He put his feet up and lay along the bunk with his hands behind his head, as comfortable as you please.

Something must have shown in my face, because he looked at

me intently, and there was something else beside doubt and scepticism in that look. Then an idea came to him.

'Mr Moore, were you an actor before you began to write for the stage?'

'No, I was not!' I said, and then, 'How did you know I was a writer?'

'It's on your passport: "Occupation, playwright".'

'Oh, of course. No, I've never been an actor, and I've not been acting tonight, if that's what's in your mind.'

'I don't think it is,' he said. 'Not seriously – more a passing thought.'

He looked at his feet and frowned at them for quite a while, saying nothing at all.

'Are you going to search the ship?' I said at last.

'No,' he said, 'I'm not. If there had been a murder in here, as you say there was, the body would be long gone. I could have a corpse off this bunk, down that alleyway and out over the rail in sixty seconds. I wouldn't look on the ship for a place to hide it.'

He looked at his feet placidly until I felt compelled to break the silence again. 'Do you think I made it all up?' I asked him.

'I tried that with myself,' he said, 'but it didn't work, not entirely. I thought of publicity for Mr Anthony Moore, playwright, but I didn't see anything in that. I thought maybe you're a bit wrong in the head. You get passengers like that, sometimes. They like to invent excitements for themselves. But you're not in that league either.'

More foot-watching; more silence.

'Then do you believe there was a body? Do you believe I saw a man killed on that bunk you're lying on?'

He turned his head to me with a glint of humour in his eyes. 'Putting on the pressure, Mr Moore?' He swung his feet off the bunk and sat up. 'Very well. Do I believe there was a body? Hardly at all. Do I believe you saw a man killed on this very bunk I'm sitting on? I think perhaps you did. I don't know that your eyes saw it, but I think maybe your imagination saw it for them.

'I'll tell you what I see,' he said. 'I see a man who's been

34

working as hard as he knows how for some months, perhaps living all by himself, using all of himself, giving it more than he's got in him to get the thing out of his inside onto paper.' He held up a hand this time, to stop the obvious questions. 'The steward who served you brings me my supper,' he said. 'He told me all about you. And I saw you having that drink at the bar before dinner. You were pale and exhausted. You were isolated and wrapped up in yourself, filled with some kind of personal triumph. But you were running on nerves. You were like one of these madmen that's just sailed the Atlantic single-handed in a 14-foot dinghy.'

He stopped speaking and looked into my eyes, nodding his head two or three times. 'You should see yourself,' he said. 'Go and look in the mirror.'

I stayed where I was. 'I spoke to that man,' I said. 'I booked this cabin after the allocation list was closed. He didn't know that would happen. He thought there was no risk, less risk than booking a cabin for himself, and leaving a trace, being remembered. He came on to this ship muffled up to the eyebrows. He wanted to keep out of sight, so he broke into an empty cabin, got that man in here somehow and killed him.'

When I'd said my piece I got up and went to look at myself in the mirror over the washbasin. I looked like the wrath of God. If I had sailed out of sight of land and back in again to a west coast port and said I'd just come over from Boston, there would have been plenty to believe it. My face was pale and thinned out as if I had been on a crash diet. My eyes were bleary, feverish and sunk deep in dark, dark sockets. Then there was my breathing, which was perhaps the worst of it. I was breathing through my mouth in short quick breaths. There was too much tension there altogether. I didn't like that face very much, and I turned away from it.

'Damn it, Mr – ?'

'Sutton,' he said. 'John Sutton.'

'Mr Sutton,' I said, 'I hear what you're saying but it's not true. If I was going to imagine something – well, I don't write that kind of play. I don't write plays with bodies that vanish and mysterious Austrians disguised as doctors.'

'What's that got to do with it?' he asked. 'You writing people can take too much out of yourselves. Look at Virginia Woolf, Steinbeck, Hemingway, Scott Fitzgerald. Woolf reached the point where she said writing each word was like pushing a heavy stone up a hill. You people go into yourselves too much. Nietzsche said something about that, he said you should remember that when you look into the abyss, the abyss looks right back at you.'

I stared at him for a long moment and laughed. I couldn't help it, there was no offence in it and he took none. 'If I'd been a musician, would you have a list of composers who pushed themselves too far?'

He smiled. 'No,' he said. 'I read a lot on this trip, that's all. I should leave it where it is, if I were you. The police couldn't do anything with what you've brought to me, and I certainly can't.' He stood up. 'I have a feeling you won't want this cabin now. Do you want another one?'

I shook my head slowly, accepting reluctantly that there was nothing more I could do to persuade him. If 'my' murderer wanted to hide, he would stay hid. I could watch for the Mercedes to drive off the boat in the morning and say 'That's him?' But what would that prove? 'All right,' I said. 'Okay. And no, I don't think I want a cabin.'

'Your ticket entitles you to a reclining seat in the sleeping saloon,' he said 'You'd be better off in company. A little comfortable snoring round about might help you to relax. Come up to the office and get your things. How did you pay for the cabin?'

'By cheque.'

'We'll tear it up and cancel the booking. Right, let's go.'

I remembered the smear of blood on the dead man's mouth and leaned over to where he had turned his face to the wall, but there was nothing to see. I followed John Sutton, purser extraordinary, back to his office – and to Madame Stephanie. She gave

36

me the scornful look that Frenchwomen do better than anyone else, handed over the attaché case, the jersey and the rainproof jacket, and on Sutton's instructions led me through the ship to the sleeping saloon where she showed me to a seat. She left without saying good night.

I sat, or rather reclined, and listened to the sounds of other people sleeping. It was half dark and soothing, in its way, that long hallway populated by sane, sleeping or almost sleeping human beings. Even the up and down, up and down, and half-roll of the ship provided a lulling motion.

Inside my head, however, wild pictures and thoughts of what I had seen in Cabin 23 kept me wide awake. My brain was racing to nowhere in particular. Suddenly, and belatedly, it occurred to me that the murderer might want to get rid of *me*, the eye-witness, but then I saw that as far as he knew my visit to what he had called the management had come to nothing. There had been no rousting of passengers out of their sleep. He had left no trace behind him, and the next thing he had to worry about was what he would find at Southampton when we disembarked. If there was a flock of policemen on the pier then he would be in trouble, but in the meantime his best bet was to lie low and leave me strictly alone.

If I turned up dead, or disappeared, it would be the one thing needed to validate my story to the 'management', and from the inaction that had followed my visit to the Purser's Office the killer must feel fairly confident that my credibility in that quarter was low. He might want to be sure my credibility was absolutely zero, but there was nothing he could do about it. All he could do was wait it out. That was my last conscious thought of the night.

I woke to bright sunshine and people moving all round me, stretching their stiff limbs and setting off for the washrooms with towels and toothbrushes. The ship was still heaving up and down, and out of the window beside me the sea was as stormy as ever, great waves frothing and breaking at their crests into foam. Across a blue sky tattered white clouds flew before the wind.

My sleep had been full of bad dreams, and I was alive as soon as

I woke to the fact that one of those bad dreams had been real, but the cheerful weather, and the anticipation of getting off the ship and driving up to London, carrying that new play to my agent, gave me the feeling that I was starting off the day on the right foot. The night before I had been caught wrong-footed, out of my ground: but with agents and directors and impresarios I knew what I was about. My own toothbrush, towel and battery shaver were in that invaluable attaché case held firmly between my ankles. My face in the washroom mirror was more like the self I liked to see, and I set off to find breakfast in a more reasonable frame of mind than I had hoped for.

I was enjoying the company of all these strangers, too, whose happy end-of-holiday chatter kept even the real nightmare of that scene in the cabin at a distance. The noise and bustle could not keep it out of my memory, but they helped my own determined effort to avoid bringing it into close focus.

The group I had adopted went on deck on their way to the cafeteria, exclaiming at the fine weather, the waves, and the appproaching coastline of the Isle of Wight, and I went along like a sheep in its own flock. When we came to the huddle that formed round the magic entrance to breakfast and coffee, I waited passively for the rest of my group to go ahead.

Then the unbelievable thing happened.

A man came from nowhere and stumbled against me. It was not a violent collision of bodies, and I said automatically, 'So sorry!'

'My fault,' he said, and then somehow one of his feet got mixed up with mine and we ended up sprawling on the deck at the side of the ship, a tangle of arms and legs – and he with my precious attaché case in his hand.

The hand moved towards the rail, and I knew at once what he was going to do.

'Don't!' I said, and hardly heard my voice, it made such a small sound. 'You mustn't! That's very valuable. It's my new play.'

'Yes,' he said, and smiled into my eyes. 'I know.' And still smiling, he slipped the case through the rail and let it go. I watched it fall down the steep side of the ship, a long way, until it splashed into the water and was swept astern, thrown about by the turmoil of the ship's passage. I watched it until it vanished forever into that wild sea.

He had reached his knees when I turned back to him. He had an odd expectant look on his face and the smile was still there, taunting me with what he had done. A yell of hopeless rage burst out of me and I threw myself at him. I grabbed him by the throat and he went over backwards, his head hitting the deck with a good resounding thump. I banged it on the deck for him again and shook him like a terrier shaking a rat. He did not fight back, except to save himself as far as he could from the damage I was trying to do to him.

In any case, it did not last long. I was dragged off him and lifted to my feet by half a dozen shocked, and very Britishly shocked, bystanders.

'Poor little devil!' I heard one of them say, as my opponent was helped up, and sure enough, he was a foot shorter than I was.

'Quite unprovoked, too.'

The small, unprovoking man disclaimed the need for further attention from his well-wishers, dusted himself down, said he was going to his cabin to clean himself up, and wandered nimbly off the scene.

'Ye'll hae tae come wi' us, mister,' a familiar voice said, and here were the bos'n's heavies of the night before, McElroy and friend, holding me fast between them.

I ended up in a small room with a desk and a couple of chairs, more like an interview room than an office in regular use. The desk was bare except for an ashtray, and there was no filing cabinet, no sign of occupancy. A place to hide the bad boys. It did not look like a cell, but it would have done.

The purser came in, and this morning he was not using his technique of long silence.

'If the man you attacked wants to prefer charges, we'll hand you over to the police at Southampton,' he said flatly. 'In any event, you'll stay here with McElroy until we've docked and cleared the ship. Give me your car keys and we'll drive your car off.'

That seemed to be it. 'Mr Sutton,' I said, 'that little bastard threw my play into the sea. That play was going to be worth £50,000 to me, and maybe a lot more.'

'It's a great loss then,' he said, 'but I'm quite sure he did nothing of the sort. The two of you fell and the case fell too. Everyone who saw it agrees that your attack was quite unprovoked.' He paused. 'I think you're in a bad way, Mr Moore. I think you should take yourself to a doctor and get advice. But that's nothing to do with me; I don't care either way. You've been a nuisance aboard this ship and now you've committed a criminal assault, and good day to *you*!' He turned to McElroy. 'Don't let him out of here until Mr Webster comes for him. I'll send in coffee and something to eat.'

With that he departed, and I felt the enormity of what had happened grow in me by the moment. The worst thing was that I had lost my play, the inspired child of my imagination: but funnily enough, in the forefront of my mind was the fact that my credibility with the purser, low though it had been, had indeed now sunk to absolute zero. That incident out on the deck had been arranged. The little man had not stumbled into me by accident, and simply thrown my case overboard out of malice. He had done it on purpose, and waited for me to jump on him.

Along with my dejection about the loss of the play, and my fury and frustration at being manipulated so successfully by these people, whoever they were, both last night and this morning, a nasty feeling of apprehension began to come over me. They were too clever for my good. If they had not finished with me, my future did not look at all bright. In fact it looked dim, very dim indeed.

The man did not prefer charges. An hour later, I was driving the Peugeot up the road to London, scanning every lay-by I passed for a black Mercedes and watching my driving mirror like a sparrow searching the blind spots for a predatory hawk.

Chapter 5

————◆————

When I had told my tale, the sergeant and I looked at each other in the torchlight and the dark, and then, by some mutual consent, at the dead face in the car with its bloody eye-sockets: and away from it again.

The sergeant said: 'This man you fought with on the deck, can you describe him?'

'Lord!' I said. 'Can we finish this somewhere else?'

'We can,' he said. 'Come back to the car, and we'll do it there.'

We started back. Kenna and Gatenby, who had stood close by to hear my statement to the sergeant, moved in to look at the body for themselves. Seddall was standing behind the Mercedes looking at the trees climbing into the dark, as if there was inspiration up there. Perhaps there was, for him. For me there were only rooks.

'We used to shoot them off, when I was a kid,' he said as I passed.

'Because of the lambs?' I asked him.

'Yes,' he said, in his drawling, accentless voice. 'And the fat ones made rook pie. Ever had it?'

'No,' I said, 'and never will.'

'My turn,' he said as Kenna and Gatenby came up, and he went down to the front of the car on his own.

The rest of us went back to the track. Policemen piled into the white car and we settled into the black one, where the uniformed sergeant wrote down what I could remember of the man who had thrown my play into the sea: small, pale, balding, dark eyes — it was curiously little. The sergeant thanked me and shifted himself into the car in front. We waited for Seddall.

The patrolman who had guided us to the wood spoke to Gatenby. 'Want a pilot?' he asked.

'To Gosport Harbour?' Gatenby said. 'Police berth? No problem, but thanks.'

'One of these days,' Kenna said, 'you'll be at a bloody loss, and that will bloody teach you.'

We went on waiting for Seddall, with the engine running to keep us warm. No one spoke. The patrolman stood by his bike smacking his gauntletted hands together. At last Seddall appeared, stopped to chat to the two men who were waiting with their Land Rover for the ambulance to turn up, made an oddly elegant ducking motion to greet, or seem to greet, the occupants of the white car, and climbed in beside me.

Gatenby reversed down the track at speed and we set off for the coast.

Kenna did not wait long. 'You know him, don't you, Harry?'

Seddall's mouth made a drooping, sarcastic smile. 'What does his passport tell us, Gerald?'

They were on Christian name terms all of a sudden, but the relationship between them seemed more distant than ever.

'Hugo Winkler,' Kenna said. 'Austrian passport, age forty-seven, doctor of medicine.'

'Hugo Winkler.' Seddall repeated. 'Well, well.'

That was all he said.

Kenna bent forward as if he had just left the funeral of someone dear and departed, and the emotion had gripped him. Seddall slouched back in his corner and produced a packet of Gauloises. He lit one with, surprisingly, a rolled gold Dunhill lighter, and a cloud of smoke drifted over Kenna's bowed head.

Gatenby reached the main road, and pounced.

Viewing a body in the mortuary at Newport on the Isle of Wight was a more clinical business than it had been in the beechwood with the rooks cawing overhead. I looked at the waxy face of the

42

man I had seen dying in the bunk on the car ferry. It was more like a deathmask now than his own face, the relic of a man long dead. I wondered who he had been, living.

I made the identification, the formalities took place again, and after that everyone seemed as keen as I was to be done with it and get back to the mainland.

On the police launch I went into the control cabin for the warmth, where Gatenby set about getting a Berlitz course from the man at the wheel on navigating at night across the Solent, so that next time he could do it himself. I went out into the cold.

In the stern of the launch Kenna was standing looking out to starboard, and Seddall was looking down into the water on the port side. I sat on the life raft. Kenna moved across and stood close behind Seddall as if he were going to make an arrest.

'Harry,' he said, 'who was the man in the car?'

'Hugo Winkler,' Seddall said to the black cold sea below him. 'Alias Otto Ullman, real name Klaus Bermendt, born in Graz, Austria, nearly fifty years ago. Medical student at Heidelberg, never qualified. Ran heroin from Marseilles to Vienna and got five years for it. Got three years for manslaughter in Potsdam, but came out after two –'

'Potsdam's in East Germany,' Kenna interrupted.

'It is,' Seddall agreed. 'We don't know what kind of manslaughter. He went on selling heroin inside West Germany after he stopped running it across the frontiers. He likes playing with truth drugs; it's his hobby. He hires out. Top man. Makes a nice little living, one way or another.'

Kenna went round to Seddall and put a hand on his arm to make him turn and look him in the eye. Seddall leaned his head over to look at the hand on his arm, but allowed it to move him; the whole movement was a shrug. The big Irish face above him was almost forlorn.

'That means you're in, doesn't it, Harry?' Kenna said.

'I'm afraid we are, Gerald. Very definitely.'

Seddall lifted Kenna's hand gently off his arm.

'Do your know something, Harry?' Kenna said. 'When you

were telling me about Winkler-alias-Ullman just now, you talked as if he were still alive. "Hires out," you said. "Makes a nice little living." Do you know what I think, Harry? I think you're sorry his nice little living is over. It's a bit of your world gone. You like the creatures who live there; they're company for you. That's why you like them, Harry, because that's where you live. But it's not life, Harry, it's death.'

Seddall spoke softly out to sea. 'You should have gone back to Ireland, Gerald Kenna, and joined the Garda. You should be riding your bicycle over the green fields after poachers, letting them go with the kind word.' He had spoken with such a pure lilt that I wondered whether he was an Irishman himself, but then the voice returned to that lazy, accentless English of his. 'We have the same enemies, Kenna,' he said. 'It's just that you feel the need of a bath if they touch you, I don't.'

'I feel the need of a bath right now,' Kenna said.

'Sure you do,' Seddall said casually, leaving us all a little up in the air.

The Harbour Police gave us corned beef sandwiches and cocoa, just as if we were on the Murmansk run during the war, and Gatenby whisked us back to London driving on the compass.

Chapter 6

When I woke the next day it was just before noon. I felt peaceful, rested, and ready to do nothing at all. Outside the window, snow was falling: it was too early for snow, I thought.

I turned the heating up, put some good strong coffee to drip while I got some clothes on. I smoked three cigarettes with my coffee, and that made it time for brunch.

I was having a wonderful day in cloud-cuckoo-land, hoping that the world had gone away for good, or at least for twenty-four hours. The phone rang. I had had an hour.

It was Joanna Lee, agent. 'What have you decided?'

'Decided?'

'About Canada, Anthony. About Canada, about adapting Dickens, about writing an opera libretto.'

'Oh, yes.'

'What do you mean, "Oh yes?" Don't hang about, Anthony. Make up your mind and call me back. Bye.'

I poured another cup of coffee and lit another cigarette, drawing on it slowly and pretending to taste the tobacco. I had made it, back to cloud-cuckoo-land. I decided that if I was going to go on smoking, I would give myself a gold lighter like Harry Seddall's. I found myself shaking my head: there was a strange man, if ever there was one. The phone rang again.

'Hullo,' it said. 'Harry Seddall.'

'Hullo,' I said, warily.

'What about dinner?'

'Tonight?'

'Tonight. It's, ah, an invitation from my boss. The three of us, just. At his club, you know the sort of thing.'

It sounded as if he had said, 'You know the sort of man.' With reluctant effort, I thought about this for a moment. If I declined, they would ask me to the Home Office, or invite themselves round to the flat.

'All right,' I said. 'Thanks.'

'Good man,' he said. 'It's for eight o'clock. If I pick you up about quarter to – how does that sound?'

'Fine,' I said.

'Then I'll see you,' he said. 'So long.'

Curious old-fashioned slang he used, like a child at prep school. The phone was by the window, and as I put down the receiver I saw a van park outside. I recognized the man who emerged from it as the messenger from Joanna's office, so I went to the front door and he gave me a parcel.

I was half unwrapping it and half shutting the door when a familiar voice said: 'Do you know what's in that?'

It was Chief Inspector Kenna, complete with galoshes and umbrella. I looked round for Gatenby and the black Rover. 'I've escaped,' he said naughtily. 'Lunch break.'

'Chief Inspector,' I said, 'are you cadging?'

'Didn't plan to,' he answered. 'But if you're offering, yes. Do you know who the parcel's from?'

'From my agent,' I said. 'Carry on up. You know the way.' He shook the snow off his umbrella and went in. I closed the door against the weather and followed him. Umbrella and galoshes were parked neatly at the top of the stairs.

I gave him some whisky to warm him up. He swallowed half of it and then stood in the middle of the room, rubbing his hands. 'Nice little place,' he said. 'Nice, uncomplicated little place.'

I finished unwrapping the parcel: a boxed set of Proust, Kilmartin's new version of the Scott Moncrieff translation. Good old Joanna. There was also a note which gave me the phone number of Marcus Nye, the composer, and to which she had added: 'Man of the moment is a stockbroker, but he's into the futures market. You may get to buy me dinner yet.'

46

This was all very pleasant and like what I was used to in my life. But here was Kenna standing on my carpet, and ahead of me tonight were Seddall and his boss. Very well, first things first.

'We'll have lunch,' I said, and I produced for us avocados, omelettes and salad, and some of the cheese I had brought home from France.

'Right,' I said to him as we sat down. 'What's up?'

'Oh, nothing,' he said. 'Nasty kind of day yesterday. Came to see if you were all right.'

I did not believe that for a moment, but if he had something to tell me he would come out with it in his own good time.

'That parcel,' I said, 'did you think I was going to be bombed?'

'Not really, not really at all. Simply that it was delivered by messenger, and I happened to be there. I'd have looked foolish if you'd been blown up before my eyes.'

'Thanks,' I said drily. Then I added suddenly, 'Who does Harry Seddall work for?'

'Oho!' he said, delving into his avocado. 'Technique will out.'

'Technique?' I said. 'What does that mean?'

'Once an interrogator, always an interrogator.'

'I was only in the Army three years, short-service, and that was over ten years ago.'

'I know that,' he said. 'My goodness, Mr Moore, you can make an omelette. But two years of that you were in Military Intelligence, BAOR. Aptitude exceptional: make every effort to retain.'

'Cut the cackle, Mr Kenna. Where did you find that?'

'Ministry of Defence; it's noted on your file.'

'That doesn't mean much. I was young, bright, fresh from the university and had an unmilitary mind. They needed a variety of types. I was just one of the varieties they needed. And they spent money and time training me; of course they wanted to keep me.'

'They made you a captain,' he said.

'And I'd be a captain yet,' I said. 'Where is this leading?'

'You know where it's leading, and you're right to be on the defensive, Mr Moore. But I'm no threat to you, not really. I'm

47

just playing at being the school bully. The real big boys are waiting for you outside the playground. I got your file this morning. They saw it yesterday.'

'Who are the big boys?'

'I can't tell you that. You'll have to guess.'

Which meant that I could guess, easily enough. He meant Harry Seddall and, by extension, Seddall's boss, who was to give me dinner that night. Why had Kenna come to give me what amounted to a warning? Irish fellow feeling could account for some of it, but if it was an emotional response of that kind, the tirade he had let loose against Seddall on the police launch the previous evening might account for a great deal more.

'You're telling me to watch out for Harry Seddall,' I said.

'He uses anyone who'll serve his purpose,' Kenna said heavily.

'I'm not likely to serve anyone's purpose except my own. But you're both working on these killings – so why should you get in his way like this, coming to warn me off?'

He did some of that face rubbing he had gone in for yesterday when I first met him. 'Policemen – whether they're called policemen or not – should do their own work. Don't let him rope you in – it's dangerous for you and no help to us.'

'Gatenby gave me a hint to that effect,' I said. 'It's not the whole story. What is up with you and Seddall?'

He stood up. 'This was a mistake,' he said. 'I've put myself out of court. People don't usually get the chance to speak like that to senior Special Branch men.' He laughed, shamefaced, and sat down again. 'Och, Mr Moore, I half like Harry Seddall and I half don't. He's a misfit, a loner, hellish to work with. He's a rude, sarcastic – well, whatever. He's no respecter of persons, either. If he doesn't like orders, he doesn't take them.'

'He must get results, then, if he's still in the civil service.'

'Civil service? Aye, well. He gets results, but he doesn't stay long under the one roof. They shunt him from office to office like a hot potato. He started in the Ministry of Defence – he was Army, he may still be for all I know. He was there about six years and at the end of it he was put on to some caper that threw up more than they wanted to know – a general got retired. I think Seddall enjoyed it too much. His father was a general; he doesn't like them. So Harry got shifted too. He's been around. Now he's at the Home Office and God knows where he'll end up. In a gutter with a knife in his back, I wouldn't wonder. He's too thick with the riff-raff. The small men, that's his hunting ground, that's where he finds the scent. He likes to start with the dregs and work his way up to the scum, you might say.'

He stopped there and looked at a loss for a moment, listening to what he had just said. 'I'm laying it on too thick,' he said. 'I'm spoiling my own case. You won't believe me, but some of this –' he waved a hand expressively in the air ' – is because I'm concerned for Harry.'

I looked at him for a long time. He sat watching the spoon stir sugar into his coffee, and his eyes did not come up to meet me till I spoke. 'Mr Kenna,' I said, 'what am I to make of this? You come here to put me on my guard against Harry Seddall, you're full of solicitude for me and then for him. You warn me that Seddall will try to use me, and you warn me not to let him. That suits me just fine – yesterday was enough for me, looking at those bodies. But I've done that now and the rest of it is nothing to do with me. So that's that.'

We faced each other over the remains of our lunch. I saw the tough Special Branch man with the hard line of his mouth and the hard eyes, and inside that the clever complicated Celt. I asked myself how far the two halves of him were at war, or how far they served each other.

'What's the rest of it, though?' Kenna asked me. 'You didn't finish, did you?'

I laughed, and heard the exasperation in it. 'You're who you are,' I said. 'I have to think there's a purpose in you I don't know about. You suggest that Seddall – or Seddall and his boss – will try to rope me in somehow. But you know I'm not likely to go for that anyway, you know what my reaction would be. So how's this, Mr Kenna? You come to see me with this supposed warning of yours, and get the reaction over with. Then in a back-handed kind of way you get me interested in Seddall so that I'll have a second reaction, working against the first one. By the time I sit down to dinner with them tonight, I'll be ripe.' I shook my head at myself. 'It makes no sense though. I've no time to play your games, and no wish to, and no talent for them. You both know that.'

His face became vastly ironic and pitying. 'They might not need much of your time, or any talent at all.' He stood up to go and looked for his coat. 'You've a terrible imagination, Mr Moore. You can't tell a staged scene from a real one. No doubt it's a hazard of your profession. Thank you for your help. I must get back, or Gatenby will think I've defected and start watching all the ports single-handed.'

Down at the front door, he said: 'It was a rare lunch, and thank you. I'd like to think we might meet again when the dust has settled on this one.'

'Mr Kenna,' I said, 'I'd like that very much indeed.'

He walked off into the falling snow. Whatever his motive in coming to see me, I thought to myself, he was a considerable man.

Chapter 7

John Heneage had all those attributes of the undesirable host that descend from snobbery. His speech and manners so assiduously flew signals of good breeding and flashed messages of gentility that if he had been a signal frigate in time of war, you would have suspected he was an enemy imposter who had stolen your own code book. I had met the curiously obsolete snobbery of the civil servant before, but I had never – to continue the Hornblower metaphor – sailed so close under the fire of its guns.

He had a meaningless face. It had the marks laid there by life which you expect on a man of fifty or so, but no marks of character emerging from within. The only interest to his appearance came from that pure whiteness of hair which you find in very old men, and more rarely in those whose hair has whitened in their youth. He wore faultless clothes and a scentless aftershave whose astringency wafted clinically under my nose as if I were meeting a surgeon fresh from the operating table.

He said he had Taken the Liberty of asking them to Open some Rather Good claret for us, to give it Time to Breathe, and Hoped I had no Objection to claret. I had spent three months in France drinking the wine from the local co-operative, and though I like good wine the stylized commercial jarred on me. When the claret turned out to be none of the classified growths but something very adequate and ordinary, I decided that his pretentious way of doing things was going to irritate me all evening. So we were off to a bad start. I hoped like hell he was not going to be so refined that we could not get down to cases till the coffee.

So I began with the soup.

'Why am I here?' I asked him.

Heneage looked startled. Seddall put down his spoon and gazed round the dining room like a man who has heard a rare bird call and is unable to locate the tree it comes from. Harry Seddall had done us proud. He was wearing a single-breasted suit of such dateless and imperceptible merit that you suspected he had stopped buying clothes from Savile Row when the foreigners moved in, having acquired everything he needed already.

Heneage touched the linen napkin to his lips punctiliously, and took some of his precious wine. 'I should very much value your judgment of this claret,' he said.

I saw that he still hoped we would stick to the rules he had set for his little dinner party, and began to feel quite sprightly at the idea of disabusing him. 'Bourgeois claret is excellent for lunch-time or business talk,' I said briskly. 'A good choice.' I drank half a glass at a gulp. 'Jolly good,' I said, and beamed at them both.

Seddall contrived, from a perfectly inscrutable countenance, to let me know that he understood I was having a little joke. Heneage, however, pressed on regardless.

'I do so agree with you, that bourgeois claret is a perfect luncheon wine. Yet I find that the wine from Moulis, if one chooses the right year, can stand comparison with classified growths of the third rank.' He thought about this. 'Not to say, the second.'

'Wine is not my bag,' I said brutally. 'I've heard Mr Seddall's news about the body in the car. What about the man who was killed in my cabin?' I had begun to wonder how these two managed to work together.

'Must we be sticklers for social formality?' Heneage said easily. You would have thought his hidebound behaviour had been imposed on him by the rest of us. 'My name is John – Harry you know well enough by now, surely: do we call you Tony?'

'We call me Anthony,' I said.

'Very well,' he said. 'Harry, tell Anthony about poor Marco.'

He gulped down the rest of the wine in his glass with a lack of connoisseurship that surprised me for a moment, and then withdrew from us to finish his soup, regarding an empty space in front of him with a fixed expression as if an invisible copy of *The Times* was propped up against the pepper mill.

'The man in the cabin,' said Harry Seddall, 'was an Italian freelance who worked for me sometimes.'

'Freelance what?' I asked him.

'An informer,' Seddall said. 'A kind of scout.'

'For Christ's sake, Harry!' Heneage said, emerging suddenly from his trance and plunging incongruously into Americanese. 'Stop pussy-footing around. Shoot the works!'

I stared at him, but he looked exactly the same Heneage as before. He went on eating soup and staring fixedly in front of him. I was no longer sure he was reading *The Times*. Perhaps he was watching one of those old 'B' movies, where the blonde doll says, 'It's been a long time, Johnnie,' and Johnnie says, 'Too long, kid,' just before he passes out on the couch with blood on his vest.

The lamb cutlets arrived. 'Have you ever noticed,' Heneage said, 'that when Perry Mason takes Della to the classiest French restaurant in town, they always order steak, baked potato and a green salad? It seems such an insufficient use of a chef.' He splashed the wine into our glasses, and gave me the dregs, just to teach me to be a good loser.

'Shall I go on?' Seddall asked peacefully, sitting well back in his chair as if he knew the answer.

'No, I'll take it, Harry,' Heneage said. 'This Marco – why should we bother you with his surname? – was an Italian who made a shady living on the edges of Italy's crooked financial world. Not that I mean to say the Italian banking world is all crooked, I refer to the shady part of it, which as it happens is rather a *large* part of it, but it is careless to generalize even from evidence that may seem at first sight to enjoy the status of universal reference.'

He stopped for a moment. 'I get carried away,' he said. 'I like to talk like Lord Curzon, the last of the great Foreign Secretaries, don't you think? Ah, well! This Marco had got hold of something hot, so hot that he was trying to bring it to Harry in person, to make himself a deal. He had a retainer from us and for special information Harry would pay extra money into a bank account, but this time Marco thought he had hit something big, and he wasn't going to show before he'd persuaded Harry to put a very big ante on the table indeed.' He paused. 'And then some,' he added smoothly.

'Just what is it you people do?' I found myself asking.

Heneage began casting about for the attention of the dining room steward. 'You tell him, Harry,' he said.

'Large movements of sterling affect the value of the pound,' Seddall said. 'They alter the balance of the economy. They exacerbate already negative situations. We –'

'We seek foresight of such movements,' Heneage said crisply, as the steward appeared at his shoulder. 'Arthur, how *good*! You never let a man go thirsty.' Arthur put on the table another bottle of wine, lying in a Burgundy basket. Heneage detached the bottle from the basket and gave the latter to Arthur, who wandered off. Heneage poured. 'I do dislike a basket in a club, don't you? If the wine has thrown enough detritus to warrant the basket, then it ought to be decanted, surely!'

Seddall smiled at him with an open sarcasm that confirmed the idea I had begun to form of an obscure and rather devious rapport between the two of them. 'It's not your best club, is it, John?'

'It's the club I like best,' Heneage answered, 'because the dining room is always half empty.' So it was. 'All the same, if you'd put me up for you-know-where, you over-connected little weasel, I could accustom myself to be less solitary in more splendour.'

'When you sack me, John, I'll propose you.'

'Don't think I don't understand you,' Heneage said, 'Il existe des services si grands qu'ils ne peuvent se payer que par l'ingratitude.'

'Who said that?' I asked.

'Dumas,' Heneage replied.

We fell into a silence, and ate. It was a good dinner, plain and successfully cooked, and I was comfortable in that large, sleepy dining room with no one else sitting near us, and quiet voices from other tables hardly reaching my ears. I was comfortable, too, with my companions. I enjoyed their double act, or rather Heneage's act, to which Seddall was merely playing the feed. I had put aside – which they doubtless intended – some of the reserve with which I came to this meeting. They would come to the point sooner or later, and I would be ready. Meanwhile I was enjoying John Heneage, and being intrigued by Harry Seddall. There was a chameleon quality to both of them which I began to suppose must be a mark of their still, to me, ambiguous and ill-defined profession.

The steward came to remove our plates. 'Shall we have,' Heneage asked us, 'the apple dumpling? What do *you* think, Arthur?'

'The name is Archibald, Mr Heneage,' the man said. He had a large fleshy face with a big nose that drooped over his upper lip and gave him the air of a French comedian.

'I can hardly believe it,' Heneage said. 'I've been calling you Arthur for years, have I not?'

'No, Mr Heneage,' Archibald said. 'Tonight is the first time. I'm not the man to advise you on the dumpling, I never eat them, they would sit like lead in my stomach.'

'Cheese, then,' Heneage said arbitrarily. 'Archibald, how can I have been so forgetful? I pride myself on my memory for faces.'

'This is a question of names, not faces,' Archibald said, 'and more of habit than of memory, Mr Hendrix, considering how often you sit at my table.' With this rebuke he departed.

Heneage said: 'Archibald and I have a lot of childish fun.'

It seemed to me that Heneage had a lot of childish fun, all on his own, and before this exchange with the steward I had begun to doubt how important his position could be in the department he served. Now I was offered a different view of his facetiousness. As his face altered from the artificial liveliness of his encounter with the steward to the state of neutrality behind which he could retire, apparently, at will, he looked at me for a few moments with an expression of deep seriousness and some show of fatigue. This was deliberate, for, before he resumed his contemplation of the imaginary *Times* or whatever movie he chose to run for his private self, a confiding and rueful smile flickered across his mouth. He used his rather hectic little games (I was to gather) simply to let off steam.

This second withdrawal of his left me to Harry Seddall, and he promptly took up the running. 'They could have been truth-drugging Marco for one of two reasons,' he said. 'Either they wanted him to share his secret with them, or it was their secret he had found out and they wanted to learn how much he knew, and if he'd told anyone else. I like the second view, because it explains why they shot Bermendt in the car: it means they have a project in view and your seeing Bermendt had jeopardized the project.'

'Remotely,' I said. 'Surely, the chance of my seeing him again was slim.'

'Not so remote,' Seddall said. 'Bermendt is photo-filed with Interpol. You'd seen him playing doctors. We might have shown you pictures of men who play doctors.'

Heneage rejoined us. 'Harry is so laconic,' he said. 'It is not a style to which we bureaucrats are accustomed. I also incline to the second view, though I retain the first in my drawerful of options. So what do we know, assuming the second of Harry's possible interpretations? We know that Marco had knowledge that suggested to him a large, a very large, movement of sterling. How large would it have to be, Harry, for Marco to be so sure this knowledge he had was worth a special price to you?'

'Upwards of two hundred million pounds.'

'We know,' Heneage resumed, 'that criminal men have an interest in this movement of sterling. Criminal men,' he repeated, 'whose interest must arise either because this money is their own, and they will derive some untold advantage from moving it; or because it belongs to someone else, and they expect to win, or steal, an advantage from their knowledge of its being

56

moved. What kind of criminal men do we contemplate?' He stopped as if to allow answers from the floor, but it was so obviously a rhetorical question that neither Seddall nor I spoke. It was simply that Heneage marshalled his thoughts in paragraphs. 'If we assume the possibility that this imminently mobile sum of sterling may not be merely two hundred million, but a massive amount, then our review of the possible class to which these criminal men belong widens to a positive panorama. A massive movement of money becomes in the vernacular of multi-national corporations and governments, an instrument of policy, which is to say, a vehicle for the general good so vital that the destruction of anyone seeking to interrupt its progress may be seen as virtuous.'

Harry Seddall completed a quite unconcealed yawn at the same moment that Heneage reached a five bar rest, and took the opportunity to translate. 'John means that we may not be up against professional criminals but any big international company, or any government.'

I found Heneage's orotund style perfectly acceptable; it offered his thought at a pace easy to digest. But the way Seddall put it compelled a question. 'You say any government,' I said to Seddall. '*Any* government?'

He gave me his singular, cheerfully sardonic smile. 'Sure,' he said.

'*Any* government,' Heneage said emphatically. 'I have known – I do know – men who would strangle their own grandmother with her own tea-towel in the name of policy. Policy is a powerful god. To some men it is a faith or at least a perfectly acceptable gloss on the Thirty-Nine Articles. I mean,' he added swiftly, seeing no doubt a querulous expression on my face, 'that they have no trouble reconciling any act, so long as it is in the name of policy, with the established religion of this country.'

'That *must* be rubbish,' I said.

'When I depart from my brief I go too far, sometimes,' Heneage said agreeably. 'Perhaps I have done so this time.' Which was as good a way as any of saying that he had no

57

objection to being contradicted, but it did not change his view.

'You don't love policy,' I said.

'But I do. Policy is precious, and must be husbanded. Of course I love it, it is a constant challenge, like an inexhaustible supply of ready-made frozen pastry of which one has to make delicious pies.'

'The other kinds of criminal men – ' he went on without a break ' – whom we must contemplate in connection with this supposed massive movement of sterling, are terrorist movements or co-operatives, a large and long-established criminal band such as the Mafia, or the half-forgotten Camorra – the unspeakable Turks have their own mafia – whichever is top gang in Marseille this year, the skilful and intelligent bank thieves of France and West Germany and, last but not least, the one man band with two or three employees.' He thought, briefly, and added, 'Or an ad hoc consortium of any of them, bound by a common interest.'

The cheese had come and gone and dinner was over. It was time for coffee. We wended our way through the long dining room, over the shabby carpet and among empty tables, until at a table near the door where three men were drinking port one of them looked up and said, 'John,' to Heneage, nodded slightly to Seddall, and moved his eyes from me back to Heneage with a perfectly polite look of inquiry.

Heneage hardly paused. '*Sir* Edward!' he said, with an emphasis and a diction that might have implied the distance owed to respect but had a palpable note of sarcasm. Sir Edward closed his eyes at the gratuitous offence and turned back to his companions.

In the smoking room Heneage moved towards the table where coffee and cups were laid out for members to help themselves, but Harry Seddall made a sign to me with a movement of his head and we left the smoking room, walked a long corridor, turned off it and climbed three steps to a door with a sign hanging from the handle saying 'Private Meeting in Progress'. Seddall opened the door and we went into a small empty library, with one window at the far end and a long mahogany table running down the middle.

Seddall took out his Gauloises and I accepted one. The pungent farmyard smell of it helped to dispel the sense of unreality that had gathered round me from dining in this dilapidated club to the accompaniment of Heneage's rarefied lunacies, and the visions he had presented of international criminals with impeccable credentials on either side of the law, conspiring to steal inconceivable quantities of money.

I peered at some of the titles on the bookshelves, protected by dust, glass and wire gratings. They were a weird mixture. There was what might well have been a first edition of the Waverley Novels under Scott's own name, 1830 was it? Next to Scott were old law books, beside them a group of novels by Charles Morgan and all around, quite covering the walls, it seemed to me, memoirs and biographies of some very old-stagers indeed of the type *With Rod and Gun to Omdurman*. The best titles, though, surpassed invention, as *Woody Taxonomy of the Federated Malay States*. I could easily imagine Heneage, when he retired, setting himself up in this unwanted library and immersing himself in the more outlandish reaches of the past.

I sat myself close to an ancient cast iron radiator, which exerted a modicum of heat on the chilliness of the room. 'Heneage is an odd bird,' I said. 'So are you if it comes to that.' I had decided to make another bid to break out of the atmosphere the pair of them created.

Seddall knew it, too. He leaned against the dusty bookcase and grinned lazily.

'Thanks,' he said.

'You make an incongruous team,' I persisted.

'Team? Not so much,' he said vaguely, so that I could not tell whether he meant they were not incongruous, or not a team. 'Heneage is a shit,' he said unexpectedly. He let the blue cigarette smoke drift out of his mouth. 'We get on all right.'

A foot kicked the door. Seddall went to open it and then sauntered back again, leaving Heneage to bring the large silver tray he was carrying down to our end of the room. He laid it on the table with a satisfied sigh.

On the crowded tray were a Queen Anne coffee-pot, cups of much finer porcelain than had been visible in the smoking room, a box of dates in an old-fashioned silver basket, a bowl of hand-made chocolates and half a dozen cigars. From the fingers of Heneage's right hand were suspended by their stems three glasses, and gripped precariously between his left arm and his ribs was a bottle of cognac.

'Do something, Harry, for God's sake!' he said.

Seddall slipped the bottle from under his arm which allowed Heneage to set down the glasses. The cognac was *Fine Champagne*, the cigars *Romeo y Julieta*, and the chocolates had ginger inside. I thought it surprising that he should be able to extort old and exquisite Sèvres porcelain from the club. He was wearing a different air now, too, not only that of the pleasant, but also the pleased and proprietorial, host.

'John,' I said, using the familiarity as part of my attempt for the initiative, 'do you live here?'

'As a matter of fact I do, some of the time,' he said, gabbling now like a university don, or a duke landed with entertaining someone from a different set. 'They do a good breakfast and it's frightfully handy for the Office.'

Seddall grinned at me, like a dog, challenging me to cut through this cloud of irrelevant witness.

'Who is Sir Edward?' I said.

Heneage chose me a cigar, gave me a cigar-cutter, and put a box of matches beside my coffee. 'There,' he said.

'Sir Edward,' I repeated.

'Sir Edward is terribly high-up,' he answered, and abandoned his act. 'Do sit down, Harry,' he said, 'I can't see what faces you're making.'

'High-up in the Home Office? Is he your senior, your boss?'

'Yes to the first; as to the second, I shall put it this way. We have a fief, Harry and I and a few others, but exactly to whom we owe allegiance is a cause of quarrel among the baronage. The

60

Treasury value our service, but find us uncouth. We are *in* the Home Office, but our work is mostly outside their interest, and indeed a great deal of it is abroad, which intrigues the Foreign Office. When there is any doubt it is always possible to raise a committee and re-distribute the doubt to the general advantage.'

'I hardly expected you to tell me all that,' I said.

'Why not?'

'Perhaps I'm wrong. I had the idea the work you do is secret.'

He said nothing, but let his face become interrogative.

He sat tilted over the table like a chess player who has seen seven moves ahead and knows his opponent can anticipate only five. I began to worry, despite myself.

'Would you tell just anybody what you have just told me?' I asked him.

'No,' he said, 'but we are all friends here.'

I thought it was not going to take seven moves. He was about to put me in check. 'Uhuh,' I said. 'What does that mean, "We are all friends here"? What does it mean, imply, remotely suggest and exactly signify?'

We drew on our cigars as if studying the board to assure ourselves of the disposition of the pieces, and of every strategic and tactical combination of possibilities contained in it. Seddall blew a long cornet of vulgar French cigarette smoke between us, and threw some brandy down his throat as if it were absinthe. So did I, down mine. I had an instinct that I was going very much to dislike what Heneage said next.

'When you were with the BAOR you signed the Official Secrets Act,' was what he said.

'So what?' I said.

'So nothing very much,' he answered, 'except that we can trust you not to repeat anything we say.'

'Yes,' I said slowly, 'you can.' It seemed to me there must be more to it than this. My earlier meeting with Chief Inspector Kenna came to my mind. This confused me, for I realized I had Kenna to thank for the idea that Heneage and Seddall wanted to use me in some way. Up to now, I had spent my whole evening with them waiting to know what they wanted of me. Yet perhaps they wanted nothing. In that case, why had we met?

I made a reconnoitring move with a knight, to see what Heneage would do about it.

'My Intelligence work with the Army of the Rhine,' I said, 'was –'

'Was elementary,' Heneage put in smoothly. 'You might as well have been in the Boy Scouts, as far as I'm concerned.'

'Still, you looked at my file in the Ministry of Defence.'

'Did I? Kenna, I suppose. Certainly I did. I should have been negligent else. There might have been a pattern in it which foreshadowed your career as a master criminal.' He relished some of his cigar and gave me a quick, rather nice smile. 'No, Anthony, all I wanted to do was know as much about you as possible, so I found out what I could at second-hand, and now we have dined together. You made a surprise appearance in what is shaping to be a very murky drama indeed, and though you did appear to be an innocent little red herring, what if you had turned out to be a big, bad predatory fish?' He set the Havana carefully on an ashtray and took up his glass of cognac, rolling it gently between his long white hands. They looked incapable of transmuting warmth to the brandy, office hands, for turning papers primly on a desk and making notes in margins; hands for forming gentle elegant gestures palely at the ends of dark sleeves.

'Yes,' he said, 'a big fish you might have been, Anthony, a respectable playwright – if that is not, forgive me, a contradiction in terms – by day, and a foul fiend by night.'

I believed him now. All he said made sense to me, except the last. I laughed a little. 'Playwrights don't make master criminals,' I said, 'or sinister agents for Foreign Powers.'

'Oh,' Harry Seddall drawled, 'I dunno. Kit Marlowe spied for Walsingham.' He had gradually made himself comfortable during this dialogue, and was lying back in his chair with its front legs off the floor and the heels of his socks, since he had removed his shoes, resting on the shelf that divided the two levels of the bookcase. His tie was loose and his jacket hung open. He had cornered the dates.

'I don't know,' Heneage said, 'that you have sufficient warrant to say that. Can you footnote it?'

Seddall smiled sarcastically, and spat a date stone into his cupped hands.

There was an assumption in the way these two behaved with me, in their free play of personal idiosyncracies and the open exchange that passed between them, that I sensed as a compliment deliberately made. They were an eccentric coterie of two, and let me feel myself accepted. It worked on my vanity, it made them likeable, and noticing it made me wary again.

'You were talking about red herrings and predatory fish,' I said to Heneage. 'What kind of fish am I?'

Heneage jettisoned a long length of ash from his cigar and blew softly on its glowing tip. 'Piscatorially,' he said, 'I perceive you as a capable trout, swimming confidently in the familiar waters of your land-locked lake, loch, or lough. Out in the great salt sea, Anthony, there are monsters beyond your fishy understanding, not so much ruthless as indifferent. To them you would be merely plankton, whom they would digest without knowing they had swallowed you at all.' He said this with no colour in his voice. He said it without looking at me, with his eyes on his cigar. Seddall was watching me, though, his yellowish eyes half-asleep, half-scornful – either of Heneage for being so heavily impressive, or of me for being visibly impressed. It made no difference to me – John Heneage had made the very opposite of a recruiting speech, and cleared my mind of doubt.

Heneage rubbed out his cigar briskly, before its time. 'I'm so sorry about your play, Anthony, and your father's attaché case, such a very personal loss. These men are simply not *safe*. One hears that you are likely to go to Canada, a good idea, you will be out of harm's way over there. I shall have a chocolate.'

There was no point in asking him how he knew about Canada. 'I might go,' I said. 'I probably shall.'

'Quite the best thing all round,' Heneage said. 'I daresay this

63

affaire will be satisfactorily concluded before you return.'

Harry Seddall emitted his soundless laugh, that jump of the head and shoulders and the mouth open as if he had something to say that was too good to share.

Heneage looked daggers at him. 'You have the most filthy manners, Harry,' he said.

It was clear that the evening was over. I thanked Heneage for having me to dine with him, he wished me the very best of good fortune, and we all stood up. Seddall took the red display handkerchief from his pocket and put a handful of ginger chocolates in it, said, 'Thanks, John, nice dinner,' and went to the door where he waited for me.

We left Heneage standing in the little library, his white hands grasping the back of a chair. I noticed how tight their grip was, the knuckles stood out. I saw suddenly that he couldn't wait for us to go, and wondered how much of his evening's performance had been run on nerves. It was like leaving an actor who had been over-using himself in his dressing room.

Seddall closed the door and wandered through the club with his jacket open, his shirt out of his waist-band and the knot of his tie on his chest, swinging the red bandana of chocolates in his hand.

We hardly spoke until we were sitting in his car. He placed the chocolates carefully in the back seat and while he was still facing towards me said, to my intense surprise: 'Do you want a woman?'

'A woman?'

'Yeah. Do you want a woman, now?'

'No,' I said. 'Do you?'

'Up to you,' he said, not answering, and started the engine.

In the environment of the evening the suggestion had come as disconcertingly juvenile, as if we had just dined with our tutor, or the father of one of us, and now it was time to be young bloods and make a night of it.

His driving was quite different from Gatenby's. He drove easily, in no hurry, as if he were sharing the driving with the car instead of using it. The snow had not lasted and the tyres hissing on the slush made a soothing sound. He drove relaxed, nothing to prove.

Seddall seemed always to be relaxed, and either to have less to prove to himself than anyone I had ever met, or a great deal more. The carelessness of how people viewed him and the contempt for general habits of human and social conduct that did not suit him, had every appearance of being inbuilt, intrinsic – to be the result of an utter absence of shared attitude and not a reaction against it. It was as if there were two ways of living, and his was the other. Yet the sardonic, scornful dispassion that held him apart was the mark of the self-acknowledged outcast, the solitary, the untouchable.

I liked him for it. With amazement I heard myself say, 'Some other time.'

He smiled forward through the windscreen, a clear, boyish unsarcastic smile. 'I've got the car, I've got the chocolates, I'll get the girl,' he said.

He let me off at the end of the mews.

'So long, Anthony,' he said. 'See you again.' It was the first time he had used my Christian name. His use of it had a lonely sound.

'Yes,' I said. 'Good night, Harry.'

Chapter 8

The plane passed over the coast of Labrador and flew south. We crossed Quebec Province above the cloud level, but the sky was clear as we started our descent to Toronto. The captain took us low across the city and turned over Lake Ontario for his approach to the airport. The air was brilliantly clear and gave me two vivid impressions of Toronto. First, a city of green parks and tree-lined streets, and just before we crossed the lakeshore a modern metropolis of skyscrapers, new and shining in the sun. Lake Ontario stretched to the horizon like a sea. As we curved back inland and lost height to run straight and steady over the outskirts of the city, something leaped inside me. It was exhilaration. I was seduced by Toronto before we touched down on Canada.

Arrival at Pearson International Airport brought no disillusion. It was modern, clean and calm. My passage through Customs and Immigration was quick and easy, and as I went through the final stage towards the concourse I saw a man holding a Stratford Festival Theatre programme against the glass wall between us. The doors opened themselves as I came up to them, and I had arrived.

'Hi,' he said. 'Bruce Baldwin. Did you have a good flight, Mr Moore?'

'Perfect flight,' I said. 'Thanks for meeting me. How did you know who I was?'

'You've got your picture in the paper. Here, let me give you a hand.' I kept my bag but let him carry the portable typewriter that travelled with me everywhere. 'I need to eat before we hit the road. How does that suit?'

'That suits me very well. I may drink coffee and watch you eat. I had an Air Canada meal an hour or so ago.'

He was a solid broad-shouldered man with an energetic face and brown eyes. The eyes were peaceful and intelligent, and his whole demeanour was calm and unhurried to a degree unusual in theatre directors. Baldwin was the associate director at Stratford who had come up with the idea of the eight hour *Bleak House* marathon, which I was to adapt. If he was as capable as he was calm, I could look forward to our collaboration.

While he attacked his steak I read the small story under my picture in the Toronto *Globe and Mail*. It was in their Saturday arts section, one of half a dozen news paragraphs that made a feature in the corner of the page. It was a good, clear photograph. The caption story ran:

> *Anthony Moore, Irish author of the play* Two for Joy *which has enjoyed an 18-month run in the West End Shaftesbury Theatre in London, England. Moore arrives at Stratford, Ont., this week-end for first discussion on the Festival Theatre's project to stage* Bleak House *by Charles Dickens as an all-day marathon production. The project, plainly a weighty undertaking, is not scheduled for the forthcoming season, but hopefully for the next. It is understood that the production is being sponsored by a leading commercial institution.*

I put down the newspaper. 'I suppose the theatre sent them a hand-out.' I said.

'Not as far as I know,' Bruce Baldwin answered. 'I guess you have a keen press agent. In fact,' he said carefully, 'we wouldn't really want to go for publicity on this thing until it had firmed up a bit.'

'Bruce,' I said, 'I couldn't agree with you more. With the best will in the world we may find it can't be done, and nothing looks worse for a theatre than grandiose plans announced prematurely and then having to be cancelled. But I don't *have* a press agent.'

Bruce frowned. 'Gossip, I guess,' he said. 'The theatre is a breeding ground for gossip. Still, it's a small story, no harm in it. Now,' he said, 'I hope you don't mind, but I have to run into Toronto to pick up some scripts and then we can go straight out to Stratford.'

His car was a Volvo, one of the old models with rounded edges that are on the way to becoming collectors' items. I complimented him on it and he said: 'She's pretty rugged, and gives me no trouble, and a good car for the winter.'

We drove south from the airport towards the lake, and then east along the Gardiner Expressway into downtown Toronto. As we went he talked to me about the theatre, about the peculiarities of the thrust stage which Tyrone Guthrie had pioneered, with audience seated round three sides, and the advantages and difficulties it created for the actors. They would be nowhere without their design department, he said. 'They're brilliant just now. And the lighting system is state-of-the-art – thank God for computers.'

He was a pleasant, positive man to be with. I could see how the backbiting and gossip that are peculiar to theatre people would irritate him. He was from Alberta originally, and had started in the theatre in Calgary, though he had taken his director's course at the National Theatre School in Montreal.

'A good school, but too much francophone emphasis now.'

'Francophone – French-speaking?'

He smiled at me quickly. 'I guess it's a Canadian term. We're anglophone or francophone in Canada, though in fact we're an increasingly multi-cultural society – Portuguese, Italians, Greeks, Chinese, South-east Asians, Sikhs, other Hindus, Moslems. It's exciting – stimulating.'

'Montreal has a right to be francophone, surely?'

'Yeah, but the school is supposed to be national, you see. The French in Quebec can go to extreme lengths with their nationalism. You'll find out if you go there.'

We were in among the skyscrapers I had seen from the air. Many of them were very new, and some of them I found actually beautiful, not a quality you expect in modern office buildings –

not, at least, if you live in Britain. The architects here had let loose their imaginations on the unpromising principle of the skyscraper and the results were, in some cases, breathtaking. This, and the newness of so many of them, which presented Toronto as a metropolis committed to a new age, suggested a freshness of approach to life uncluttered by the past, that to an Irishman born was revelatory and to an adoptive Londoner a keen delight. It is absurd to over-value first impressions of a new country, but mine were borne out for me later when I stayed in Toronto: and reinforced. The European sense that history will inevitably digest the future as it has always done, so that everything will be always the same, and which in Europe is part of the general state of mind, was quite absent here.

I pointed to a building that shone golden in the sun, an effect gained by the colour of the glass, the copper-toned frames of the windows, and the texture of the concrete, 'What's that, Bruce? It's a beauty.'

'That's the Royal Bank of Canada building.'

'Is Toronto a big financial centre?'

'Yeah,' he said. 'Very big indeed.'

He parked outside an apartment building. 'I'll just be a couple of minutes,' he said. 'You might like to stretch your legs. It's pretty cold – there's a down-filled jacket in the back you can borrow.'

I strolled up and down in his warm, light-weight jacket. The bright air was sharp with cold on my face, so cold it bit through the hair to my scalp. Many of the people walking the street wore woollen hats or anorak hoods pulled over their heads, or both. I would have to do some shopping for my stay here.

Bruce came out of the building with a bundle of scripts under his arm and we set off again, bound for Stratford, driving through a mixture of pine forest and farmland.

The Baldwin home was in a quiet street lined with trees. It was a plain brick house with a large wooden porch, and inside it was as warm as toast. Bruce's wife Sandy came out of the kitchen to meet us, a pretty fair-haired girl in jeans and plaid shirt wearing glasses. While Bruce introduced us she took the glasses off to look at me. 'Hi!' she said. 'Your fame has preceded you, Anthony. I've been reading about you.'

The kitchen table was awash with books, notebooks and sheets of paper with typing on them. A typewriter sat in the middle of all this clutter with a newspaper lying on top of it. A mug of coffee and a cigarette smoking in an ashtray said that Sandy had been taking a coffee break and reading the paper when we arrived.

'We've seen it,' Bruce said. 'Is that the *Globe and Mail*?'

'Nope, it's the *Beacon-Herald*. Here.' Sandy gave me the paper, pointed out the article, and sat on the table smoking and swinging her legs.

'Hey,' Bruce said, 'have you eaten anything since breakfast? Are you going to get something for you and Anthony? I ate at the airport.'

She slipped off the table and gave him a hug. 'Sure you did,' she said. 'I've been working all morning and I'm hungry, and we're going out.'

'American women,' he said.

'I'm Canadian now,' she said.

We took the paper with us and went out to a greasy-spoon not far away where Bruce, this time, drank coffee and watched Sandy and me eat. We had hamburgers and French-fries.

'He's quite attractive,' she said to her husband while I scanned the article about Anthony Moore, playwright.

'He's okay. He's too big for you.'

'Nothin's too big for me,' she said.

I put down the *Beacon-Herald* and joined in. 'This,' I said, 'is rather different from life in swinging London.'

'What a cute English accent he has. Besides, I've been to London, and it isn't swingin' at all.'

'He's not English,' Bruce said. 'He's Irish.'

'They all look alike to me,' Sandy said. Then she put an arm round my waist. 'Relax,' she said. 'I'm not wanton. Is he going to stay with us?'

'I doubt it, now he's met you.'

Bruce had put it to me in the car. They had booked me into a hotel, provisionally, in case I preferred to be on my own, but I was warmly welcome to be their guest.

'What are you working on,' I asked her. 'Are you writing a book?'

'Yup. Medieval banking. What's the matter – don't you think I'm old enough?'

'You're a scholar?'

'Getting there. I took my Master's, but I don't want to live on campus all my life, so I'm trying to write *the* book on medieval banking and make it on my own. You look impressed, Anthony.'

I was impressed, with both of them, and with my first sight of the way they lived. I liked her working at her book in the kitchen instead of preparing a meal for the visitor. I liked them for bringing me to this sort of place to eat, and for the way they were with each other. I had not been sure about staying with the man I was going to be working with – and working hard – but it seemed now that home life would be home life, and we would be able to leave our work behind, at Bruce's office in the theatre. In any case it would only be for a few days, before I got down to it by myself in Toronto.

Sandy laughed. 'You stay with us,' she said. 'I'm just giving you a hard time. I'm not always like this. How do you like your publicity?'

I looked at Bruce. 'I don't quite understand it,' I said. 'This is a full-blown article with a two-column picture. There's not that much to write about me but they've milked what there is. Do you think this one was inspired by the theatre?'

He looked over the story. 'I didn't know all this about you,' he said. The article covered plays of mine that had been produced in Dublin and others staged from Pitlochry in Scotland to the Avignon Festival in the south of France. Yet in those years I would have called myself a struggling playwright; it was only the successful run of *Two for Joy* in the West End that had started to make my name – and that process had only started. My career was not worth all those inches of type and neither, even to the local paper, was the business that had brought me to Stratford.

'I don't get it,' Bruce said. 'We don't scratch around for publicity out of season – and we're closed now, we close over the winter. It can't be from our Press Office, but I'll check. Maybe I'll give Sheila a call – the girl who wrote it – and ask her where she got all this background.'

He called for the check and said to me, 'Do you want to work today, Anthony, or do you need a rest after the flight?'

'Let's work,' I said, 'and see where it takes us.'

It took us a long way, off to a good start. For the next three days we broke the book up into scenes, charted plot-lines through the scenes, shed characters and sections of plot, reinstated some of them and lopped off others. We became wildly artistic and abandoned the concept of time, and became practical again and decided time was essential to the structure, if we were going to hold the audience in their seats for a whole day. We started with a running-time of sixteen hours, and got it down to about eight, we hoped.

Every now and then we went out onto the apron stage and walked ourselves as characters through this scene or that, to give me the feel of the stage and a sense of the complex sight-lines that come from an audience watching from three sides instead of just one.

On the afternoon of our third day the lighting designer came in and showed me what their miraculous computerized lighting board could do. He made curtains of light, roofs and levels of light; he made the light dance, fall like rain, and flew thunderbolts of light that flickered like lightning and landed smoking on the stage. Finally, for an idea of pure melodrama that we wanted, he hunted Bruce about the stage while I sat and watched in the huge auditorium. They kept it up for five minutes and I was enthralled. I had never worked in a theatre with such virtuosic technical equipment, and had not imagined it could be handled with such mastery.

I was by that time fascinated by the problem of putting *Bleak House* onto the Stratford stage, which meant I was already half committed. That afternoon completed my commitment: I knew I was going to write the adaptation, and I knew it would work. I told Bruce so and we went back to his office in a mood of elation. I had already said I would like to take him and Sandy out to dinner that night, which would be my last night with them on this visit. Now, against his protests, I said we should eat at the best restaurant in Stratford – we had something to celebrate. He said he would reserve a table for us at the Church, extremely chic and pricey, if that was what I really wanted. I said it definitely was.

We bundled all our notes, stage plans and charts together and went home. When Sandy heard where we were going for dinner, she said 'Talk to ya later,' vanished into the bathroom and turned on the shower. I went to change and left Bruce to call the reporter who had written the article about me.

In fact I was too pleased with the amount of work we had done, and the successful outcome it promised, to care any more about the source of the article. I supposed they sent snippets of news about the arts across the Atlantic along with news about everything else, and that maybe Joanna, who knew a vast quantity of people, had been chattering to someone at a dinner party.

On the way to the Church I was preoccupied with quite another aspect of existence, and Bruce too was preoccupied, I supposed with the same question as myself. This was Sandy Baldwin's appearance, which was marvellous, beautiful, seductive and outrageous.

We sat on three sides of our table at the Church, and as Bruce went off to dispose of our coats, after lifting Sandy's from her shoulders, I saw a man dining nearby miss his mouth with his soup-spoon and sit staring. The man with him had better manners and self-control; he turned to see what was up, blinked and turned back again.

Sandy was wearing a dress of fine, dull gold thread that draped itself to her body. Her arms and shoulders were bare, so was her back, and the low cut of the dress displayed most of a rich, soft and beautifully rounded bosom, whose only restraint was that yielding gold fabric. This was not all. The devastating effect was completed by gold lip-gloss, gold nail polish, and gold eye-shadow. She looked breathtaking, and my breath was taken.

'Hi, cutie,' she said to the man who had spilled his soup, and was still staring at her. She turned back to me. 'What are *you* thinking?'

'I'm thinking,' I said, 'that you don't look like an academic.'

'Come on, that's an evasion. Tell the truth.'

'I think,' I said, 'that you are the most seductive creature west of the Urals.'

'That includes the Caucasus,' she said, 'which makes it a compliment.'

I offered her a cigarette with a deliberately shaking hand, and she lit mine, her bright blue eyes full of sex and mischief.

'You're an evil woman,' I said.

'She's that all right,' Bruce said. 'Is this seat taken, or do you two want to be alone?'

Sandy wriggled inside her dress, watching my face while she did so, and giggled.

'That's a little unfair on the man,' Bruce said mildly. 'You'll take away his appetite for dinner.'

A waiter came with Scotch. 'Bring more,' I said to him, and drank mine at a gulp.

Sandy said: 'I've got you going, Anthony. You'll have to find yourself a good warm body when you get up to Toronto.'

'Choose your nice dinner,' I said coldly. 'Avoid fish, eggs and spicy food, and with luck we'll get through the evening.'

'That doesn't leave much,' she said. 'I can't have soup in this dress either. I fall out of it if I lean over.'

'She does too,' Bruce said, and they both laughed like children. I envied them, both of them, and tried hard to concentrate on the lavish menu.

We had a glorious evening. Bruce and I were full of ourselves with the progress we had made and Sandy sat there, luscious and increasingly ribald as we got through two bottles of champagne, and enjoyed the game she played with both of us. I thought the game would not get out of hand. They were too much in love for that.

I thought this the next day, on the train to Toronto. That last evening with them I simply relished her, and the generosity of them both, and the fact of this new friendship.

At the station on Saturday evening Sandy hugged me and said, 'Come back soon, Anthony.'

'Three or four weeks,' I said. 'Then I'll come down and report to Bruce.'

'You'll report to *me*,' she said. 'I love you too, you know.'

I had only known them for three days but I found it hard to say good-bye to them. Sandy put her arms round her husband and held him tight, and then looked up at him smiling.

'Come on, buddy,' the porter said. 'I gotta put these steps away. You get yourself a seat.'

I took a last look at them. I had never seen two people so – the word that came to me stopped me for another moment – so daringly happy. I took one more second of that last look, and climbed up the steps onto the train.

Chapter 9

———◆◆———

I spent the week-end in a hotel. I had been working with Bruce Baldwin at a high pitch of concentration, and I did nothing for those two days except wallow in hot baths and showers, swim in the hotel pool, take in a movie, and read a little. I slept long hours, and the combined effects of jet lag and three days of hard labour at Stratford had left me by the time I woke on Monday morning.

After breakfast I phoned round the property agents who advertised immediate short lets, and by that evening I was making myself at home in a furnished apartment high above Gerrard Street, and had begun to know my way about downtown Toronto. My temporary home was well equipped, well heated and spotless, but it lacked the Moore touch. I went out and bought myself some house-warming presents. I went to the World's Biggest Bookstore, two blocks away, and came back laden with books, maps and assorted notebooks and pads. I went out again and picked up a stereo cassette player-recorder and some taped music. On that journey I felt the temperature drop about five degrees, so I went out again and bought myself a down-filled waistcoat to wear under the skiing anorak Bruce had lent me, found a bright red woollen hat called a toque (pronounced 'took'), and, dressed like ninety per cent of my companions on the bitter and windy sidewalks of Toronto, I set off to walk to the Art Gallery of Ontario. I emerged from the gallery with three large reproductions of paintings by Canadian artists and a handful of smaller copies on cards of various sizes.

Back at the apartment I hung the large reproductions on the

walls and distributed the cards along the shelves and window-sills, made a last expedition in the now biting cold for food and drink, and finally closed the door of the apartment against the outside world as darkness fell.

I knew I must spend a few hours on *Bleak House* that evening, in order to light the fire under the boiler, so to speak, but when I tried to get down to it I found an irritating want of inclination. I sat at a table in the window, in front of me all my newly acquired stationery, a stage-plan of the theatre, several editions of *Bleak House* variously marked, dismembered and rearranged, and a sheet of paper in the typewriter. I read the notes I had made on the guidelines that Bruce and I had thrashed out together, to refresh my memory and slip my mind easily into gear – and twenty minutes later found myself without a useful thought in my head, looking out on the bright, inviting lights of Toronto.

I indulged in some deliberate displacement activity: made myself coffee, put on piano music by W. A. Mozart, adjusted the thermostat that governed the temperature of the room, and sat down again. It was no good. Instead of returning to the characters of Charles Dickens in their nineteenth-century world, where it had moved so willingly the week before, my mind focused insistently on my present-day world, on the events and people I had met within the past two weeks.

There was more to this than the familiar manoeuvres of the artistic temperament doing its utmost to avoid starting a piece of work. I wanted to examine Heneage–Seddall–Kenna behaviour in the light of Bruce and Sandy Baldwin behaviour; to balance the life and works of the one group against those of the other. Not so much to strike a balance of morality between the two, but the balance of reality. It was not that their natures and their attitudes to life were utterly opposed – they were too far different even for that. They were so distant from each other, that it seemed to me if the one lot were real, then the others were merely fantastic: if one lot were living in the real world, then the others were simply at play.

I poured another cup of coffee and phoned the Baldwins.

Bruce answered. 'Bruce, it's Anthony. Let me give you my phone number.'

He took it down, we exchanged a few idle remarks, and then he said, 'I meant to tell you before, but I forgot. I spoke to Sheila Smith on the *Beacon-Herald* about her article on you. It seems a man from your High Commission came down from Ottawa, took her to lunch – at the Church – and fed her all that material she based her story on.'

'Oh,' I said, a little blank. I had forgotten about this free and superfluous publicity. 'Very keen of him.'

'I'll say – Ottawa is over three hundred miles from Stratford. That's a long way for a diplomat to go for lunch.'

Three hundred miles: I looked at the telephone as if it had made a mistake.

'Well it is, yes. Maybe he had some other calls to make in your direction.'

'Not according to him. He stressed that to her – said there was a lot of action coming up from the High Commission to emphasize the cultural link between Britain and Canada.'

There was a short pause before Bruce spoke again. 'You know, Anthony, no offence to you, but Britain is just another foreign country to most of us now, so I don't get this cultural link business. Diplomats are just not that naive.'

'I suppose not,' I said. 'Let's not think about that. We have worse problems.'

'Yeah?'

'Yeah. I'm sitting here trying to work, and all that happens is, I keep thinking what a good time you gave me in Stratford.'

Bruce's voice had a smile in it that came right along the wire. 'Well, Anthony, we've been thinking what a good time you gave us. Hey, can you hold a moment?' I heard him put the phone down, and half a minute later he spoke again. 'That was Sandy – she's in the bath, or she'd come to the phone. She says if you find you can't work there, come right back here. She'll share her kitchen with you any time.'

It was my turn to laugh. 'That *is* an offer. No, seriously, this is a good place. I just need some advice and stern encouragement.'

'I'll give you advice; you don't need the other. Take tonight off – go out and get yourself a drink, come back, read your opening passage in *Bleak House* and go to sleep. It'll work on your dreams and you'll start off in the morning with no trouble. I've got your phone number, but where's the apartment?'

'Gerrard Street. West. The south side.'

'Okay – then take a right outside your front door and drag yourself along the street to the Chelsea Inn. They have a nice dark piano bar. It's not exciting but I guess it might simplify your mind. Or do you want some real night life?'

'No, no, I don't. I want the right therapy to get me working.'

'Well, there you go then. I might be in Toronto next Saturday – if you feel like a meet we could have lunch and do a couple of hours in the afternoon?'

'Let's do that. I'll take your advice, Baldwin. Meanwhile, put your mind to words of stern encouragement in case they're called for.'

'How about, "No work, no pay"? Talk to you later.'

The Chelsea Inn was a large, long North American hotel, about twenty floors high, but it had some conscientious touches of English decor. The doormen wore the uniform of Chelsea Pensioners, there was a bright red cast iron mailbox in the lobby, acres of wood panelling and, as I learned later, they served afternoon tea just like Fuller's used to do.

The long dark bar, however, might have been in New York or Chicago. A girl was singing torch songs with a small band, and though the place was busy, I found a table ideally placed for what I wanted. It was not too close to the music or surrounded by noisy neighbours. I could hear the girl sing, and myself think. I ordered a drink and the girl began to sing 'Please Don't Talk About Me When I'm Gone'. She knew how to sing, and how to sing torch; she sang it straight and sad, without making a production of it. The thoughts that had been too active in my mind back in the apartment begin to drift about in it again, but at a more negotiable pace. I took stock of them, and of myself.

I recognized that by coming to Canada I had made a sudden jump from the macabre episode which had begun on the Channel crossing and ended with dinner in Heneage's club. Looking back on it, I saw the dinner as creakingly stage-managed, though with what effect in mind I could not tell; but also as being heavy with an atmosphere of which the stage managers were either unaware, or to which they had become so inured that it had become their natural element, the only one in which they could now move and breathe. It was an atmosphere of exhausted cynicism, in which they could believe men capable of anything; themselves included, no doubt. Why not?

Why not?

My face grew stiff, with my eyes wide, and I sat slowly forward, until I was bolt upright on my chair. An unbidden thought was working its way forward and had almost found words, was on the tip of my tongue, when a voice spoke.

'What can I get you?'

It was the waiter, who had translated my involuntary movement and the look on my face as a request.

'Scotch again, please,' I said. 'A large one.'

Whatever it was in my mind, whose imminent arrival had begun to startle me, had slipped away again to hide. There was no point in chasing it; it would venture out again in its own good time. I took in my surroundings. Singer and band were taking an intermission. There was a slow coming and going in the bar all the time, and one of the newcomers who had not been there when I sat down, was looking at me with a kind of careful diffidence. I wondered if I knew him, but then the singer came back, with the band, and I turned to watch her. She was worth watching. She had changed into a black satiny shining dress that sheathed her body and was cut low and moulded to her breasts. Her hair was ash-blonde and fell straight to the white shoulders, like starlight on snow. She looked round the crowd in the bar for a moment or so, meeting a few eyes, mine among them, smiled faintly at something far away over the mountains, and began to sing 'I Get Along Without You Very Well'. I tried not to take it personally.

My whisky arrived and as I picked it up I noticed again the man who had been watching me. His eyes were on the girl and had got their metaphors badly mixed: they were licking their lips. I knew who he was now – it was the man whose first sight of Sandy in her gold dress had made him pour soup all over himself. I did not think it much of a coincidence, seeing him there; it happens a good deal when one travels abroad. At least we had not met – he would be a hard man to like. I turned back to enjoy the singer, sight and sound.

What a guy! she sang. *What a fool am I, to think my breaking heart could kid the moon!*

She sang long pure, legato notes, no tremble in the voice and no dramatics, singing only the song. Wonderful. The waiter brought me another drink without my having to ask for it. Wonderful! He refused my money and pointed to the man who spilled soup and who mixed metaphors with his eyes. The man lifted his glass, sprang from his chair and sat down beside me all in one line of the song.

My new friend and I watched her. She looked straight at me, cool and detached, but I could tell she was hurt. I was anybody's for a shot of Scotch. She tossed the starlight about on the snow-white shoulders and sang out the song. *No – it's best that I stick to my tune*, she ended firmly and bowed, the hair falling like a curtain over her face. The band struck up again after the applause, and she began to move her body, little and languorously, but to great effect, and went into 'Body and Soul'.

'I join you,' the man who had joined me said. 'You forgive me.'

'Why?' I said, taking a tough line. I did not want to speak to the little berk. His manners were bad, his appearance unprepossessing – he had greasy hair, a Zapata moustache, fleshy lips, shifting eyes and too much of him was round: nose, chin and suit, which clasped him like a barrel holding a tun of wine together. Not that he was fat, he was just too snug altogether. He smelled of chypre and he had a foreign accent. It was still my first week in Canada

81

and I was taking to it like a duck to water. If ever there was an un-Canadian activity, it seemed to me, it was talking to this relic of old Europe.

'We met in Stratford,' he lied grossly. 'You were dining with the lovely lady in the gold dress.' Unmentionable movements took place inside his eyes, which were an unpleasant brown, like the edges of burnt eggs.

'We did not meet, we did not speak, we were not introduced,' I said chillingly.

'I introduce myself,' he said, cutting through all this red tape. 'I'm Franz Lehar.'

I began to laugh – who wouldn't – and knew I had lost my campaign for Lebensraum. 'Franz Lehar?' I said.

He gave me a snug little bow. 'From Mejico.'

'Lehar is not a Mexican name,' I said.

His smile lost size. 'It is my name, and I am Mejicano.'

This was incontrovertible. 'Still,' I said. 'Lehar – '

'My grandfather was Hungarian.'

I decided not to ask about his father. He had shown a Spaniard's pride when I impugned the connection between his name and his nationality, and I rather like that sort of thing.

'Mr Moore,' he asked with slightly wrinkled suavity, tinkling the ice in his glass. 'Who was the lovely lady with you in Stratford?'

'The wife,' I answered repressively, 'of a business associate. How do you know my name?'

'I see your picture in the paper. I ask about your party of the waiter in the restaurant. They tell me the other man is of the theatre also. I hope maybe the lady is an actress.' Evil thoughts flourished in those over-fried eyes. He swung his glass again. 'You know – actresses!'

This was true. I did know actresses. I decided to make the best of my undesirable acquaintance: at least he had character; unlike most of the encounters that are forced on you when you travel abroad, this one was ludicrous rather than boring. 'Actresses, I said, 'are very expensive.'

'You think your friend is very expensive?' He meant it; his eyes were intent.

'Sandy? Look, I've only known her three days, and she has made it clear that she is very, very expensive indeed!'

I wondered if Sandy Baldwin's ears were burning. I looked guiltily at the stage, as if this disgraceful dialogue must somehow be getting through to the singer. Far from it: I knew she was mine just for the taking, she sang encouragingly. She would gladly surrender herself, body and soul.

'Besides,' I said to Franz Lehar. 'Sandy's husband is very jealous.'

'Bah!' he said, and pouted. 'In Mejico we beware of husbands. Among the Anglo-Saxon races, there is no need.' He meditated. 'Sandy is a lovely name. It is a name one could speak.' He spoke it. 'Sandy, Sandy.'

The movement of his red juicy lips saying Sandy's name made me, all of a sudden, very old-fashioned. I wanted to punch Señor Lehar on the mouth. Instead, I gulped down a good deal of his unsolicited whisky at a swallow.

He sighed. 'Still, a woman is only worth so much. You think she would be too expensive?'

I downed the rest of the drink. 'She wears gold,' I said. 'It is symbolic.'

'Symbolic? Ah – a symbol! Like your sex symbol. A sex symbol in gold!' He laughed boisterously and slapped his round snugly trousered thigh, loudly. People looked at us. The singer had taken her applause and left.

'I must go,' I said.

He looked startled. 'So soon?' he said.

'Lots of work to do tomorrow. In any case,' I said, for I was sure he had not been sitting alone, 'you will want to rejoin your companions.'

'Oh, they have gone to bed. I am what you call a night mouse.'

'Night owl,' I said. 'Well, I'm not. Enjoyed our meeting.' I stood up. 'Oh, and thanks for the drink.'

'Nothing,' he said. He seemed reluctant to let me go. 'You live in an apartment, Mr Moore?' As soon as he said this, the smile fell off his face as if something had gone wrong.

'How did you know that?' I asked him curiously, pulling on my down-filled waistcoat and anorak.

The smile jumped back into place. 'You have your outside clothes – I may say you are not staying in the hotel, so probably you have an apartment.'

'Yes,' I said shortly, 'I do.'

I was growing irritated at his imperviousness to my own wish to depart, so I began to leave anyway, pushing my chair into the table to make room for my exit.

'You are – interested in apartments? Is that why you live there?' This last question made no sense to me at all. Neither did his expression, for his face had grown less round, the smile inverted, and the normally vagrant eyes were fixed on mine. He had me stopped for the moment. 'Yes. No. I like them to live and work in.'

'You are not interested in them as property?' Again he made an odd hesitation before, presumably, the key word.

'Property?'

'Property.' He nodded in a slow continuous rhythm.

I had had enough of Franz Lehar. I found my woollen toque under my seat and left him there nodding. The band were packing up, anyway. My torch singer had finished for the night.

When I entered the lobby of the apartment building a man was dialling at one of the wall telephones. He left the lobby while I was waiting for the elevator. A man in business clothes came out of the elevator, brushing me with a strict, self-engaged look as he passed. I went up to the twelfth floor and unlocked my door.

Things were not as I had left them. All my notes, and the copies of *Bleak House*, both whole and cut about by me and Bruce, were gone. I went into the bedroom. There was no damage done, but the mattress was on the floor and the bed-clothes piled on the bed.

I called the manager of the building, who came carrying a heavy flashlight and a perturbed air, went through the apartment holding the flashlight like a club, and relaxed when he found the place unscarred. He said he had called the police. 'House rules,' he said. He was a thick-set man in his thirties with a big, capable face and a slow smile. We heard the police siren belling up into the night. 'I was watching *The Maltese Falcon*, he said. 'Musta seen it twenty times.'

'It's a great movie,' I said.

We had left the door open, and a policeman came in before we knew he was there, holding his gun at his side. 'Hi, Bill,' he said to the manager.

'They've been and gone,' the manager said. 'You made good time, Stewart.'

'Sure,' the policeman said, and went through the apartment for himself. 'Okay, Doug,' he called out, and another policeman came in from the corridor.

I gave them coffee and they took notes, but there was not much for them to write down. It was an odd crime, to say the least of it, and we did not try too hard to make sense of it. The senior man, stepping gallantly onto unknown territory, asked me if there could be inter-theatre rivalry at work – an attempt to slow down the adaptation of the Dickens novel.

'No,' I said, smiling only slightly. 'And it wouldn't work. I can get photocopies of everything we've done so far sent from Stratford.'

'Makes no sense, does it?'

'Not to me,' I said. A fanciful thought came into my head, but instead of passing, it stayed, and fleshed itself out with characters: one man to keep me talking in the hotel bar, one to watch the lobby and phone upstairs when I returned, and the man who came down in the elevator. It seemed absurd, but they had noticed it in my face, so I told them. The notebooks came out again and they took descriptions. They liked the sound of this hypothetical team of apartment thieves. It had a professional ring to it.

'If they read about you in the papers, maybe they thought you had something worth stealing,' Stewart said.

'Well, I don't,' I said, 'even at home. A couple of paintings, maybe. My stereo, that sort of thing.'

'Mr Moore,' Stewart said, 'I'll pass this on, but I can't promise you very much will happen. You reckon no more than fifty dollars' worth stolen. To us it's small potatoes.'

'I know that,' I said. 'I don't see what you can do, unless you catch them at it somewhere else.'

'Franz Lehar,' he said. 'That's quite a name. It didn't seem phoney to you?'

I smiled at him. 'It's the kind of name that happens,' I said, and gave a shrug.

He nodded amiably. 'True enough. I sometimes wonder why we don't hear more of Mozart's great-great-great-great-grandchildren.'

Emboldened by this historic-cultural reference, the young cop struck in. 'Maybe this Lehar's Hungarian grandfather went from Austria to Mexico with the Emperor Maximilian. Austria-Hungary was one state then.'

'Doug's a university graduate,' Stewart said to me. 'When I took you on as my partner, Doug, you promised not to throw your education in my face.'

'Come on, Stewart,' Doug said cheerfully. 'You brought up Mozart. I wonder where they are, all those little Mozarts.'

'We'll call it quits, then, till next time. I guess we'll call it quits here too, Bill – Mr Moore. Thanks for the coffee.'

The policemen and the manager went away, and I put the chain up on the door. I switched on a table lamp and sat in the dim light, smoking cigarettes and thinking evil thoughts.

The crime rate was getting on my nerves. The criminals of the world had apparently united to stop Anthony Moore writing for the stage. It was a severe form of criticism, I thought – and at that thought smiled sourly at myself. The smile did not last but the sour feeling did: what exercised me was the question, *were* the men who had broken into the apartment united with criminals I had fallen foul of on that ill-fated crossing from France to England?

It seemed far-fetched, and I hoped it was too far-fetched to be true; I would much rather believe that the break-in was the work of professional apartment thieves, than that I was being drawn back into the sinister and anarchic world where normality was represented by the callous, functional murders of Marco and, in his own turn, of the man in the Mercedes; I had no liking, either, for the part of that world where John Heneage and Harry Seddall walked their mysterious paths. Yet in the bar earlier that night, I had begun to smell a faint whiff of Heneage and Seddall in these stories and pictures of me planted in the newspapers; and since then, since the break-in, I had been toying with a scenario in which the lecherous Franz Lehar (if that was his name) picked up my trail in the restaurant in Stratford and followed me to Toronto. If that scenario was not as fanciful as I hoped it was, then the barefaced way in which Lehar had kept me talking in the bar this evening while the others calmly raided my apartment, had an unpleasant echo of the brisk, spontaneous style displayed by my enemies on the Channel ferry.

An elusive passage from the big-game hunter's manual·that had been flying around in my head came home to me at last, and very nasty it was. It said simply: tether a goat in a clearing, and you will bring the tigers out of the jungle into the open.

I thought that maybe Heneage had put the finger on me, had set me up, with the help of the Cultural Attaché in Ottawa, to flush his unknown enemies out of the undergrowth.

I went to bed at last, but I did not rest easy. The night sounds of Toronto assured me that I lay in the heart of a civilized modern metropolis, and the occasional wail of a police siren affirmed that the law never slept: but every hour I woke with my ears straining to hear the heavy body brush through the tall, dry grass; to hear the leaves rustle as the displaced twigs sprang back into place; to hear the snarl in the throat of the tiger.

Chapter 10

First thing in the morning I called the car-hire companies until I
found one that could rent me a European car. They offered me a
Renault 18 and I said I would pick it up after breakfast. My
master plan for the day was a simple one. I would drive to
Stratford, collect copies of everything that had been whisked off
my desk the night before, come straight back to the apartment
and start work.

That was my practical campaign strategy. To back it up I
would impose a régime of negative indoctrination, which is to
say that every least thought that came into my head about the
recent intrusions into my life by criminals high or low, international or local, would be ejected forthwith. Today would see the
turn of the tide, Moore's El Alamein. All I had to do was go to
Stratford and fetch the tanks.

I showered, shaved and dressed in short order, and went to
breakfast with a newspaper in the coffee-shop on the corner. I
read that the bank robbery business in Montreal was on the skids,
they were down to one a week; that the RCMP had raided a barn
in northern Ontario and found enough marijuana to keep the
entire province, as one of the Mounties quaintly expressed it,
looped for a week; that there had been yet another kidnapping, or
at least an unexplained disappearance, of an entire family called
Monteith, and that in two separate incidents, a man had been
shot dead and a woman injured by hunters who had mistaken
them for deer.

'Hi,' a voice said. 'Join you for a coffee?' It was Bill Godwin,
the manager of the apartment.

'Morning!' I said.

He sat down; the waitress came and cleared the remains of my breakfast. 'Last night didn't spoil your appetite any,' he said.

'What you see before you,' I told him firmly, 'is Anthony Moore putting last night out of his mind.'

He looked at me half amused, a little interrogative. 'That simple, huh?'

'Yes,' I said. 'Also, no, but I came here to work, and work is the only item on my agenda.'

'Good for you,' he said.

I laughed and handed him the paper.

'I don't like hoodlums pawing over my things,' I said, 'but that was small-time compared with what else has been going on.' I nodded at the paper he was holding. 'Sudden death, kidnapping, the great pot raid, bank robberies and what have you.'

He scanned the front page. 'Yeah,' he said. 'The hunting season's opened. You want to take care if you're out in the woods this time of year. Some of these guys shoot anything that moves.' He raised his eyebrows. 'The Monteiths,' he said. 'Well now. That's old Toronto money, and still at it. He owns a lot of Canada.'

'Land, you mean?'

'I guess, but I don't mean that. He owns a lot of real estate, here in Toronto, Montreal, Vancouver; mostly office buildings.' He finished his coffee. 'Toronto's full of money,' he said. 'Time I went to earn my share of it. I hope you have a good stay with us, anyway, and no more hassles. See you later.'

I went back up to the apartment and phoned Bruce Baldwin at the theatre to tell him I wanted to borrow his notes. 'Sure,' he said, and after a short pause, 'what happened to your own set?'

'Lost them,' I said. 'I'll explain when I see you.'

I drove to Stratford under a clear blue sky. The road ran in long straight stretches through the Ontario farmland. I kept my mind as clear as possible of the ideas that had disturbed my sleep. The car was almost new, a pleasure to drive, and as I approached Stratford the sun shone brightly. It became possible to believe that all was right with the world. I even thought I might write the lost play sooner than I had hoped. I could do the adaptation in the mornings, and the play in afternoons and evenings, or the other way round.

When I reached the theatre Bruce was up to his ears. 'I've a meeting in ten minutes,' he said. 'We'll be at it most of the day. I'm having my set of notes copied now and they're promised for one o'clock. The books you'll have to cut up yourself, I guess – can you buy some new ones in Toronto and duplicate what we did with them? Bill me at the theatre, right? I'll be in Toronto Saturday, I could collect these from you then, see how you're getting on. Is that good?'

'Good,' I said. He thrust the books which we had marked up, cut to pieces and revamped, into my hands.

'How'd you lose them?'

I told him. He sat down, slowly. 'That is the damndest thing,' he said. 'It's crazy. Who'd want a bunch of notes on *Bleak House*?'

'God knows to me,' I said. 'I've decided not to think about it. I just want to get on with the work.'

'Look, the notes will be here, on my desk, one o'clock. Why don't you lunch with Sandy, she'd like it. I told her you'd be here.'

'I'd like to see her. I don't know about lunch. I feel I should get back, get started.'

'Tell her that, she'll give you an early lunch. She'd like to see you. She's having one of her downs.'

His square, rugged face was anxious, full of his own business but worried about her. It was an appeal. I could not refuse him, and this haste to be at it, which I was riding on, could afford to take a breather.

'I will,' I said. 'I'd like to. What's this about Sandy having downs?'

'Usual thing,' he said. 'She has a lot of ups, but now and then she gets a deep, deep down.' He gripped my arm. 'Thanks, Anthony, thanks a lot.'

He reminded me how to get there – down over the bridge, a

left and two rights – and was gone, clutching a bundle of papers and a clipboard and lighting a cigarette as he went.

I crossed the bridge, took all the lefts and rights, and turned into the driveway of the Baldwins' house.

Sandy met me at the door; old blue jeans, big fisherman's Aran sweater, blue eyes looking at me through cloud, and a fast flickering smile. She shut the door, led me by the hand into the kitchen, and said: 'How good are your hugs, stranger?'

I put my arms around her and hugged her. 'Hold me tight,' she said into my chest. 'Break me in two. Squeeze the tension out.'

I pulled her close against me, tightening my arms round her more and more until she nodded once, and held her like that for a long minute or more until I felt a big sigh rising in her. I held her loosely then so that she could let it come shuddering out. She stood still with her arms round my waist. I combed her mussed-up blonde hair with my fingers, and rubbed her gently on the small of her back. I watched my hand stroke the faded seat of her jeans, feel the tight swell of her buttocks.

She put her arms round my neck and looked at me, leaning close. 'You give good hugs, sailor,' she said, 'but what are you doing now?'

'Getting carried away,' I said. My voice was husky.

'You sure are,' she said. 'I can feel it. I think that's very nice of you.'

She kissed me softly, rubbed her lips against mine, and said, 'Thanks, Anthony.'

I held her head in my hands and then let go of her. 'Any time,' I said. 'How are you doing?'

'Better,' she said and stepped back, looking at me. 'Oh, shoot! I'm glad you're here. Do you want a beer?'

She gave me a can of Molson's, and we sat on each side of the kitchen table which was littered with her books and papers, drinking beer and smoking cigarettes.

'I go for weeks,' she said, 'and suddenly I get so low, so damned low and useless, and then I get shaky inside, breaking up inside.'

'The black dog,' I said.

'Yes,' she said. 'I've heard it called that.'

'Have you looked for the cause?'

'Analysis, you mean? Yeah, I've looked. I never finished looking. Stratford's not hotching with transactional therapists, either.'

'Toronto's not so far,' I said, pushing her.

'Damn you,' she said. 'Stop there. I know all the answers too.'

'No,' I said. 'They're always clearer to someone else.'

'Holy cats!' she shouted at me. 'What is this – *Destry Rides Again*? Leave it alone for now, just leave it.'

'Consider it left,' I said mildly.

She put a foot up on the table and scowled at it, then she looked at me, speculating. 'It's all right,' she said. 'I just shout. It's all right – if it's all right with you?'

'It's just fine with me. Once an hour. More than that and I'll smack your pretty bottom.'

She opened her mouth and squinted at me through her hair. 'You just said that so you could talk sexy.'

'Probably,' I said. 'But I'd do it.'

'Yes, you would,' she said, still summing me up through her hair.

'Yeah.' she ran a hand down her thigh. 'You like the gams?'

'The gams are just terrific.'

'What else do you like?'

'Every last living bit of flesh you have, Sandy.'

She gazed at me again with that mouth-open look. 'You're really something, Anthony. I'm not a nymphomaniac – do you think I'm making a pass at you?'

I shook my head. 'No. I know what you're doing.'

'Giving you a hard time?'

'More than that. Getting it out in the open. Drawing the limits. Setting the ground rules.'

She nodded slowly and then began to laugh, threw back her head and laughed more. 'Oh God, Anthony,' she said. 'Great, great corny dialogue. I don't deserve you turning up today, but

I'm sure glad you did.'

She lifted her foot off the table, put her arms above her head and stretched, relaxing more of the tension out of her. 'Here it is,' she said, and wiped the hair out of her eyes so that I could see her clearly. 'I could fall in love with you, maybe, but I'm all in love with Bruce, and all of this' – she sketched her body with a gesture, frank and curiously moving – 'is his.'

'I think all of us know some of that,' I said, 'and each of us knows enough.'

'Well, you pompous bastard, what about *you*?'

'Oh, I'm half in love with you,' I said. 'What's for lunch?'

'You goddam playwright,' she yelled. 'Lines, lines, lines!' She threw herself at me and hugged me fiercely.

For lunch we had pastrami sandwiches on rye, pickles, cheese and more beer.

Chapter 11

———◆◆———

I started work as soon as I was back in the apartment, and this time I swung into a routine, working like a Trojan for twelve hours a day and stopping only to eat and sleep. It is perhaps an unusual way to go about things but it suits my temperament if I am in a thoroughly good frame of mind to start with.

The last had been hard to come by recently, and the work was well under way before I acknowledged to myself that the impetus which had thrown me into action had sprung from my encounter with Sandy Baldwin.

I suppose I had not let myself admit it sooner because, though it is hard for an Irishman to resist flirting with other men's wives, there had been a lot more than that to the meeting with Sandy. Instinctive reciprocity was one thing, but the depth of recognition that had passed between us was another: and although the emotional excitement of it was still with me, in the very act of acknowledging how much it lifted my spirits and acted as a stimulus to my work, I had made myself accept the sense of guilt, and the risk and wrongness of it.

For I was too much of an Irishman not to feel the truth that runs in Celtic legend, where a man becoming enamoured of his friend's wife brings the three of them to a sticky end. Yet the work was going well, and I laid the dilemma on one side and kept at the typewriter.

I wrote scene after scene at a tremendous pace until by midday on Friday I began to slow down and found my thinking had gone stale. It was time for a break. I packed it in and went for some fresh air.

It was fresh all right, with a strong north-east wind blowing across the city. I walked along Gerrard to Yonge Street and set off briskly through the lunch-time crowds. If any street in Toronto is the main stem, it is Yonge Street. It runs north from the lakeshore; for a short stretch becomes the Soho of Toronto, wearing its strip clubs and sex shops with an air of conscientious decadence as if secretly aware that Sin, like Patriotism before it, has lost its innocence and is therefore no longer enough; enters a phase of boulevardian respectability; crosses Bloor Street where the classy stores are; and travels on forever through the city.

I had turned north bound for Bloor Street and Britnell's bookstore, which is to Toronto what Hatchards is to London or Blackwell's to Oxford. I wanted copies of *Bleak House* to replace those Bruce had lent me, and I wanted to browse as well. A good bookshop is a companionable place and I had hardly had my nose out of the typewriter all week.

As I gasped at the cold wind that whirled out of one of the cross-streets, I remembered that at the start of the week I had firmly resolved to put the apartment break-in and all the implications I had attached to it out of my mind. Well, I had more or less succeeded. My life had resumed its normal course. I told myself that I had made more of the mutual spontaneity of my meeting with Sandy than it warranted: all that had happened was that it had helped me to a saner perspective and that, being so highly charged, it had acted as a buffer between me and the exotic events that had recently come my way. I must take more care for my friendship with Bruce and Sandy; be more circumspect.

Grafting these moral contemplations onto my sense of achievement, I battled across one more windy canyon and turned into the warmth of Britnell's bookstore. Halfway down the store I saw White Denver.

It was years since I had known him; he was a Canadian and had been a Rhodes Scholar when I was an undergraduate, had won the Newdigate Prize for a long poem about Byzantium when he was at Oxford. He was now a considerable poet. He was more esteemed by the critics than in the marketplace, but that's poetry for you.

He had become more English than the English at Oxford, and his style of speech confirmed that this progress had continued. 'My dear Anthony,' he said, 'what a pleasing surprise!'

He was a long narrow man with a narrow head topped by thin, wavy hair already grey. He wore an enormous fur coat over tweed jacket and flannels, and was wearing, I was distressed to see, our college tie. His observation of social comment was acute; he detected the frisson that crossed my face. 'Don't fret, dear boy,' he said. 'I never wear it in England, but it adds a little something to my sense of *self* at U. of T.'

'What precisely is U. of T?' I asked him.

'How very civilized not to know!' he said warmly. 'The University of Toronto, Anthony. A monolith of education. We teach them not in regiments or in divisions, but in whole army corps. You must come home with me this instant for tea: it is essential. We shall toast bagels instead of crumpets.'

'That's very kind, White,' I said, thinking fast. Did I want to have tea with him, or would it be too long a break from my work?

'Now or not at all,' he said, reading my hesitation. 'I fly to Europe on Sunday on a God-given sabbatical. This evening I must receive the hypocritical good wishes of the men in my department, not to mention their excellent wives, all of whom look forward to an air disaster so that I may vacate my Chair prematurely. I would take you with me but you would hate it. I am sure you have nothing in common with universities. So come and have tea, Anthony. We shall talk about England,' he said, as if he were Rupert Brooke at the Dardanelles. He corrected this impression at once. 'As, for example, who you know in television, and who are your many friends in the BBC's cultural and artistic enclaves.'

'I know,' I said cautiously, 'a man who reviews books occasionally on the BBC World Service.'

'There you are,' he said, 'I do not in fact envisage, or even wish for, an increased reputation among the Highlands of Zimbabwe

96

or the marshes of the Nile Delta, but I am sure you will come up with some seriously useful names. You can come back with me in the car.'

It was a pleasant afternoon. I liked his home. It was an immaculately kept nineteenth-century house in a tree-lined street, with a wide porch, floors of gleaming birchwood, old polished furniture, shelves of books and good paintings – three of them by painters of the Group of Seven.

I began to appreciate White Denver. He was obviously well off but the house was a plain house in the Canadian tradition. His affectation of Englishness was hardly skin-deep, probably no more than a personal armour against the communal – and often competitive – nature of academic life. It occurred to me to wonder how he managed to make time for his poetry. I gathered from what he said that running a department in a big university was a taxing and highly political business.

'My cottage, Anthony, and the vacations. I hardly write a line during a semester. I have a cottage up north, a regular pioneer's cabin, in fact – they're quite rare, you know, not many have survived. Very small, built of squared logs: a perfect poet's hideaway. I don't know what it's like being a playwright, but I do need to be off by myself to write poetry.'

'If the play is pretty clear to me when I'm ready to start,' I said, 'so do I. If it's still forming, I need distraction as well.' As I said it I thought to myself, the play you have to write again *is* pretty well there.

'In that case,' he said, 'you would love my cottage, Anthony. When I'm in the thick of it here, correcting papers, writing for the journals, deflecting the masterstrokes of the university Machiavellis, I think of the simple life up at Little Duck Lake and the vacation to come.'

We talked about cooking, university politics, poets and playwrights, and life in Toronto. As he talked it dawned on me that despite the quiet, industrious style in which he lived, and this comfortable but plain house he lived in, White Denver had some of the indefinable attributes of the extremely rich.

'White,' I said, over the coffee, 'are you what is described in the words "Toronto Money"?'

'We have been,' he said elusively. Then, 'To be candid, Anthony, I am.'

'Does that mean you're an old Canadian family?'

'Hell, yes,' he said. 'My cottage was built by my mother's grandfather and great-grandfather. It's called White's Landing. It's an original log cabin – did you know the size of them was dictated by the length of log two men could lift between them? That's why they look so small to us nowadays. They were made of very thick timber, squared off tree-trunks. My father's family had a hardware store in old York – before it grew into Toronto. They grew with the city.'

'White,' I said, inexcusably perhaps, but I had been taken by the phrase "Toronto Money", and what it implied did not seem to match his very moderate life-style, 'what do you do with it?'

'Wealth?' he said. 'I haven't decided what to do with it yet. Isn't it strange?'

'It's unusual,' I said.

'I'm very conservative about it,' White said. 'It's mostly in with other Toronto Money's money, if you follow me. Like Johnnie Monteith – did you read about him in the *Globe*?'

'The man who's been kidnapped?'

'Oh, I'm sure Johnnie has *not* been kidnapped. I think he's hiding – he has a big deal on just now.' I realized I was looking at him with a smile of curiosity on my face. 'I know, I know,' he said. 'Why do I keep on with the hassle of university teaching? I like it for one thing – it's a trade I'm good at. You are wondering why I don't just take off to White's Landing or some snug mini-chateau in the sun and write poetry? Because I really think it would go wrong. No more poetry or something. This is a good life I have, don't you think?' He wore a slightly anxious expression now.

'It looks to be absolutely excellent,' I said. 'You seem to be flourishing.'

'There you are then,' he said, back to his cheerful and sardonic manner. 'Don't worry about me. I'll be all right.'

I laughed. 'I've been very rude,' I said. 'At least you have an imported car in the driveway.'

'The Volvo? Alas, no. They make Volvos in Canada.'

'I thought I'd seen rather a lot of them.'

'Good winter cars, and we have long winters.' He gave me a thoughtful stare, and then went out of the room and came back almost at once with photographs of his cottage.

It was a tough-looking little house with a front door and a window on either side of it. It was variously pictured in a wilderness of snow with bare birch poles scattered around, and in the summer with the leaves bright in the sunshine and the big blue lake throwing back the colour of the sky. There was an extreme clarity in the air that gave a curiously primitive look to the place, more than the sense of wilderness, as if the country there had hardly been touched by man; was ancient but still on the edge of creation. It was as if being there, you would feel the span of time between today and the origin of the world suddenly shortened.

'You feel it, don't you?' he asked me. 'It's almost a kind of fear. My great-grandfather found it too isolated up there – he left it and came down to Toronto, but it stayed in the family and I resurrected it.'

'Yes,' I said. 'I see what your painters are about.'

'You ought to go there, Anthony. Here's the key.' He threw it onto the couch beside me. 'Do you ski?'

'A little,' I said. 'Not for a while.'

'You want to get cross-country skis. The place is provisioned – tins and dried stuff, flour and so on – but the snow has come early up there and seems to be lying. You may need to ski-in about a mile, and back-pack whatever you carry from the car. Good exercise for you. You'll have to start the generator for power supply, and after that the water pump – it draws water from the lake. Boil it before you drink it.'

'White,' I said. 'Thanks. I'll go even if only for the odd week-end.'

'Use it any way you like,' he said.

'Will you use my apartment in London? It's no bigger than your cottage.'

It turned out that he would be spending his sabbatical at Cambridge; a *pied-à-terre* in London would be perfect. He told me to take the Volvo up to Little Duck Lake – it was a station-wagon, easy to load all the supplies and tackle I would want with me. 'And you're better with a heavy car, driving in snow,' he said. So we exchanged house keys and car keys and felt absurdly pleased with ourselves.

'For God's sake, Anthony,' he said. 'Respect the cold up there. Take the right clothes, the right boots. I'll make a quick list. I'll give you a map to show you how to get there.'

He furnished me with lists, maps and instructions about the water supply and I finished the afternoon in a state of pleasurable anticipation. As I was driven back to Gerrard Street in a taxi I thought a good deal about that cabin waiting for me at Little Duck Lake.

That evening I worked diligently, marking and cutting up the copies of the Oxford paperback edition of *Bleak House* that I had bought at Britnell's bookstore, until I had an exact replica of Bruce's originals. At ten o'clock I set out to find myself some dinner.

Downstairs a taxi was disgorging its passengers onto the sidewalk, so I asked the driver to take me to an Italian restaurant.

'Plain or fancy?' he asked. Plain, I told him.

Plain turned out to be a long low room with booths up each side. I ordered antipasto and pasta and a bottle of wine, and was tangling with the spaghetti when another man joined me. The place was pretty full and at first I thought nothing of it. I gave the man who had come to my table and was divesting himself of hat and coat a cursory glance and returned to my pasta and the book I had brought with me.

Then I looked again.

The coat was a long beaver fur with a military cut to it, the brown hat an old-fashioned homburg, but when they were off he was just a man in a business suit: he was also the man who had come out of the elevator in the lobby when I was on my way up to my apartment to find that it had been broken into.

He had a narrow face with a trim moustache and dark sombre eyes, and they were looking at me as much as I was looking at him. He slid along the seat to put himself opposite me, produced a wallet and took a card from it, and laid the card on the table.

The card said he was Mr Ivar Voster, and that he was an importer of fine wines, with an address in Toronto and another in Bordeaux. 'It is pronounced "Eevar",' he said. 'An Icelandic name. My mother was Icelandic.'

I closed the book I was reading, using his card to mark my place. 'Hallo!' I said, and filled my mouth with spaghetti, which left the talking up to him.

Vertical lines appeared above his nose and down his face. They gave him a stern and melancholy look.

'I have come to make my apologies,' he said, 'and to see if we cannot come to be on better terms.'

He used a curiously archaic style of speech, but I understood what he was saying well enough. It was what he meant that baffled me. My mouth was too full for words, so I revolved my fork in the air in an inquiring manner and raised my eyebrows.

He sighed, and the lines on his face became sterner and more melancholy. I wondered if he imported stern and melancholy wine, and if so where he found a market for it.

'An employee of mine entered your apartment,' he said.

I had swallowed. 'I thought so,' I said. 'Why did he do that?'

He flicked the edge of the card sticking out of the book. 'I supply restaurants with wine, Mr Moore.' He knew my name – but of course he knew it, if someone of his had been rummaging through my things. I went on eating. He nodded, as if he had read what was passing through my mind. 'One of my competitors is trying to cut me out. They are preparing a list of fine wines to match what I provide to these restaurants, at prices to undercut mine. I need that list. By an absurd mishap we mistook your apartment for that occupied by their representative.' He shrugged. 'You will think it dishonourable of me to attempt to steal from my competitors, but for my part I find it dishonourable of them to seek to steal my business. It is plagiarism, is it not, as if a rival were to copy one of your plays and sell it as his own?'

This was pretty close to home. 'Or as if you were to steal the notes I was working on?' I suggested.

All the time he had been telling me this tale about the wine he had been eyeing me in an unpleasantly thorough way, looking at my hair, my hands, my arms, my upper torso, and at ears, nose, chin, neck and every bit of me he could see as if he were taking me into his memory piecemeal so that he could assemble a complete picture of me afterwards. And this general reconnaissance was punctuated by sudden penetrating glances into my eyes calculated, it seemed to me, to catch me off guard and surprise me into betraying my reaction to what he was saying to me.

I thought I could put paid to that, at least: 'Why are you telling me this nonsense?' I asked him rudely. 'The working notes you stole from my apartment don't look in the least like a list of wine prices. And how did you know I was here, in this restaurant? Are you following me about Toronto, or what? Did that man Lehar follow me to Stratford on your account? Did you have Lehar keep me talking in the Chelsea Inn to give you time to burgle my apartment?' I took a glass of wine in two swallows. 'What's your interest in me, and who the hell do you think you are, Mr Ivar Voster, to clutter up my life with your unwelcome presence, and what makes you think I'm not going to call the police and get them to take you off my back?'

He showed me some tobacco stained teeth and some gold fillings. I was surprised that his mournful countenance could smile at all, and I could not think what I had said to make him smile. 'Oh, Mr Moore,' he said. 'The last thing you would do is to go to the police.'

'I called the police first thing after you raided my apartment, Voster,' I said.

The moustache closed down on the teeth, but then it lifted

again. 'Perhaps you did, but it is one thing to call the police for an affair like that, and another to encourage them to inquire into such . . . shall I say, such meetings as this?'

I poured the last of the wine into my glass and slid it and myself to the end of the booth next to the aisle. Voster raised an arm and twiddled a hand in the air above the partition, as if to summon a waiter. What came was little Lehar, carrying a package, and with him a man twice his size dressed like a chauffeur, even to gaiters and a peaked cap. Voster gestured and the package was put in front of me.

'I make restitution, Mr Moore,' Voster said. 'These are the papers that Martin inadvertently took from your apartment.'

'Then Martin', I said, looking a long way up at the chauffeur's cold green eyes, 'can keep them. I've already replaced them.'

I did not expect that this generous offer would make Martin step back and unblock my way to the exit, and he didn't expect it to either, but then a man and a girl came down the room and stopped at our table. The girl walked over his feet and said to me: 'I sit beside you, okay?' She did this by sitting on me while I was still moving to make room for her. She was a black-haired, black-eyed beauty in jeans and a black leather jacket and high-priced perfume, but it was not her beauty or her trampling all over his feet that made Martin move back, it was the man she came in with.

He was a man with black hair brushed back from a widow's peak and a hard dark Mediterranean face that gave a dark shave. He wore a black topcoat and a red silk scarf and could have been a successful banker or lawyer; he had that sense of acquired authority. But he had something more. There was a grim power in him which was no doubt masked most of the time by his decorous exterior, but it was moving in him now as he read the picture we made.

I saw the bleakness of it settle on his face. It was a shock to watch it happen to that perfectly groomed modern urban man, as if some old inheritance of the blood that ran in him, deep and undiluted, had risen like a pike to break the still surface of a pond.

So, Martin stepped back, and the newcomer nodded at me gravely and said: 'Hi, pardon the intrusion.' Then he looked at Voster and stood there, waiting.

Voster, who had been chewing his moustache, joined us at last out of a preoccupied silence. 'Mr Moore,' he said, 'this is Mr Tozzetti.' He sighed. 'And this is Miss Zangarini.'

Little Lehar, who had melted into the background at Tozzetti's onset, returned to the scene now that the amenities were being observed, and addressed himself to Miss Zangarini's voluptuous bosom. 'I'll sit beside you,' he told it, but the proud owner spoke up in its defence.

'No,' she said. 'No-no-no-no!' She flourished a lot of blood-red fingernails at his stomach until he moved it away.

Tozzetti sat down opposite her and said to me: 'How do you do, Mr Moore. We shan't need Mr Lehar or Mr Martin.'

I returned his greeting, and left the second part of his speech to the self-styled wine importer.

Voster sighed again, and merely hooded his eyes at his henchmen, at which signal they departed. 'Well,' Voster said when they had gone. 'What now?'

'We have to talk,' Tozzetti said agreeably.

Voster frowned. 'It is business?'

'Yeah, it's business.'

Miss Zangarini stopped eyeing me, looked across at Voster and spoke nastily in Italian.

Voster replied in the same language, but he had no fluency in it and had to struggle to find words to stem her increasing eloquence and growing temper. I have no Italian and could make nothing of it: I caught Tozzetti's eye, and saw him recognizing this fact. He let them wrangle for a little and then ended it.

'Gabriella,' he said gently. 'Shut up!'

She shut up, and then for some reason looked at me coyly and contrived, even in that confined space, to move a great deal of herself about in her own devastating version of a shrug.

'We cannot impose a business discussion on Mr Moore,' Tozzetti said. He stood up. 'Mr Moore, we apologize for intruding upon your evening.'

As Voster followed along out of the booth and Gabriella stood up too, there was one last phrase of Italian from him which had a peculiarly unpleasant inflection about it.

'Ha!' she said, and became voluble again. Despite knowing no Italian at all, I recognized a word I did not want to hear.

So did Voster. 'Quiet, you little fool!' he hissed in English, and even before he spoke had slapped her hard across the face to silence her. She yelped, put a hand to her cheek and glared at him, but she had taken his point.

All three of them stayed silent. I looked with most interest at Tozzetti, surprised that he had not reacted to Voster's assault on his young protégée – or whatever she was – but perhaps he thought she had it coming to her. There was a spark of life in his bleak eyes, a gleam of humour like a spot of shining coachwork on a dirty car. He stood there and waited for them to join him.

I watched them go, then picked up the package which was still on the table, and left. It had been an odd and irritating encounter from the start, from the moment when Voster sat down, but with the arrival of Tozzetti it had become positively disturbing, and the girl's final outburst had set alarm bells ringing in my head.

In the taxi back to my temporary home my mind was racing, and when I got there I sank back into a chair with a stiff whisky and tried to make sense of it all, but no sense came. I left the day to bury its dead, and turned in.

Once in bed, the thought of that hideaway of White Denver's, to which I had the key, came to me like a lifeline. I fell asleep to dream of an isolated cabin beside a lake.

Chapter 12

The telephone rang. I knew there was no phone in the cabin, so I laughed in my sleep. Then I woke up. The phone was still ringing. I picked it up.

'Anthony,' a voice said, 'do not, repeat not, speak my name. Remember me? We once talked about rook pie; you said you didn't care for the idea? I'll give you five minutes to wake up then I'll call you again. When I do, don't speak my name, just listen. You could start getting dressed.' The phone clicked and hummed. He had hung up.

His timing was ominous, in view of the ideas that had been worrying me before I fell asleep, but the way people were breaking into my private life these days, he was right on cue. I had made myself a cup of instant coffee and was back in bed when the phone rang the second time.

'Are you awake?'

'No.'

'Leave your apartment in fifteen minutes, walk south on Yonge to King Street, turn east on King and keep walking. Wrap up well, it's a good few blocks and it's cold out here. South on Yonge, east on King.' Click. Hum.

I looked at my watch. Four o'clock in the morning, just the time for a walk on the wild side. I was glad I was pre-conditioned to resist the invitation. Every time I read the report of a spy-trial I was irritated by the demented secrecy spies went in for and the way this obsession led them to call attention to themselves. They met in public parks, used mail-drops in graveyards, and told each other to walk south on Yonge and east on King in the middle of the night: not a chance! I twiddled my toes and watched them moving snugly under the covers.

Ten minutes later I was cold and cross and walking briskly down the Sohoesque section of Yonge Street. The lights were going out, the strip-joints had closed and the girls had retired to do their homework of one kind or another. The party was over and as often happens with a long, hot party, the end of this one was surreal and depressing. A few cars went by, curb-crawling. One or two individuals sat desolate on the sidewalk, here and there a couple wandered by, and there were vignettes for the artist: a man disguised as Zorro stood like a statue gazing proudly over the desert, an old woman and a pretty girl counted their money, and a happy group of boys and girls squatted round a miniature bonfire which they were feeding carefully with cigarette packs, chequebooks, and anything that came to hand. I liked the bonfire group and stopped to watch them for a moment. I remembered that kind of fatuous dedication to an absurd object from the days of my wasted youth.

A car drew up beside me and a door opened. 'Hop in, Anthony,' said Harry Seddall.

As I sat down beside him one of the girls called to us, 'Hey, you guys got any paper?'

Seddall handed me a newspaper from the back of the car and I passed it on. Cries of 'Gee, thanks,' 'Great,' and 'Now go easy with it,' sent us on our way.

'What happened to King Street?' I said. 'I wasn't halfway there.'

'Disinformation,' he said, 'in case your room's bugged. I doubt if it is.'

'Even if it is bugged, would anyone just go to King Street and wait for me to turn up?'

'Some would, some wouldn't. No harm in shortening the odds. I really wanted to see if you're being followed.'

'Am I?'

'Not this morning. You're clean, Anthony, and so am I up to now.'

'All right then,' I said. 'What's going on? Where are we going? Are we going to see Heneage?'

'Ah!' he said obscurely. 'Not unless we're very unlucky.'

I gave myself a cigarette and studied him. He was the same figure who had driven me home from St James's that night in London. Slouched in his seat, two fingers on the wheel, sloppily dressed but with a fur hat set rakishly on his head. He was smiling a little. I thought he liked doing this, driving at night in a sleeping city.

'The hat's new,' I said.

'Yeah. I'm with a trade delegation. We buy ourselves presents, you know, when we go conferencing. Tell me some things.'

'I'll tell you one thing,' I said bluntly. 'I'm full of mistrust.'

He nodded quite deeply, once: an acknowledgment. 'Sure you are, but tell me why?'

'You set me up to draw these Vosters and Lehars into the open. That stuff about me in the papers here, you arranged that – pictures and all.'

'Nope. Someone saw to it, not me.'

'What difference does that make – it was someone of yours, in your set-up.'

'It makes a big difference to *me*,' he said, with a sarcastic thrust in his voice. 'I knew nothing about it.'

I said nothing. I was too tired to work out what it might mean, even if he was telling the truth. Instinct told me he was, but reason gave me nothing to support it. We went slowly through the empty streets among the dark skyscrapers of the business world.

'I could tell you a thing,' he said at last, 'but then you'd be in some of the same trouble I'm in.'

He waited. 'Tell me this thing,' I said.

'I'm not here officially.' The lurking smile stretched into a reckless grin, as if he were taking a corner too fast on purpose. 'No one knows I'm here, except you. At the Office, they think I'm in Italy.'

'Then why are you here?' I heard a good strong note of

disapproval in my voice, as if I were Authority, and we were all getting tired of Seddall's irresponsible ways.

He flashed a mocking glance at me. 'I'm showing initiative in the field. I'm out of touch with base. I'm bringing maximum destruction to the enemy.'

'Heneage doesn't know you're here? Not even Heneage?'

'Nope.'

I thought about this. 'Harry,' I said. 'That doesn't work with me. How could you get yourself onto a trade delegation with none of your people knowing about it?'

'Hah!' he said, and thumped the heel of his hand on the steering-wheel with fierce pleasure. 'It's a *German* trade delegation,' he said.

'How come?'

'Friends in Bonn.'

That meant, presumably, that West German Intelligence had helped him to get a place on the delegation. His shorthand was hard to follow. 'So who are you working for?'

He put his foot down and I saw we were running onto the Don Valley parkway that goes north out of Toronto. '*Fiat justitia, ruat coelum,*' he said.

'Put it in English, for God's sake! Spell it out, Harry.'

'A loose translation would be "May God defend the right."' He slid me a quick embarrassed look. 'Right with a small "r" – I'm defending the right, Anthony.'

I lit another cigarette. 'All by yourself,' I said. 'Against orders with no backup. I can see it in lights: "Seddall Runs Amok." Marvellous! Why? Just for fun?'

'No,' he said in a flat voice. 'Not for fun. Not for fun at all.'

We fell silent after that, until at length he pulled off the highway to find a service area. There were only one or two cars there besides ours, and once inside the restaurant we chose a table in a corner with no one else near. Seddall ordered himself a hamburger. I settled for a coffee.

'Now you tell me,' he said. 'just what's happened with you since you got here.'

So I did. I was still not sure of him, but what harm could it do? I told him everything, from my arrival at the airport where Bruce Baldwin showed me the story about myself in the *Globe and Mail*, to last night's bizarre gathering. The only fact I left out was my meeting with White Denver. Maybe Seddall knew about that already – I could not tell how close he had been keeping to me – but at least he would not know that White had offered me a cottage in the wilds. It seemed to me I might be glad of a bolt-hole.

When I reached the point in my story where Voster had smacked Gabriella Zangarini, I had another impulse to keep something to myself, but I had gone too far and he spotted my hesitation.

'Come on, Anthony! What did she say, that Voster wanted her silenced?'

'I don't understand Italian.'

He studied me, humorous and sceptical and bored. He fished a pack of Gauloises out of a pocket and offered me one. He bent over the table and shook his head slowly, sat up again and sighed. We smoked.

'She said "Monteith",' I told him.

He leaned far back, tilting his chair till I thought it would fall over backwards, leaving me stuck with the check. He came forward again. 'Did she, by God?' he said quietly.

The waitress came and gave us more coffee. We smoked some more. He thought his thoughts, and I thought mine. I thought about the Monteith family; father, mother and daughter, who had disappeared almost a week ago.

'Back at the ranch,' I said, 'back in London, you have a problem?'

Seddall said, 'Yeah,' and stared out at the night through the window. 'Someone's gone wrong.'

'Who?'

Even Harry Seddall was surprised by this directness. He peered at me over the top of imaginary spectacles, like a schoolmaster who has been asked one of those questions that shows you have neglected your work.

He said, 'Excuse me,' and went away to the washroom. Out on the highway headlights went by. Two of them led a car into the service area and its occupants slammed doors, came into the restaurant and sat at a table near us. They were men fresh off the night-shift, big and hearty and making an early start to a hunting week-end; bound for the woods to kill deer.

Seddall came back and put dollars on the table.

We drove back into Toronto. The streets were no longer empty.

'My plan for today,' I said suddenly, 'was to have breakfast while I thought out what to say to the police – '

'The police!'

' – and after breakfast to go and tell them about Voster and company, about their Italian friends, and about Monteith's name cropping up.' I succumbed to a huge yawn. 'And then to try and get on with my work.'

'Your work?'

'Yes,' I said with surprise, 'my work. What's so funny about that?'

'Bugger your work!' Seddall said. 'You think about your work too much.'

'How would you know? Who says so?'

'Your profile says so, that's who. The purser on that boat had ideas about it too.'

'Well, he was wrong about his ideas, wasn't he? He thought I was imagining things.'

'Wrong about that. Not wrong about the way you go at it. Living alone, working away by yourself. No ties, no close friends, little social life. Here a woman and there a woman. Yeah, you think about your work too much.'

I listened to this. It was an arid description of my life. 'You're different?'

A pause. 'My work's different,' he said.

'Thank God for it, too!'

'Forget all that,' Seddall said. 'This business about the police –

no bloody way are you going to the police.'

'I'll decide that, but why not?'

'Don't be cross, Anthony. Because it will get the Monteiths dead, that's why not. This mob you've been mixing with, half of them are stupid and the other half are trigger-happy.'

'What about the RCMP – they're federal, aren't they?'

'The Mounties? Not bloody likely to that too. The Mounties run security over here, I don't want them peering into our little domestic problem. We don't want to wash our dirty linen in public, do we, Anthony? Sit back and think of England, old man, and let's leave it to Seddall.'

'I see,' I said sarcastically. 'I'm not only to trust you, I'm to expect you to sort this whole thing out on your own, with a little amateur help from me.'

'As to the last, sure – why not? And you know perfectly well you can trust me, as you put it.'

'Harry, how in hell can I know that?'

'Christ! Can't you tell?'

'I don't know, Harry. I just damn well don't know!'

We travelled in silence for a bit. There was light in the sky and I saw cloud low and heavy overhead. It looked like snow.

Seddall spoke again. 'Well, Anthony, give it a try. I'll be letting you off soon. Think it over, and see if you can't end up believing that Harry Seddall may have a rough exterior, but his heart is pure.'

I laughed at this. 'I'll say one thing for you, Harry – you're not over-sophisticated in your approach.' Exasperation came out of me in a kind of sigh and made a whistling noise through my teeth. 'I'm up to my ears in shady characters. I don't have the faintest idea why or what it's all about. I'm right out of my depth. I don't want to know about it.'

He stopped the car and gave me one of those lazy smiles, loose-lipped and mocking. 'I dunno,' he said. 'Up to your ears isn't out of your depth, is it? We'll see. I'll call you. Time to go, Anthony. You'll find Gerrard two blocks down.'

I put my hand on the door handle, and questions came out of

me all at once. 'Is this the financial deal you were talking about in London? How did you know Canada came into it? They *are* the same crowd that killed . . . ?'

He cut across me. 'Not now. I'll tell you next time. Let's not hang about.'

I opened the door reluctantly and stepped onto the sidewalk. He drove off, turning the first corner he came to. As I walked along Gerrard Street to the apartment, snow fell out of the clouds in big, big flakes. It had come early to Toronto too.

The days grow short when you reach November, and I woke to a later afternoon giving way to dusk. I was on my third cup of coffee, still undecided whether to start the evening with breakfast or go for an early dinner, when Bruce Baldwin turned up. I had quite forgotten he was coming and was oddly embarrassed that he should find me just out of bed, bleary-eyed and still half awake: I had a confused sense of guilt about being involved with Vosters, Tozzettis and Harry Seddall to the detriment of the Dickens adaptation, until I remembered how much I had done on it in the course of the week.

Bruce, however, was preoccupied with a problem of his own. He took off his anorak and I dumped it in the bedroom. 'This is a flying visit,' he said when I came back. 'I've got to go out to north Toronto before we can talk. How about dinner? Say two hours – seven o'clock?'

'Dinner suits me – suits me very well, in fact.'

'I want to snare an actor. Would you mind if he joined us?'

'Not in the least. I talk to actors.'

He showed relief. 'That helps – it means I don't have to feel I should be in two places at once, and I won't keep you waiting. Can I call a cab? I left the car for Sandy and came up by train.'

'There's no need,' I said. 'I've hired a car. Take it. Sit down and have a cup of coffee. You'd have to wait five minutes for a taxi anyway.'

He smiled and fell into a chair 'You're right. I want to slow

113

down, I'm behaving like a theatre director, I guess.' He took the coffee. 'Sandy sends her love.'

He had a lot of tension in him and he knew it showed. 'You know theatre, Anthony. It can be long on temperament and short on temper. We're in the thick of it again, setting up next season.'

'I know theatre all right. I like making plays for it. I wouldn't work in it. How are you both?'

'Good, thank you. Sandy's doing wonders in the kitchen – with her medieval banking.' He laughed. 'She's cooking well too, every now and then. How is it with you?'

'Better than I'd hoped, I think. Done a good deal this week.'

He glanced at the table beside him. 'You got yourself two sets of notes? Taking precautions, hey?'

'Not exactly,' I said. 'The men who stole them brought them back.' He raised his eyebrows. 'It's a strange story, Bruce, I'll tell you over dinner.' I thought, as I said it, that I would have to prepare a tailored version that would accord with Harry Seddall's notions of security.

He finished his coffee and went into the bedroom for his anorak. I gave him the car keys and pointed out the Renault to him, in the parking lot across the street. 'That's terrific, Anthony,' he said. 'Thanks a lot. See you later.'

I went back to the window. The snow had stopped but the city was transformed; the streets white, some of the cars on the lot with thick snow on their roofs, snow on the window ledge. I had disliked seeing the strain on Bruce; I thought it was not like him. I wondered if it was really the pressures of the theatre or if it was something between him and Sandy. I watched him cross the road, sweep the snow off the rear window and the windscreen and stand back to brush the snow off his gloves.

Then he jumped at the Renault and threw his arms on the roof, on the snow there. A big American car drove past on its way out of the parking lot. His arms slid snow off the roof and he knelt on the ground as if he was searching for the car keys. He rolled on to his side and lay still.

Two people came up and bent over him: a man and a woman. They stood up slowly and stepped apart, back from Bruce and from each other. They looked about them. The women pointed, and the man ran. He ran to a phone booth. The woman waited, lit dimly by the light reaching into the parking lot from the street lamps.

I stood at the window and watched. I could not move.

I had not remarked on it when Bruce picked up my anorak, the anorak he had lent me, the blue anorak he had lent me instead of the red one he came in, and had put it on to go down to my car in the Toronto dusk.

It should have been me lying there on the snow.

Chapter 13

It was a good modern office painted in magnolia white, with clean-cut furniture, a coffee machine and bright red filing cabinets.

Now, with the recording session of question and answer over, at least for the time being, I was surprised how easy it had been to lie to them. I had simply sat there looking troubled and upset – because troubled and upset was what I was – smoked endless cigarettes, chewed my fingernails, scratched my head, shifted my position uneasily, fumbled answers and corrected myself. And although my conscience was restless and I had been forced to test every answer against the dilemma I was in, I had felt remarkably little guilt about what I was hiding from them.

What I was hiding, of course, was Seddall, Heneage and the whole recent history of violent death I had been caught up in that had culminated in my heedless dash across the traffic of Gerrard Street to the little group in the car park gathered round the body of Bruce Baldwin. I had found him lying face up and peaceful. There was no wound that I could see, just a few patches of blood on the snow.

I knew Seddall would have wanted me to lie to the police, but I was not so sure it was what I wanted. I did not even know why I was doing it. I owed, and felt, less loyalty to Harry Seddall than to Bruce Baldwin, who had been killed in mistake for me. I was sick and bewildered, trying to come to terms with the fact that someone who wanted me dead had shot Bruce instead: and I knew that not knowing this would make it harder for the police to find his killer.

At the back of my mind was the hope that soon my dilemma would be resolved, and that at any moment – now that an innocent, uninvolved human being had been killed – Seddall would walk in the door waving official credentials and start making discreet explanations.

There was more than one reason I hoped he would do that: for also at the back of my mind was the spectre of Seddall as the killer, a spectre which would vanish like a ghost with the coming of day if he turned up now.

But Seddall did not walk through the door.

'Mr Moore,' the inspector said. His name was Terry, and I realized that Inspector Terry was staring at me with bad temper in his narrow face. All he said though, was: 'Are you with us again, Mr Moore?' It was the harshest thing he had said to me, in the two hours I had been sitting there, cheating him.

'Yes,' I said, 'I'm with you again.'

'Not entirely,' he said ambiguously. 'Not entirely, I'm afraid. I have no more questions for you, but I'd like you to hang around for a half-hour or so. Gary, why don't you type that up, and we'll have Mr Moore sign it for us.' The constable who had taken down what I said in shorthand, despite the tape recorder working away on the desk beside him, went away. That left the inspector, Staff Sergeant Bratchpiece, Sergeant Ableman, and me.

Inspector Terry walked round the room, poured fresh coffee into our cups, emptied ashtrays into a wastebasket, and sat down again. He put both feet up on his desk and an unlit Marlboro in his mouth and looked at the ceiling. He waited until the staff sergeant had stirred the sweetener in his coffee and then canted his head towards him.

'Bratch,' he said round his cigarette, 'what you thinking?'

The sergeant's red face, red moustache, red hair and round blue eyes looked at me as if I was a used car he was about to insult so that he could get a better price on the one across the lot he really meant to buy.

'I think it goes to 1300,' he said. 'I think you should give it to us.'

'Yeah,' Terry said, and lit the cigarette with his real, old-fashioned desk lighter. 'So do I. Make the call, will you?'

The staff sergeant activated his phone and waited.

'What happened in 1300?' I asked Inspector Terry.

Humour visited his eyes, briefly, but he let it leave without introducing me to it. I was not a man he cared to share laughs with.

'The Homicide Squad,' he said to his feet, 'is at 1300 Yonge Street.'

'You're not Homicide?'

'We ask the questions, Mr Moore,' he said, and he meant it too. He had been politeness itself while he was questioning me. Now he just left me, drew on the cigarette, took coffee, and became unaware of the corner of his office that had me in it.

'Yeah,' the staff sergeant said into the phone, 'this is Bratchpiece. I'm at 52 Division. Inspector Terry wants us to take the shooting on Gerrard. Yeah, it's all going by the book. The body's at Grenville. Yeah – pictures, measurements, the lot. That's right: here now!' The round blue eyes made sure I was still there. 'Yeah, I'd say so, promising but complex. You'll find out. Yup, we'll be over; no, not long.' He put down the phone. 'I guess we'll eat,' he said.

'You know the way,' Terry said, and Bratchpiece and Ableman left us alone.

Terry said: 'The break-in at your apartment – do you connect it up with Mr Baldwin being killed?'

'No,' I said, too forcibly to convince either him or myself. I desperately wanted the two crimes to belong in separate worlds. I wanted Bruce's murder to be no part of the entangling web I had sensed gathering round me.

'No,' I said again, without belief.

A bleak silence lay between us.

I rose and went over to the window, and looked out at the street. People down there moved fast in the cold night. I was alone in the room, isolated by the inspector's dislike, friendless in limbo and thinking of death. I saw myself in the glass, out there

118

in the cold watching me. The sight jolted me from self-absorption.

'Godammit!' I said and turned round. 'What about Mrs Baldwin?'

'She's on her way, Mr Moore. Due any minute, I guess.'

'Is a friend driving her?'

He took his feet off the desk and looked at me as if I were beginning to show recognizable human features. 'No. She wanted to drive herself, but that was unwise, we thought, in the circumstances. We suggested the weather was bad – there could be whiteout on the highway with this wind – and we arranged a ride for her with the OPP, that's the Ontario Provincial Police. She said she'd rather that than a friend. She didn't want to talk to people she knew. They'll bring her here.'

His eyes on me were alert with new interest, and I felt myself frowning to repudiate the connection between us. Something had begun to happen in me when I looked out at the empty night. I felt myself poised, on edge, as if I were going into the first day's rehearsal of a new play of mine: but this was not theatre. This was real life in an alien land and with the new winter coming in. I thought it was strange that I would add that, about the winter coming in.

'They killed him in the snow,' I said sternly, and began to walk up and down the office.

'Take it easy,' the inspector said. 'Mrs Baldwin will be coming in here soon. This is a bad night for her. We want to make it as easy on her as we can.'

I sat down for a few minutes and then stood up again. 'Where will she spend the night?' I asked him.

'Mr Moore,' he said. 'We have a hotel room on standby, if that's what she wants, and if she wants to go back to Stratford, the OPP boys will take her home again. We have a doctor waiting, in case she needs medical help. Now you take it easy, or I'll have to ask you to leave.'

That brought me up short. 'You mean you're not holding me here?'

'You're not in custody, Mr Moore. You're an eye-witness, a friend of the dead man, the last to speak to him in his life, so far as we know, and he was killed with the key of your rented car in his hand. So we asked you to help us, that's all: and you have helped us, haven't you?'

He went over to the coffee maker and took the heatproof jug out of the room with him, leaving the door open. I heard a tap running, and an exchange of words. When he came back he ladled coffee into a paper filter and set the machine up again. 'The OPP car's on University Avenue,' he spoke with his back to me. 'They'll be here in five minutes.'

It was too late to say it now, but somehow he had dragged it out of me. 'I think he was shot in mistake for me,' I said.

You could have heard a pin land on the carpet.

Still with his back to me he watched the first drops of coffee fall into the jug. 'It seems reasonable,' he said. 'You're the guy with the offbeat social circle. How would they make a mistake like that?' He turned round and came over, standing that six inches too close that makes a threat of it. He offered me a Marlboro, I took it and he lit it, and lit his own. We used small movements in the little space between us, blew the smoke from the corners of our mouths, held the burning ash away from each other's clothes. I told him about the anoraks, the red and the blue.

'So they marked you for the guy who had rented that car, and wore a blue anorak. So they'd been keeping tabs on you, tailing you even. Why, Mr Moore?'

I drew on the cigarette and blew smoke sideways; but some of it went in my eye. 'I don't know,' I said.

'Sure,' he said. 'That fits with what you've said all along. You don't know where these guys all came from, or why they came over all interested in you. They just started coming out of the woodwork and multiplying.' There was no irony in the voice, only in the words. He brushed ash off my coat sleeve and moved away, to settle on the end of his desk.

'I guess maybe you're in danger, Mr Moore. Maybe you're still a target. We'll have to think about that.'

Bratchpiece and Ableman came in at the open door. 'Hi!' he said to them. 'You heard that little bit extra Mr Moore gave us?'

'I heard,' Bratchpiece said. 'Ableman was getting the dutchies.'

Terry was leaving us. I said: 'What about Mrs Baldwin?'

'I'll look after Mrs Baldwin,' he said, and went out.

So I had dinner with the Homicide team: dutchies and coffee – dutchies being pastries like danish, but different. Each of us paid his share, but the entertainment was free; while we ate we listened to the recorder playing back my answers to Terry's questions.

When Ableman first switched it on I thought the food would stick in my throat, hearing my voice describe Bruce Baldwin's murder and then doling out to them half the truth of what I knew. But then I became fascinated, listening to his patient inquisition, to the absence of comment in his voice as I failed to provide an explanation of a link between me and Voster, and Voster's Italian friends. I thought, too, that my side of it came over quite well. The reticence was there, something was missing, but I did not hear in my voice the note of a man lying.

When the tape had finished speaking Ableman turned it off. 'Well, well,' he said to Bratchpiece. 'There's a lot of experience in that interview.' He gathered the remains of our meal onto a tray and put it outside in the corridor.

Bratchpiece opened a briefcase and drew out a cardboard file, and from the file a sheet of paper. 'This is a telex from London,' he said to me. 'Moore, Anthony J. Nothing known against. Criminal record stroke associates negative repeat negative. No previous inquiries Moore, A. J. any source. Writer, theatre and TV. Army service 3 years BAOR, captain, Intelligence Corps.'

That word again: Intelligence. When policemen heard it, little bells rang in their heads. Bratchpiece was looking at me just as Kenna had looked at me in London. He seemed to think I should say something.

'That sounds right,' I said.

'You were in Intelligence,' he said.

I frowned a well judged frown, to show that I could not see any relevant implication in the question. 'Yes,' I said.

'Would you mind telling me what kind of Intelligence?'

'Oh!' I said, seeing the light. 'Army Intelligence, nothing very secret. Keeping records of Warsaw Pact communications systems, that sort of thing.'

'Nothing – investigative?'

'No cloak-and-dagger stuff, if that's what you mean?'

'It's one thing. Could be others, there was quite a black market in Germany at one time, I recall.'

'It came my way sometimes, but mostly that's police work. I was seconded to Special Investigations Branch for a time.' He let the silence grow, and I let myself break it. I was tired, and out of practice. 'So you could say I was on your side of the fence,' I said.

I smiled, and he smiled back, letting Ableman take it. Ableman was a mildly plump man with a hooked nose, a shaggy black moustache, shaggy black hair, and a lazy look. 'It doesn't take long,' Ableman said, 'to move a fence.'

'I don't know, Charlie,' Bratchpiece said. 'You ever tried digging up a fence post? Easy enough to jump over, though.'

They looked at me pleasantly, relaxed and good-humoured, as if they were assessing my chances as a hurdler.

I lit a cigarette, sipped coffee, and grew wary. It had been a long time since I sat where they sat, but the reflexes were beginning to work again. I tried for a change of pace 'I'm in theatre,' I said. 'I'm not in espionage, and I'm not in crime.'

'You know that, Mr Moore,' Bratchpiece said earnestly, 'and we know that.' He turned to Ableman. 'But do you know what puzzles me, Charlie?'

'What's that, Bratch?'

'They musta got our telex on Mr Moore here, over in London, England about seven p.m. our time, which is midnight over there. Now if we got a telex about a Canadian playwright at midnight we could come up with everything like they sent us about Mr Moore, except for one thing.'

'Well, share it with us, smart-ass!'

'Come on, Charlie! Have you ever tried to get a man's armed service record at midnight on Saturday? That's civil service stuff. You'd wait till Monday.'

I had thought this double act was being staged, but now I saw that Ableman was, if anything, more puzzled than I was.

Bratchpiece smiled at the two of us and shook his head. 'Okay, you guys, what puzzles me is this. They get our query in the middle of the night and shoot the answer back inside the hour. So-o,' he said slowly, 'that little fact about Mr Moore being in Army Intelligence must have been sitting in their computer already. So someone over there in New Scotland Yard has already been interested enough in Mr Moore's service record to look out that one little fact.'

I cursed Heneage, Seddall and Kenna for running an inefficient combined operation. Then I saw no reason on God's earth for them to foresee that I would be investigated by the Toronto Homicide Squad.

Or that the squad would include a man like Bratchpiece. This was too sharp an instinct and too quick a mind on the other side of the desk, for me to play against. He was big, broad, comfortably relaxed, with a tanned outdoorman's face. It made a good disguise.

I found myself looking full into his eyes, and saw them speculating. 'What are you thinking, Mr Moore?'

'I don't know what to think,' I said. 'I know nothing about police records.'

'Well, you sure used to,' he said, 'and you can take it from me, we policemen don't hoard information for no purpose. Someone in the Metropolitan Police in London has needed to know about you. Can you account for that?'

'No. I can't account for it. I expect they can.'

'Oh, we'll ask them, don't worry about that.' He got up and gave us fresh coffee, and stayed on his feet. 'And we'll find the man who killed your friend, or the men, won't we, Charlie?'

'Why not,' Ableman said. 'We got enough leads to paper the walls.'

123

'Right,' Bratchpiece said. 'And we have an 87.7 per cent clearance rate on homicides in this city. You won't leave the country yet, Mr Moore.' He was telling me, not asking. 'And I want you to stay in Toronto, or talk to me or Sergeant Ableman personally if you think of leaving town. Have you got a card to give him, Charlie? Ring that number or call at 1300 Yonge Street if you think of anything you've forgotten to tell us. If they come at you again, let us know. We've got a security problem there, Charlie. We'll have to talk to the division about that.'

'They're not going to be able to bodyguard him,' Ableman said.

'We'll talk about it, anyway.' Then he picked up the phone, dialled, and said: 'We're ready now.'

The two Homicide men stopped smiling and composed their faces, so that I almost knew what was going to happen. But not quite.

Sandy walked into the room, her face taut with unshed tears. When she saw me she stopped. just inside the door.

'Oh, well,' she said. She looked down at the haircord carpet and shook her head. She looked up again and came towards me. 'It's because of you,' she said. 'He's dead because of you.'

'Yes,' I said.

'Well, Anthony,' she said, and her voice was soft and sad, 'damn you for that.'

Then she hit me hard across the face.

Chapter 14

———◆———

I tried twice to telephone Sandy in the next five days, and each time was answered by a young, courteous and incisive male voice which turned out to belong to her brother. On the first call he asked me to hold, and then came back to tell me she was not well enough to come to the phone; by the time I made the second call, two days later, he was briefed and ready. 'I don't know what it's about, Mr Moore, but my sister asks me to say she doesn't want to hear from you.'

'Yes, I can understand that,' I said. 'Thank you.'

There was a slight pause and then he said: 'Okay, Mr Moore.'

On the fifth day I went to Bruce Baldwin's funeral. I owed it to Bruce to go, and I owed it to Sandy, on the face of her brother's message to me, to keep out of the way. The night before, I was still debating this problem with myself but in the end I decided that it could be managed, and in the morning – the police had impounded the rented car – I took a taxi to North York where the service was to be held at – I presumed – the Baldwin family church.

The notice in the papers had said eleven o'clock, so I arrived half an hour early and from a café across the street watched the cars drive up. Sandy, and what I took to be members of the two families, arrived promptly five minutes before the hour. She was not bowed under a veil or wearing black, but erect, wrapped in a coat of deep burgundy and with her hair uncovered. She climbed the steps a little ahead, a little apart, from her group and walked into the church. It was a big turn-out – 'a good house', Bruce would have said – and it was another fifteen minutes before the last late-comer went in.

I left the café and crossed the street. There was a path running down the side of the church to the next road and I walked up and down there in the bright wintry sunlight, in the crisp windless air, making my own personal rite for the man I had known so briefly but come to like and respect so well. It was a gaunt granite building very much like a Scottish Border church, and as I heard the minister's voice rise and fall in eulogy and prayer and saw that the dates on gravestones by the path in the filled churchyard went back little more than a hundred years, I had a strange feeling of guilt that in coming to this young country, made and still being made by people who had come here to carve out new life for themselves, I had brought in my wake the worst of Old Europe, some inherited evil compound of centuries of intrigue.

I abandoned this gloomy retrospection and came down to earth. I had been so preoccupied when I was interviewed by Inspector Terry and his Homicide colleagues, with keeping Seddall out of the picture, that I had forgotten that as well as keeping them in the dark about a vital aspect of Bruce's murder, I was perhaps concealing information about a kidnapping. There had been no more stories about the disappearance of the family Monteith, and I did not know if they had been kidnapped or not, but I had not mentioned to the police that Gabriella Zangarini had brought out the name Monteith and been silenced by the slap in the face from Voster.

Seddall I had tried to trace and failed, calling round the downtown hotels until the Sheraton told me there had been a West German trade delegation staying there, but it had left. Of the Voster stable I had seen neither hide nor hair. The police had left me to myself.

'You weren't in the church, Mr Moore?'

My eyes had been unfocused, staring at nothing. They focused now on Inspector Terry.

The funeral crowd were walking off down the sidewalk and getting into cars. I started up the path to the back of the church and he came with me. 'Why are you here?' I asked him. 'I thought you handed the case over to Homicide.'

'He was killed in my division. We don't have that many killed in the division, or in Toronto for that matter. Not murdered.'

That told me nothing. People came up the path behind us and we stood at the end of the church, I with my back to them and he watching them pass. 'She won't come out this way,' he said.

It had grown chilly. A little wind had begun to blow and dropped the temperature about five degrees; what they called the perceived temperature. Even to scientists, life can be a subjective experience. I pulled up the collar of my overcoat.

'They've had no more questions for me,' I said. It sounded cross.

'Are you feeling neglected?' he said. 'Don't tell Homicide. Sometimes men who kill feel neglected, after the excitement's over.'

I looked into his thin face, but he was still watching the path behind me. He was here on business, I thought. 'Homicide have enough ideas about me already,' I said. 'Right?'

'Ah, don't let that lean on you. An investigation like this is full of ideas, at the beginning.' His eyes touched mine for a moment. 'It's like trying to think up a new thought, one of these tricky cases. Full of uncertainties you try to get the taste of before you let them even sit on the tip of your mind's tongue, in case they're irrelevant.'

'What did you read at your university?' I said. 'Zen?'

He grinned suddenly, not too like a weasel at all. 'Not only Zen. Mostly politics and history.'

'Dear God,' I said. 'I thought crime detection was all forensic science and computers these days.'

'You forgot to mention polygraphs,' he said.

'Polygraphs? Oh, lie detectors.'

He was looking at me now, and I was looking at him. 'I think that's the last of them,' he said, still looking at me looking at him. 'Come on, I'll give you a ride back to town.'

We walked down the side of the church. 'You knew I came in a cab?' I said.

'Sure,' he said. 'I might have guessed, since we're holding your rental car, and that'll make it hard for you to rent another. But sure, I knew.'

'Do you have me followed?'

'You get seen, at least. I don't say all the time.'

'Feels unpleasant,' I said.

'Don't let it, Mr Moore. Think that maybe we're protecting you – some of the time.'

No one was left now at the front of the church. Terry lifted an arm and a car across the street made a U-turn and came down the curb towards us. Then it braked suddenly, as a dark green Lincoln backed up towards it. 'Look who's here,' the inspector said.

The back door of the Lincoln opened and out came a lot of expensive broadcloth and a familiar Italian face. Mr Tozzetti said: 'I thought I might find you here.'

'Both of us?' the inspector asked.

'I meant Mr Moore, Inspector, but it's a pleasure to see you too.'

I was at a loss. My instinct was to accuse him outright of killing Bruce, but some instinct told me it would be mistimed. My confusion did not last long. We had a distraction.

The police driver came up and said: 'That's a hell of a way to back up. I nearly ran into you.'

'Then we're about even,' Tozzetti said cheerfully. 'An illegal U-turn is naturally unpredictable to other road users. I came to invite you to luncheon,' he said to me. He actually said luncheon. Nobody was talking the normal language of cops and racketeers this morning.

'Thanks,' I said roughly. 'Inspector Terry is giving me a ride downtown.'

'Well, we wouldn't want to stand up the Metro Police,' Tozzetti said. And waited.

'Why don't you go with Mr Tozzetti,' Inspector Terry said. 'I'll be lunching at my desk today.'

So I went with Mr Tozzetti.

It was a car for crossing continents in all weathers. It was air-conditioned as well as heated, and the smoke from his panatella and my cigarette vanished as soon as it was formed.

'You're on good terms with Inspector Terry,' I said accusingly. I said it like that because I was confused, and I had to blame somebody for that. I was confused because I had cast Tozzetti in a leading role of the conspiracy to murder Bruce – or rather to murder me; but I could not quite suppose that Terry had sent me off to be fed a poisoned lunch.

'I hear distaste,' Tozzetti said. 'You are an innocent, Mr Moore. I had nothing to do with killing your friend, and Mr Terry knows me too well to suppose anything of the sort.'

'Who are you, Mr Tozzetti?'

'You allow yourself great licence, Mr Moore. The tone of your question is not quite polite. To you I am Italian, not Canadian. Probably you think I am a member of some criminal group; a gangster like in the movies; a capo da Mafia, maybe. Just because we met in the company of some unsavoury characters, you cast me in such a role. In the theatre you call it typecasting.' He used some of his panatella and let the smoke out slowly. 'I am right, eh?'

'How else would it look to me?' I asked him.

'Okay,' he said. 'How would you look to me? I first see you dining happily with those same doubtful characters, but I do not assume you to be a criminal. In England you say a man is innocent until he is proved . . .' He waved his cigar in a slow circle, as if he was at a loss to finish the phrase.

'Guilty,' I said. 'Innocent until proved guilty.'

Tozzetti nodded thoughtfully, as if absorbing the idiom into his vocabulary. He pressed a switch on his armrest and said: 'Back to Rosedale.'

The driver said: 'Yessir.'

'Put it another way,' Tozzetti said. 'You might say a man was innocent until proved adult.'

The Lincoln picked up speed and at the next intersection we left the lunch-hour traffic, and the sidewalks crowded with office workers making for their favourite eating-places. As we drove across town the roads grew quieter and the houses bigger until we entered a street of sizeable mansions each with its acre or two of garden, and the car slowed down.

Tozzetti extinguished his panatella. 'Equally,' he said, 'you could say a man was innocent until he was proved.'

He took me by surprise. I had been turning over in my mind what he said about typecasting. He was right about that.

'Oh, yes.' I answered at last. 'Yes, you could say that.'

He watched me with some speculation in his eyes, and then the car turned into a driveway and stopped before a house as imposing as any of its neighbours and more graceful than most. The scrolled ironwork on the porch that ran along the front of the building, the mansard roof and the fine proportions suggested a house in a Paris suburb. I commented on this as we got out of the car.

'Second Empire,' Tozzetti explained. 'There is a French influence in our Ontario architecture.'

The house was warm and in the drawing room a wood fire blazed. It was a long room full of light from the tall windows. The winter sun brought out the honey glow in the maplewood floor and the rich colour in the rugs, and woke memories of summer in the Impressionist paintings on the walls. In pride of place, between the two windows at the far end of the room, hung one of Pissarro's paintings of the Seine.

'The Seine at Suresnes,' I said.

Tozzetti was delighted. 'You like the Impressionists – you like Pissarro?'

'I like them,' I said, 'and Pissarro is often my favourite.'

He smiled, a polite moment of a smile, but he was watching me with the same intent speculation he had shown out there in the car.

'Why should you ask me here at all?' I said. 'You have something in mind.'

'Yes,' he said. 'I have something in mind. We share a problem in the man Voster. I thought that perhaps we might be able to

130

help each other. Now, I think we can.' He moved down the room. 'Let us discuss it after luncheon. You will have something to drink? My wife will join us soon. Also the impetuous Gabriella.'

'Gabriella?'

'My niece. You met her the other night.'

It did not seem to me that Gabriella was a girl who luncheoned, and I was right. By the time she wandered into the dining room with her book in one hand and a cigarette in the other, the Tozzettis and I were eating apple pie.

My hostess was a crisply elegant and vivacious woman whose talk ranged from sharing the cultural insights of *Atlantic Monthly* to defending the case for keeping her native province of Quebec as French as possible, and I expected Gabriella's untidy incursion to raise at least an eyebrow if not a rebuke. Instead, when the self-absorbed beauty plumped herself down at the table without a word, and discarded the cigarette on her side plate, Mrs Tozzetti addressed not her but the woman who had served our meal.

'Get her a hamburger – with everything – and an ashtray,' she said calmly, looked at her watch with a pretty cry of dismay, and left us to go and raise funds for the Toronto Symphony Orchestra. She should have no trouble about that. The plain woollen dress she was wearing would have bought her a return Trans-atlantic flight on *Concorde*.

Tozzetti's way with his niece was different. As we left the table he got her attention by seizing her neck in a firm grip and said: 'I would like you to join us for coffee, mia cara. Okay?'

She gave him a not too sulky smile. 'Okay. Riccardo,' she said. She regarded me with one of those long speculative looks that ran in the Tozzetti family, said, 'Ciao, lover,' and went back into her book.

Coffee was waiting for us upstairs. We passed through an ante-room where a young man sat at a desk talking into a phone, and into Tozzetti's office.

'My office downtown has the same layout. Duplicate files. Everything. Neat, eh?' He expected an answer.

'If you want to be in two places at once, then it's neat,' I said. 'What do you do in your offices?'

'I'm a developer. I project an office block, raise the money, buy a piece of ground, build the office block, and sell it.'

'Do you sell it piecemeal or in bulk?'

'One or the other. I have a staff of five.'

'Five!' I said.

'Only five. I keep them up to five years, then I turn them loose. I hire ambitious little bastards and teach them how to be ambitious big bastards. I tell them that if they cheat me I will break their hearts. But you cannot break an ambitious big bastard's heart, so when they have grown into big bastards I send them on their way.'

'You're training the competition,' I said.

'Sure! But all over town I know how the competition's mind is working.' He cut the end off a cigar. 'And development's a big town. It runs from here to Texas.'

The boy from the outer office came in and laid a sheet of paper on his master's desk. He was perhaps twenty-one.

'Mr Moore writes plays, Bentley,' said Tozzetti. 'He's an intellectual, you should get on well together. Except that only one of you could trust the other.'

'Hi,' Bentley said to me pleasantly, and then mildly to his boss: 'Damn it, Ricky.'

'Tell us, Bentley, what kind of intellectual prefers Pissarro to Degas and Monet?' Ricky asked him.

Bentley grinned. 'One who has a mind to buy, not to sell.'

'Okay, smart-ass,' narrowing his eyes on the match flame at the end of his cigar. And then: 'Mr Moore and I have a common problem. If you see him again or he calls you, give him anything he needs.' He held out the piece of paper Bentley had handed him. 'Shred this. Tell me when the men get here. You can listen to us talk.'

Bentley went out, leaving the door open.

'Pissarro is often your favourite,' Tozzetti said to me. 'You're an emotional Irishman with English training. It was your friend

132

that got shot. They shot him in mistake for you.' He took smoke into his mouth and let it drift out again. 'You have vendetta in you.'

At the abrupt reference to Bruce anger warmed me but I let it cool. 'Vendetta,' I said. 'That's fanciful. Vendetta is in your history, not mine.'

'Vendetta is just the word. Sure, it is in my history, and in my family. My family came from Gragnano near Naples. Whether you are Irish or English you have Irishness in you. The English cry is for justice, the Irish for blood. That is vendetta. You are coasting just now, in neutral. You don't know what to do. Your friend's body is lying where your body should lie, and you feel yourself to have become an effete playwright, impotent to bring retribution on his assassins. Impotent.'

I began to shake. My coffee cup rattled into the saucer as I got rid of it. He got up and closed the door and crossed the room to stand looking out of the window. A sharp pain hit me in the chest and intensified until huge, shuddering breaths came up in me and the fit passed. The shaking stopped.

I felt Tozzetti's hands on my shoulders and his thumbs dug into my shoulder blades, forcing pangs of agony out of the knotted muscle there. 'You are full of tension,' he said. 'You need a good masseur.' His thumbs stopped working but he kept his hands on my shoulders. 'You okay?' he said.

'Okay,' I said.

He opened the door again and sat down at his desk. 'Anthony,' he said. 'I don't know who shot your friend, and I don't think the police will find them. I think they came over the border on a contract and will be back in the States by now. But somebody ordered it done, and that must be somebody who knows you, or somebody who knows somebody who knows you.' He waited, but I waited too. 'So it's somebody *you* know,' he said at last, 'or somebody who knows somebody you know.'

It was my turn to get up and look out of the window. It was snowing again in big, slow falling flakes. A man would spend a lot of time in Canada looking out of the windows at snow, remembering. I thought of the man dying in the ship's cabin and the dead man in the black Mercedes; of the police boat crossing the Solent in the night, and of that dinner with Seddall and Heneage in London; of my work with Bruce Baldwin and the pleasure of knowing him and Sandy – Sandy who I liked too well and who blamed me for Bruce's death; of Lehar spying on us all in Stratford, and of Voster's invasion of my apartment. I thought of something else too: of a couple of paragraphs in a newspaper about a family called Monteith disappearing, and of the way the mere mention of the name Monteith provoked Voster to slap Gabriella across the face.

A black limousine came into the driveway through the snow and stopped outside the front door. Four men got out of it, and the car went off round the side of the house. I watched them climb the steps and disappear from view under the porch roof.

Tozzetti spoke from behind me. 'You know something, don't you, Mr Moore? You know *somebody* outside of Voster's gang who connects with Voster and with your friend's murder.'

'I may not tell you,' I said, 'but I have some questions for you.'

'Try me,' he said. 'But for God's sake come and sit down again. I can't talk to a man's back.'

I sat and looked at him across the big desk. He had stubbed out his cigar. He looked, suddenly, a little tired. 'You don't seem to think Voster killed Bruce,' I said. 'Why not?'

'I've been to see him,' he said. 'I can tell. He was scared, angry and worried. Somebody had rained on his parade. Somebody else did it.'

Bentley came in. 'They're here,' he said.

'I'll come down,' he told Bentley, who went away. Tozzetti stood up. 'Next question,' he said to me.

'What's your connection with Voster?'

'Later,' he said. 'Any more?'

'One more. Just a name.' I paused. 'Monteith,' I said.

His face changed and he sat down again. 'Yeah,' he said. 'Monteith. Johnny Monteith.' His face lost colour and at the same time the lines on it deepened. He stared at me for a long time. His eyes were busy on me, but behind their activity was a slow, calm meditation. I felt it cover my face. The back of my neck grew chill. 'You leap in the dark, don't you?' he said. 'I can see why someone thought of having you killed.'

He stretched the sinews of his face and shook his head like a dog and got to his feet.

'Come on downstairs,' he said. 'You ought to see this. It will begin to answer some of those questions of yours.'

Chapter 15

We went into a room off the hall, where Bentley and the men who had got out of the car were waiting. We sat round a long table and I took it that I was sitting in on a meeting of Tozzetti's business staff, but I was wrong.

'Which of you is the top man?' Tozzetti asked them.

'I am, Mr Tozzetti. Bernard Collet.' He had the kind of black slicked-down hair you only see nowadays when an old Herbert Marshall movie is shown on television, a long pointed chin, a long pointed nose, and a long thin mouth. He also had cold grey eyes and the confidence of a croupier working a rigged table.

'What am I getting for my money, Collet?'

Nothing changed in the man's face, or in the man, at Tozzetti's pointed use of his undecorated surname. 'You get what you agreed with Mr MacIntyre, Mr Tozzetti. Four men in the house, two in the grounds, which is where they are now, and two in the outside car.'

'The car is in the road?'

'No, sir. The car is – '

He was interrupted. 'I want the car out there in the road,' Tozzetti snapped.

'No, sir, not while it's snowing like this. You can't see out of a car with snow covering the windows, and a parked car with the snow cleared off the glass looks unnatural.'

'So?'

'So the car is around a couple of corners. When the snow stops they'll park down the street.'

'Mr MacIntyre said the car would be – ' Tozzetti stabbed a

finger through the wall – 'out there, in the street. Who decided different?'

'I did,' Collet said, as cold a fish as never rose to the bait.

Tozzetti had his hands clasped on the table with thumbnails uppermost. He looked down at his thumbs for a while. When he spoke it was without the Big Man's hectoring rasp. Instead he slid his anger softly along the polished table. 'Tell me, Collet, do you intend to make any damn changes you like to the arrangements I made with your boss?'

Collet's answer came in the same hard-edged voice he had used throughout. 'Yes, Mr Tozzetti, that is what I intend. I will make any decision that ensures the security of your family.'

'And how tight can you make that security?' Tozzetti lifted his look from the thumbnails to the inflexible hireling across the table.

'Just as tight as a cow's ass in fly season,' Collet said coarsely.

Tozzetti's eyes widened. Collet gave him the neutral gaze of a croupier at a gambler having a run of luck – good or bad, it meant nothing to him. I looked at his three subordinates. The young one's mouth had fallen open. He was a blond ugly tough-guy. Beside him a short bald man smiled at the ceiling with bright blue eyes, and only with his eyes. The next one, a man of jaundiced complexion, with a vivacious look to him nevertheless, let a forefinger tap the table in a private round of applause.

Bentley was watching eagerly. This was a seminar to Bentley: he was learning how men handle each other in the real world.

Collet stood up. He had a lot of height.

'Where are you off to?' Tozzetti demanded, as if he thought Collet was quitting on him.

'We've been on the job twenty minutes, Mr Tozzetti, and we haven't started work yet. It's time I posted my men.'

Tozzetti sighed in a satisfied way, as if he had just completed a good job of work. 'I don't ask what weapons you carry,' he said. 'There are shotguns and rifles in that cupboard if you need them.' Bentley reached in a pocket and placed a handful of keys on the table. 'There's a key for each of you,' Tozzetti said. 'Take them.'

The young man, the bald man, and the yellow-faced man looked at Collet. He nodded. They picked up the keys. The yellow man, who was nearest him, passed one to Collet.

Tozzetti stood up. Everyone was standing now except me. 'Bentley eats in here,' he said. 'You can eat here, or in the kitchen, or have it brought to you.'

'We'll mix it around,' Collet said.

Tozzetti turned to go, and I stood up and followed him to the door. When he was there he turned to Collet. 'I asked MacIntyre for the best,' he said. 'And the best seems to be what I've got.' Collet said nothing, but when Tozzetti favoured him with a nod, he nodded back.

We went back up to his office where Gabriella was sitting in his seat with her feet on the desk and the book on her thighs.

'Move it, kid,' her uncle said. Even men like Tozzetti could learn from a man like Collet.

She moved it. She was wearing blue jeans that fitted her like wallpaper to a wall, except that nothing inside them was flat. She was also wearing a navy sweater, and though the sweater was cashmere, she looked more like a Canadian uncle's niece than the stormy Italian girl I had first met.

'I need a drink,' 'Tozzetti said. We all needed a drink, and we all had Scotch whisky. Tozzetti sat behind the desk, I sat where I had sat before, and Gabriella threw a cushion on the floor and sat against the wall.

She leered at me like a fresh kid at a party. I smiled attractively and drank whisky.

'Quit that stuff!' Tozzetti told her, and said something vigorous in Italian. She shrugged and pouted and adjusted her position on the cushion, so that for a few moments a lot of her was in motion.

When that was over, Tozzetti sighed. 'At least she's got guts,' he said.

'She's got more than that,' I said.

'Listen – lay off!' Now he was annoyed with both of us. 'If you knew the trouble she was in! Why do you think I've got these security men crawling all over the place?'

'I don't know. Why have you?'

'To protect her,' he said. 'God knows, kids are different these days. I've got two – I ought to know. I've got one herding sheep in Australia and one singing with a rock band in Morocco. Morocco, for God's sake. What's wrong with Canada?'

'Well, Canada's home,' I said.

'Okay,' he said, 'okay, my kids are great, I like my kids and I'm not worried about my kids. It's her I'm worried about. The kid was in her first year at university,' Tozzetti went on. He stopped there and started again. 'Look, I have to tell you, Anthony, I've had a report on you. I hired an agency to get a run-down on Anthony Moore, playwright. I know a lot about you, that I've no business to know. Who your father was, where you went to school, what they thought of you there, I know about your time in the army, your theatre and television writing, I know about your credit-rating.'

I said: 'Much good may it do you. Go on.'

Tozzetti had been a bit tense while he told me this, and now he relaxed again. 'I had to know who you were, where you connected with Voster.' He shook his head. 'So far as I can see, you don't connect with Voster at all.'

'Not on purpose, I don't,' I said, gliding smoothly among the snags and shallows of the half-lie.

'Yeah.' He looked at me sceptically. 'I have to trust you.'

I blinked at this. 'You have to trust me?'

He sighed and looked at Gabriella, who was keeping a low profile, or as low as could reasonably be expected of a girl of such ebullient composition. 'Yeah,' he said again. 'Because of her.'

So I looked at Gabriella too. There we were, staring at her. Tozzetti with a grim, brooding look and Moore contemplating all that ebullience and wondering at the same time how this dynamic teenage bundle of fun could have put her high-powered uncle into his debt. The beautiful texture of her lightly olive-skinned face darkened sweetly as she began to blush under the two pairs of eyes, but her own eyes grew angry at the mixed messages they received from our scrutiny.

'Che dici?' she spat at her uncle.

'I am going to tell him what a fool you have been, and how you have brought disgrace on me,' Tozzetti said with a kind of gloomy relish.

I had not thought her English was up to this, but she knew what he meant. She threw her head and arms about and said in sarcastic agreement. 'Oh, si, si! What a fool I 'av been, what deesgrace!' She glared at both of us, which I felt to be unfair, then pulled her legs up and put her head down on her knees so that her face was hidden.

'You know of the *Brigate Rosse*?' Tozzetti asked me.

'The Red Brigade?'

'Yes, though we say it in the plural. The Red Brigades. It is a movement but there are several of them. *Brigate Rosse*.' The girl was pressing her face onto her legs like a child, with her hands on her ears.

Tozzetti was having trouble. He emptied his glass and rubbed his hands over his face. Then he took out a handkerchief and wiped his face again, finally blowing his nose as if to discharge some of the emotion that filled him.

'I ask you to believe – I am still trying to believe it myself – that this child has come to Canada, with a group that calls itself one of these brigades.'

By the time he said it, this news was no longer a total surprise. In any case it astounded me less than, obviously, it shocked him. If one is in the *Brigate Rosse* business, there is no reason why one should confine all one's business to the home country.

I did not want, however, to seem to take Tozzetti's mortification too lightly. I did not know, yet, what exactly had happened that made him take it so badly. It must be something more than social inconvenience, or shock at Gabriella's fall from bourgeois grace. A niece, after all, was not a daughter. As it turned out I was only partly right: I was underestimating the Italian sense of family.

I got up and went to look out of the window in order to

conceal the fact that my reaction was insufficient to the occasion. It had stopped snowing. A car was parked far up the road, with no snow on the windscreen. I sat down again, and Tozzetti nodded his head at me, slowly, as if it had grown heavy. He was satisfied that I had not been able to contain my stupefaction at what he had told me without that bodily movement to and from the window.

I had proved myself a good listener. Now I had to say something. 'How old is she?' I said.

'Eighteen.'

'Uh-huh. Just eighteen.'

I looked at Gabriella as I said it. She was with us again, sitting up against the wall and smoking a cigarette, her face sullen and wary. I would be sullen and wary myself in her situation. I took a heavy glass ashtray off the desk and slid it across the carpet to her. I got a look to acknowledge receipt of same.

I remembered that Tozzetti had phrased his message with care. 'You said "a group that calls itself" a Red Brigade. You think it may not be?' I asked him.

'I'm not sure,' he said. 'She thinks it is. I don't see why a Red Brigade would do this . . . what they've done.'

'What have they done?' I knew he had not meant to come so near to the point, not so soon, but Tozzetti the businessman was showing signs of behaving like a character in an opera, beating round the emotional bushes to give the music a chance instead of getting the story across.

He gave us more whisky, even Gabriella. 'They kidnapped my friend Johnny Monteith, and it was Gabriella who put the finger on him,' he said like any old Al Capone, and having swallowed his medicine put the whole glass of whisky down on top of it.

All at once I was in the opera myself now, shouting my head off. 'You mean she . . . you mean they shot Bruce!' This time I found I was on my feet without any conscious act of will. I was standing over Gabriella who was staring up at me, tensed and wary like a dog expecting to be whipped. I stopped shouting but my voice was still loud. 'You came to his funeral to get me here and tell me this . . . schoolgirl is in the gang that shot him!'

The bald man with the blue eyes came quickly into the room. He looked at the girl, me and Tozzetti in that order. 'What's the problem?' he asked.

'What the hell are you?' Tozzetti growled at him. 'A personnel consultant? This is family business.'

The bald man went away, closing the door softly behind him.

'She had nothing to do with killing your friend,' Tozzetti said. 'I don't think her gang did either. Settle down, for God's sake.'

Gabriella watched darkly as I sat down, then hissed a question at her uncle in Italian. He gave her an impatient answer. She hissed again, gesticulating in my direction, and whatever he said then silenced her. She sat back again and glowered at nothing in particular on the floor, between her knees.

'Tozzetti,' I said. 'What's going on? This Red Brigade kidnaps your friend Monteith. Voster's brigade raids my apartment and then joins me for supper to apologize. Bruce Baldwin gets shot on his way to my car. How does it all tie together?'

'I don't know that,' he said. 'I only know half of it, no, only a third. I don't know much about Voster and about the shooting I know zilch, except that I hear you were supposed to be the target.'

He said that before, about me being the target. 'How do you know that?' I demanded. 'Who told you I was the target?'

He looked at the ceiling for a moment. 'Please, let me talk. Don't react all the time. If you must know, the police told me. Now listen. Calm down and just listen, right?'

'All right.'

'I had a lunch date with Monteith to talk over some business he was doing. A deal, a very big deal he was working on. He wanted to talk it over with me before he completed. It's a property deal; I deal in property; he wanted my advice on it; he trusted me.' He took time out to glare at Gabriella, but she took no notice. She was staring glumly into space. 'We were going to meet and talk about this deal, right? So, this kid's only been over here a month but she knows Johnny, she's met him here and she's met him at his own house – she was a guest in his own house, for God's sake!'

'Settle down,' I said gently.

'Yes, touché,' he said with a sigh and picked up the story. 'She calls him on the phone and says "Hi, Johnny, this is Gabriella, Ricky Tozzetti's niece, and he's going to pick you up outside your office at 12.15 in his Jaguar." I've got a maroon Jaguar – it's an English car; you know them. Maybe he thinks it's funny I'd have her make the call to him, maybe not. As it turns out, he just accepts it.'

It seemed that Gabriella knew enough English to know where Tozzetti had got to in his narrative. She caught my eye and looked away again.

Tozzetti sighed again. 'So, Johnny comes down from his office in Bloor Street. He sees the Jaguar, Gabriella pops out of the back and holds the door for him. He gets in beside a man in a black topcoat and grey fedora – that's a hat I wear sometimes – she shuts the door and walks off, the guy pulls a gun on him, and the car drives away.'

'She gave them your car for this?' I asked.

'No. She gave them my grey fedora. The car they hired.' He used that stabbing finger technique, but this time he was stabbing the top of the desk to make his point. 'They had to hire the car in New York. They couldn't find that model maroon Jaguar in Ontario so they went over the border for it. Now to hire a car like that you need to show pretty good ID and a good credit situation. These jerks are all students or drop-outs, all kids, all from Italy. Even if they had a bundle of money, or a good credit card, they'd still have to show an ID the hire company liked. They couldn't do it, you can take my word for it. But *someone* did.'

'You're telling me something,' I said, 'but I don't know what.'

'I'm telling you that someone of good financial standing with a convincing ID is in the picture somewhere.'

'How does that help us?' I asked.

Exasperation forced a vexed laugh from Tozzetti. 'I don't say it helps us,' he said. 'What it tells *me* is, someone is using these kids, and maybe using Voster too. Probably someone who seems very respectable, either a "respectable" individual or group of individuals, or maybe even a "respectable" corporation.' He paused and went on thinking aloud. 'Now, I guess there are big men in crime who have that kind of respectability, but why would they employ a bunch of imported amateurs? They'd use professionals, grown-ups who know their way around.'

I said: 'The Red Brigades are professionals.'

'Come on, Anthony! They're professional terrorists motivated by politics. If my business was crime and I wanted to snatch Johnny Monteith, and Bentley said let's use one of these red brigades, what kind of answer do you think he'd get?'

Suddenly I heard what he was saying. Two figures from my recent past, two unseen presences, joined us in the room. Tozzetti could not see the two men in my mind's eye, but he saw my mind's eye seeing them.

'Think about it,' he said carefully. 'What sort of man would use Gabriella's bunch, and Voster's little gang, and hire a team of pros to kill you – but not such hot pros at that, since they shot the wrong man?' He sat back and threw a gesture across the desk, giving me the floor. 'Tell us,' he said. 'What sort of man? Describe him.'

'You're getting ahead of yourself,' I said. I was playing for time. Inchoate patterns were trying to form in my head, falling apart and trying again. I was not sure I wanted any of these elusive patterns to settle into a shape while I was with Tozzetti. 'Why ask me? Ask the girl. She's mixed up in it, for God's sake.'

He shook his head. 'She was mixed up in it, but all she knew about it was doing what they told her to do. The group leader – '

'Who's the group leader?' I interrupted him.

He shrugged. 'I don't know, she won't give me names. Whoever he is he's a close-mouth.' He grinned, suddenly and surprisingly. 'She says they operate on the need-to-know principle. You'd think she'd been caught up in the CIA.'

The patterns in my head did some re-forming. They had been acting like a bunch of raw recruits trying to learn complicated parade ground drill on a misty night. The mist was showing signs of lifting a little.

I looked Tozzetti in the eye. 'The whole thing is on a need-to-know basis, isn't it?'

'Go on.'

'There are three separate groups here, in your view of it. Three groups for three functions.'

'Yes,' he said. 'I'd noticed.'

'That describes whoever's behind it, a little. He – or they – is staying well in the background. He's staying out of sight. He must have a strange list of phone numbers in the back of his diary. It's not only who would use the sort of people he's using: it's who would know them.'

'Yeah,' he said. 'Or who would know *of* them, and where to find them.' He had a funny look in his eye, and the look was thinking about me.

'What's on your mind?' I asked him.

'I was joking about the CIA a minute ago. But you know what this sounds like? It sounds like something the CIA might put together on the worst day they ever had.'

'They've had bad days,' I agreed, 'but nothing like this.'

'No,' Tozzetti said. 'It's not them. But they have what it would take. They don't have phone numbers in the back of a diary. They have computers, and in the computers they will have Red Brigades and hit-teams and whatever kind of free-lance middleman Voster is turning out to be.'

'What do you mean, "turning out to be"? Have you hired the entire Pinkerton Detective Agency?'

'As good as. Voster they're still learning about, but he's done some industrial espionage in his time. He is also an importer, wine and fancy foods from Europe. He goes to Europe three or four times a year. They're tracing what he does there.'

He was spending a lot of money, one way and another, with bodyguards here and detectives there. I asked him why, and he got angry, angry not with me or even with Gabriella, but with something inside himself and outside that room.

'She's family, you understand? She is a girl of my family and she betrayed my friend, my daughter's godfather, so that he is kidnapped and maybe dead.' He was very controlled. The anger was in his voice and in the blood that rose to his face, but his hands lay still on the desk, his body was motionless. For a man who gestured a lot the stillness was expressive. 'I must wipe out what she has done. I must get Monteith and his family back.'

Gabriella was responding again. She had hold of her head with both hands and was banging it on her knees. I began to see why she was in the room with us. She was here to take her punishment, to have the enormity of what she had done to the family honour beaten into her not with blows, but with repetition. And perhaps, in that role, to demonstrate to me why Tozzetti himself was in such grim earnest.

But it had another effect on me as well. Tozzetti put into the air a lot of the atmosphere of nineteenth-century Italian melodrama. Gabriella, though, did not quite complement him: she was doing a good number as the erring child of the family grieving for what she had done, but she was also fulfilling a more up-to-date cliché, the crazy mixed-up kid taking a turn to herself.

She reminded me that this was nowadays, where people did not go around vindicating the family honour in the implacable spirit that her uncle was showing

I said it mildly, but it would have been all the same if I had slapped him on the face with it. 'Don't you think the police, the RCMP?' I left the question hanging.

Tozzetti sighed. 'I am not an overwrought Neapolitan camorrista,' he said. 'I am an overwrought level-headed practical businessman. These kidnappers are idiots, half children, and this is their first exploit, they will be excited and nervous. Also they have a cause, they are at war. God knows what their cause is – who they're at war with – but their manhood will be on the line. If I go to the police they will know, and they will kill the Monteiths. That is their threat.'

I don't know what my face registered, but he smiled at me ironically. 'Yes, Mr Moore. They have told me all this through Gabriella. She is their intermediary, and it is to me they will put their demands. She has finished with them, she is repentant and ashamed, but still she will have to speak to them when they telephone. It is what they insist upon. They are to phone here sometime tomorrow to speak to me, but first they will speak to Gabriella. Look at her. If I had passed this – this dilemma – on to the police, do you think she could hide that from them?'

He spoke to her briefly in Italian, and I made out the words *polizia* and *telefono*. She looked startled and indignant, and then frightened, and came back at him with much flashing of eyes and some fine fluttering hand movements at shoulder level. She said 'No, no, no, no,' a great many times, directing the last sequences at me, and finished.

Into the respectful silence that followed, one of the phones on Tozzetti's desk began to purr.

Gabriella gave a little scream and put some fingers in her mouth. I jumped in my chair. Tozzetti for a moment looked more overwrought than level-headed, then he said: 'After all, it is still today. They will not phone till tomorrow,' and picked up the phone.

He listened, said, 'Put him on,' and almost at once his eyes flicked to me. 'Yes,' he said. 'Uh-huh. Yeah. Would she care to speak to him?'

Then he leaned forward across the desk and handed the phone to me. 'It's Mrs Baldwin,' he said. 'She'd like to talk to you.'

Chapter 16

————◆————

'What's going on?' she said. 'I need to see you. Who's this guy here?' Her voice was agitated, pitched high with strain.

'Sandy,' I said. 'Where is here?'

'I'm at your apartment,' she said. 'Well, downstairs, in the lobby. I was leaving a message for you and this man came up and said he could get you on the phone at Mr — ' Her voice became fainter. 'Mr Who?' I heard her ask. She came back to me. 'Mr Tozzetti's house?'

'That's right,' I said. 'I'm with Mr Tozzetti now.'

'Are you all right? I mean have they . . . are you . . . ?'

'I'm fine, Sandy. Mr Tozzetti's a sort of friend of mine. Are *you* all right?'

'Oh, sure, sure. I'm okay, well . . . ' There was a break in her voice and she started again. 'I'm okay, Anthony, but I need to see you. Where are you? Can I come there?'

'Yes,' I said. 'Hold on a moment. She wants to come out here,' I said to Tozzetti.

'Fine,' he said. 'Tell her to put that guy on the phone,' and he opened the office door and beckoned. The bald man came in. I held the receiver out to Tozzetti, who took it and passed it on to the bald man.

'This is your man at Mr Moore's apartment building,' Tozzetti said. 'Tell him to drive Mrs Baldwin out here.'

The bald man took the phone, but said, 'That will leave a gap. Collet won't like it.'

'This is more important,' Tozzetti said. 'The name's Mrs Baldwin. Tell him to drive Mrs Baldwin up here.'

'Right,' he said, and did.

When the bald man had gone out again, I said to Tozzetti: 'You have some special reason for running surveillance on my apartment?'

'"Running surveillance",' he said, repeating the words ironically. 'Sure, I'm keeping an eye on your apartment, and yes, I have some special reason. I have a special interest in knowing who calls at your apartment – and so do you. Don't get dramatic about it – at least it turned up Mrs Baldwin for you.'

What he said made sense. He leaned forward over the desk. 'So?' he said.

I looked at him. 'So?' But I knew what was coming.

'Yeah,' he said. 'So what do you make of it all? And, I've told you what I know, so what do *you* know?'

'Not much more than you,' I said, 'and even what I know from you doesn't fit together. What I know doesn't fit either, so maybe it doesn't belong. I'll need to think.'

'So will I,' Tozzetti said. 'So tell me what you know and we can think together.'

We looked at each other for a long time.

'You're not going to tell me,' he said.

'I can't,' I said. 'Not yet.'

'You know what "I can't" sounds like?' Tozzetti said. 'It sounds like "Name, rank, and serial number."' He looked a hard man, all of a sudden, and an idea was showing in his eyes. 'Name, rank, and number,' he said again. 'But that war's over. Korea's over, Vietnam's over. Why do you say "I can't", that's what I ask myself.'

'I said not yet.'

'You said "I can't", all stiff upper-lipped as if you were serving the Flag. I don't like the thoughts I'm getting from that. I don't think we're going to be the friends I thought we were going to be.'

'Tozzetti,' I said. 'I'm a playwright. The only reason I came over here was to write for the theatre.'

There were sounds of a slight disturbance outside the door of the office. He glanced over his shoulders but the door stayed shut.

Scuffling noises came through the door of the office. Suddenly the door jerked open and Bentley stood holding it. He looked at me before he spoke to Tozzetti. 'There's a Mr Schmidt here to see Mr Moore,' he said. Then he lost his grip on the door handle and Harry Seddall shoved past him into the room. The bald man slipped in after him and placed himself like a shield in front of Gabriella.

Seddall was still being a member of a West German trade delegation. He was being a German who had taken his first degree at Heidelberg and a doctorate at Oxford, and when he spoke he sounded like an English version of Henry Kissinger.

'Mr Tozzetti,' he thrust out a hand, 'you will excuse this intrusion. It is of great importance to me to see my friend Moore before I leave Toronto.' His hand was still in the air in front of him, with Tozzetti glaring at it, so Harry raised it to me in greeting. "My dear Anthony, I am glad to have found you. I am flying home tonight; it is vital that we finish our little piece of business.' While he spoke he was making himself at home, shrugging out of his coat, a massive hooded garment of wolf's fur which he doubtless wore at his shooting lodge in Bavaria, and was just the thing for visiting Canada in November. He handed it to Bentley as if he had ten more like Bentley back at Essen (or Dortmund), and Bentley took it in the same spirit. 'Coffee, please,' he told Bentley, 'no milk or sugar,' and sank into an armchair. 'I have security at my own house,' he said to Tozzetti, 'but nothing like yours. I almost had to fight my way in.'

This was more a challenge than an inquiry, with the familiar Seddall sneer trailing at the end of it, and his host found it hard to take. Tozzetti had glared at all of us in turn except Gabriella, who was blocked off from him by the bald man, and now the angry eyes focused on me again. 'Friend of yours?' was all he could come out with.

'Oh, yes,' I said. 'Good to see you, Heinrich.'

Seddall's eyes closed for a moment, but he took coffee from

Bentley with a steady hand.

Collet bounded into the room with slush on his boots and a gun in his fist: he looked at Seddall as if he was seeing a centipede on his salad. 'What the hell's going on here?' he demanded.

Tozzetti was calming himself again, and Collet's arrival helped him complete the process. 'I don't know who you're asking,' he said, 'but it seems to me that's a question I might reasonably put to you.'

'I was outside, down the back,' Collet said, and his face changed colour as he realized he had made something like an apology; instead of turning red, he went a little pale.

'He forced his way in,' the bald man said.

'He *forced* his way in?'

'He's forceful,' the bald man said, unruffled.

That made it Tozzetti's turn to be forceful. 'Collet,' he said, 'conduct this autopsy outside of my office. The room's getting crowded.' He was able to aim that last line at Seddall as well, but an ironic smile was all he got in return.

Collet turned on his heel and the bald man followed him out. Bentley went with them, carrying the wolfskin, and the door closed.

Tozzetti kept the initiative. 'What business are you in, Herr Schmidt, that you have to discuss it with Mr Moore? Are you an impresario?'

Seddall ignored this. 'Hallo,' he said to Gabriella, as if he was noticing her for the first time, and added something in Italian.

She liked his style, so she leered at him in the way she had practised at school. Harry spilled some coffee and ash on his suit, loosened his tie, relaxed into his stained and rumpled persona, and leered back at her.

'That's my niece!' Tozzetti barked.

Harry dropped the German accent. 'And she's caused us all a lot of trouble, hasn't she?'

Gabriella may not have understood all the words, but she heard the news between the lines and began to look a little anxious. Tozzetti was very still, and his eyes were calculating fast. His right hand was out of sight under the desk.

Harry shook his head lazily. 'I'm no threat to you, Mr Tozzetti, or even to your niece. Or even –' he smiled a crooked smile – 'to your friend Monteith.'

Tozzetti's face was a gathering storm. 'Who is this man?' he asked me in a cramped voice, his lips hardly moving.

'What have you told him, Anthony?' Seddall went on looking at Tozzetti.

'He hasn't told me a damn thing!' Tozzetti had broken the stranglehold on his voice, and the noise he made was almost a shout.

'Stout fella, Digby,' Seddall said to me, straight out of *Beau Geste*.

'How did you know I was here?' I asked him.

'I saw you get into his car outside the church.'

As if on cue, car doors slammed outside, and I went quickly to the window. Sandy was starting up the steps under the porch with a man at her elbow. 'Mrs Baldwin,' I said, and made for the door.

'Mrs Baldwin,' Seddall said in a carefully uninflected tone. 'I daresay you'll want to be alone with her for a bit. Perhaps Mr Tozzetti and I could talk together.'

'Why not?' I said, and opened the door.

'Hold on a minute,' Tozzetti said. He jerked his head at Seddall. 'Do you vouch for this man?' he asked me.

Seddall hooded his eyes and grinned at Gabriella. She blushed.

'No,' I said. 'But then I wouldn't vouch for you either.'

I went out and shut the door, passed between Bentley and the bald man, and ran downstairs. One of Collet's men was standing by the front door and a maid was putting Sandy's coat away in a closet.

'Mrs Baldwin?' I said to the maid.

'The lady's in there,' she said, and nodded at the room where the paintings hung. I went in and found Sandy warming her hands at the fire.

'Hallo, Sandy,' I said.

'Hi,' she said, still looking at the flames. Then she said: 'Well, don't I get a hug?'

She turned as I reached her. 'I want a real hug,' she said, and I held her tightly until I felt her body relax and she said: 'Okay. I feel hugged.'

She sat on the arm of a sofa and looked up at me. 'I couldn't see you,' she said.

'I know.'

She was as beautiful as I had ever seen her, with the desolate beauty of grief. She was far away from that room, in the world where she and her man had been growing a life together.

'He was killed because of you,' she said.

'Yes,' I said.

'Instead of you,' she said.

'Yes,' I said. 'Yes, he was.'

'Yes. So in the end,' she said, 'I thought it would be better if I did see you.'

'Well,' I said. 'Well . . .'

'Let's not say any of the things, not right now.' she said. 'I don't want to cry just now.'

She was holding her eyes wide open to stop them crying, and she pointed with her head at the table with drinks on it. I poured her a stiff drink and she swallowed most of it in one mouthful.

'Wow,' she said. 'What's this?'

'I don't know.' I went back and looked at the bottle. 'It's a twelve-year-old Scotch malt whisky.'

'Well, wow.' She shook her head and drank the rest of it. 'How long do we have to stay here?'

'We don't have to stay at all. Do you want to go?'

'Yes, in a minute. Will you take me? I don't have a car. That man brought me in his car.'

'Neither do I, I'll get a cab.'

I found a bell-push and when the maid came, asked her to call a taxi, and she said she would.

When we were alone again Sandy said: 'I want to go away someplace. I want you to take me someplace simple.'

I blundered. 'What about your family, Sandy?'

'Damn it!' she said. 'They understand. Why can't you?'

'I do understand.' I said. 'We'll go.'

'You're not even saying sorry, are you?'

'I said a foolish thing,' I said.

'Don't say sorry,' she said. 'You'll say other foolish things. It won't be your fault.'

'We'll have a few problems about getting away, by ourselves.' I put stress on the last two words, and she caught it.

She looked at me carefully. 'You mean the police, and like that?'

'Mostly "and like that",' I said.

'You'll have to tell me where you'd like to go,' I said. 'It's your country. You know the places.'

But I knew where to take her. There was no point in saying so in Tozzetti's house. When security outfits are in, walls have ears.

We saw the taxi come into the driveway and went out to the hall. The maid appeared and helped us into our coats, and then went to open the front door. Collet's man there hesitated, but the maid looked at him with astonishment and he moved aside. He pulled the inevitable machine from his breast pocket and spoke into it nervously. If he was the man Seddall had brushed past, he was not having a good day. I asked the maid to thank Mr Tozzetti for his hospitality and we went down the steps to the taxi.

'Hey!' The shout was Tozzetti's, and it came from above. He was on the balcony above the porch. Harry Seddall was beside him.

'We should talk, Anthony,' Harry said.

'I'll take a raincheck, Harry. Thanks for the lunch.' But Tozzetti had already gone back inside. I joined Sandy in the back of the taxi.

'Where to?' the driver asked.

'Yonge and Bloor,' Sandy said, and we drove away.

Chapter 17

———◆◆———

Sandy drove the last stage. She woke me at the turn-off to White Denver's ancestral log cabin, and as she put the car warily to the unswept track and the tires gripped and went on gripping up the slope, she gave a little smile of relief. The snow was less than a foot deep but the clouds were low and ominous, making an early dusk.

'They're calling for more snow,' she said. 'We'd better empty the car tonight and take it back down to the highway, or we might not get it out again.'

'Aren't you tired?' I said.

'I'm tired as shit, mister, but when you're a pioneer, that's how it is.'

The car topped a ridge and there below us were the cabin and the lake. The wind had bared large stretches of the ice, but the pine trees that came close to the back of the cabin and spread round the lake were laden with snow, frozen there till the thaw. When Sandy had backed the car up to the door and we got out the cold and the loneliness of the place hit me with equal force.

Sandy was watching me. 'Yes,' she said. 'This is how it was. I'll turn on the power and the water pump and get the heat going. You can start unloading, tenderfoot.'

The car was packed to the roof with winter clothes, sleeping bags, snowshoes, skis, boots, books and provisions enough for a month. Sandy soon joined me in portering the load into the cabin, but when the car was empty I fell into one of the long, cushioned chairs with flat wooden arms, a cup of coffee steaming on one arm and an ashtray on the other, and began to relax. The air inside was still chill, but we were wearing down-filled jackets and ski boots and the warm clothes and the effects of the recent exercise had put warmth into my body. The coffee helped too.

'This is more like it,' I said.

'On your feet,' Sandy said. 'You're not finished yet. You've got the stove to light and the supper to cook.'

I stayed where I was. Sandy was sitting straight-backed on a bench against the wall, but she looked as I felt, ready to drop.

'What will you be doing?' I asked lazily.

'I'll be taking the car down to the highway.'

'No you won't. I'll be doing that. It will be all of a mile, walking back again. Or we can do it tomorrow, in the daylight.'

'Look outside,' she said.

In the last of the light I saw the snow falling; thick, slow flakes that looked as if they would add another foot to the height of the snow by morning, maybe more.

'I see what you mean,' I said. 'The car might be stranded up here by the time we wake up.'

'For the winter,' Sandy said. 'So I'll take it down to the highway, okay? I'll do it because I can snowshoe back, and you can't. So you get some wood into that stove and get the supper ready. I'll take some of that chocolate to keep me going, and you just better have a drink ready for me when I get back.'

I thought about this. 'Is it safe for you to do this? I don't know about this country. What about getting lost, or bears and things?'

'I won't get lost,' she said. 'And any bears round here will be living off the garbage on the town dumps.'

'Pioneering is not what it was,' I said, and stood up.

Sandy stood up too. 'Give me a little hug and send me on my way,' she said.

We put snowshoes back in the car along with a flashlight, and Sandy drove off through the snow, munching chocolate. I watched till the bright rear lights vanished, waited a moment or two longer, and went inside.

It was one room, dominated by the big wood stove which had some corded wood piled beside it, and stood at the east end of the cabin. There was kindling too, so with newspaper and the help of the rising wind I had the fire blazing in no time, the dried out logs snapping and crackling as they caught. I opened tins and put soup in a pan to heat on the stove, and put out bacon and eggs so that I could start them cooking as soon as Sandy came in the door. And I routed out the whisky.

These duties done, I took stock of the room. The log walls had a dull, oily sheen as if they had been waxed, and I wondered if this was natural or if White Denver had done it. Probably he had, because without taking away its original character he had made it conform to his style. There were four prints on the walls of the early voyageurs braving the wilderness; a single bed at the far end from the stove, made like a long box, of beechwood, with deep drawers in it for storage; a good rug beside the bed to put the Denver feet on in the morning and a shelf of books above it; the two lounging chairs; and a small table opposite the door made of thick unvarnished pine. The kitchen sector was at the east end of the cabin, and was provided for by a porcelain sink with a teak draining board on the north or lake-facing wall, and a small electric cooker against the south wall. Between them stood the stove, but there was a good space between the stove and the end wall, presumably because of the heat it gave off. It was cunningly planned, plain and comfortable, and everything, in Denver's way, was of the best. The only change to the structure was a bathroom built on to the north wall at the bed end of the cabin.

He had been right to tell me it would be a perfect place to work. It was also a perfect place to hide out. We had come in White Denver's Volvo. In the taxi, leaving Tozzetti's house, I felt frantically in my pockets to see if I had the keys with me. Keys to car and cabin were on the same key ring. I had them.

I asked the driver to stop, gave him twenty dollars, and sought a favour. 'If your controller should ask you where you dropped us off, say we changed our minds and went down to Gerrard, will you?'

He looked at the twenty-dollar bill and said, 'You got it,' and drove off. I told Sandy what we were doing, where we had to go to pick up the car, and we started walking, taking a lot of corners. We walked till we came to a bus route and took a bus down to Bloor, and we took the subway out west, walked a lot more, stopping now and then to make sure Collet's men were not following; waited a long time near White's house, but not too near, looking and listening; then we opened the garage, got in the car and Sandy drove us into north Toronto. We had time to kill, because we planned to equip ourselves the next morning for our stay at the cabin, and Sandy had pin-pointed North Bay, which was two hundred miles from Toronto, as the place for that. So we went to a movie in the suburbs, followed it with a late supper, and set off again after midnight. We took our time, but even so we reached North Bay well before the stores were open, and had to sit around in a greasy-spoon over a long breakfast.

But I was content. We were free and clear. None of the people I had wanted to cut loose from knew about White Denver, his car, or his cabin.

When the stores were open Sandy cashed a cheque – credit cards can leave a trail – went on a shopping spree and bought everything we needed from the skin out. Then we drove for the cabin. We spelled each other driving, the passenger sleeping or dozing, and reached the lake after more than fifteen hours on the road.

It was the first effective initiative I had taken since I found the dead man in my cabin on the Channel crossing, and though we were running away, I felt good about it.

Then I found myself frowning. Sandy was five days widowed. There was nothing to celebrate in that. I wondered if she was all right, opened the door to look out into the swirling snow, and saw her flashlight coming down the slope to the cabin. I shut the door behind me and waited there in the dark till she was at the foot of the slope, and went to meet her.

'See, I made it!' she said.

'You did, didn't you?'

'Let's get in there,' she said, and brushed the snow off her hood with her mittened hands. So we went inside.

I treasure that evening. The tears came later, after the whisky and the simple meal. She just stood up from the table and said, 'Come here,' and I held her close at first, and then loosely to let the big, shaking sobs come out of her.

'Your sweater's damp,' she said at last. It was, soaked with her weeping.

'I'm sorry about that,' I said.

'You goon. Give me a cigarette.'

She opened the door of the stove and looked into the flames, kneeling there until her face was reddened by the heat. She threw the cigarette into the fire and put a couple of logs on and shut the door again.

'It was an accident, really. That it happened to Bruce, I mean. It was like a car accident, wasn't it?'

'Yes,' I said. 'It was an accident.' I was glad she was thinking of it like that. It was healthier for her, and it might ease the guilt I felt, with time.

'But someone did it,' she said.

'Yes, someone did it,' I said. 'That's what's on my mind too.'

'Good,' she said. 'It's important. Let's sleep now, we'll talk in the morning.'

I neither watched nor avoided watching while she undressed and put on the pyjamas she had bought in North Bay. When she was in bed I kissed her good night and got into a sleeping bag, using the other one as a mattress on the floor. I lay awake for a while listening to the wind and wondering how high the snow would be in the morning.

'Sleep well,' Sandy said, and I heard her turning over in the bed, snuggling down for the night.

'You too,' I said, and fell asleep.

I woke to the smell of coffee and the sunlight bright in my eyes. I shut them and yawned like a giant. Then I turned my head the other way and opened my eyes again. Sandy was squatting down beside me. There was a touch of colour in her cheeks and she looked as bright as a new penny.

'Roust out, old-timer,' she said, 'There's wood to be chopped and mouths to be fed!'

'Good God, Sandy!' I said. 'We're halfway to Hudson's Bay. This isn't an American Western.'

'Mebbe so,' she drawled. 'But I'm an American, in case you've forgotten.'

'Of course I'd forgotten. I've just woken up. I'm not thinking about you, I'm thinking about my breakfast.'

She gave me a long look with a hint of the old caustic light in the blue eyes. Then she asked: 'Did you hear me weeping last night?'

'No,' I said. 'I slept like a log.'

'Uh-huh,' she said. 'Except that you snored, you slept like a log.'

'You're still weeping.'

'I thought it wasn't showing.'

'It's not showing. It's just there. How about some of that coffee?'

'When you're out of that sleeping bag, mister, you'll get some coffee.'

'Turn your back then. I sleep raw.'

'Why the hell should I? I didn't last night. Neither did you.'

I looked at her. She looked at me. I began to get out of the sleeping bag.

'You're blushing,' she said. To my great indignation this was true. I got to my feet and she said: 'Now give me a hug.'

She was wearing jeans and a wool sweater over a plaid shirt, as she had been the first time I saw her, except that these were brand new. I took all this into my arms and gave her a hug. Her hands on my back were cool.

After a bit she stood back. 'Well, well! It was supposed to be just a hug. You better make yourself decent, mister.'

The glint in her eye was wicked.

'You're a tease, Sandy Baldwin,' I said.

'How do you know?' she came back, as if she had been waiting for me to say that. She stood with her feet a little apart, poised on her toes, as sexy and mocking as all hell.

'That's it!' I said, and I grabbed her, wrestled her to the door, got it open and threw her outside into the snowdrift that the night's wind had built up. I shut the door again and locked it and dressed in peace. I poured myself a cup of coffee, hot and strong – delicious. There was a knock on the door, and I opened it.

'Can I come in?' she said. 'I'll cook breakfast if you'll let me in.'

'My house is yours,' I said, and she came back into the cabin, still dusting snow off her clothes and hair.

She put bread into the toaster and began to scramble eggs. After a bit she said: 'Come here!' I went over and she went on stirring but put one arm round my waist. 'You're a nice man,' she said. 'Go and set the table.'

After breakfast we put on the short cross-country skis and set off round the lake. It had been noon when I woke, and the sun had begun to sink, so we did not plan to go far. In the event we were out for little more than an hour, because the snow was not good for skiing. It was too powdery. To the north the sky was a bright pale blue, but as we made our way back, more snow-clouds were coming up from the south-west.

There was a feeling off the landscape, that white desert of snow and ice running north to Hudson's Bay, north to the Arctic and the edge of the world, that moved a strange excitement in me; the pale sky and the fading sun were part of it, and the freezing air that bit into your throat; and the log cabin, bleached by time and weather and planted there solitary beside the lake. As we came back to it, home again, I became aware of the illogical belief growing in me that somewhere in my past I belonged to this. It was so strong that I actually felt as if this place had been part of my childhood, a part that had been lost to me and was now being given back.

I tried to describe this to Sandy. 'It happens to people,' she said. 'Some kind of primal hook, I guess.'

'Then you have it too,' I said.

'I have it too.' She grinned at me. 'Maybe it'll help you through tomorrow when we go out on snowshoes. That will hurt till your legs get used to it.'

'Anything in a good cause.'

'You mean keeping my mind off Bruce,' she said with tears suddenly in her eyes. 'Damn you, Anthony!' But she hit me painfully on the arm with her fist, to let me know she forgave me.

'I didn't mean that, Sandy,' I said. 'I meant getting myself fit to move around in the snow.'

'I know, I know!' she said. And she clung to me in a clumsy embrace, each of us with one ski off, in a passion of shaking and silent grief. She let go of me. 'I don't want to cry now. Let's get that coffee on. You're going to tell me why he was killed. You're going to tell me what followed you from England that got him killed.'

This was the hard word, as my father used to say. Her eyes that had been soft with tears a moment ago were as bleak and strong as the landscape settling into its bitter dusk.

So we went into the cabin, built up the fire in the stove and made coffee. Sandy sat in one of the long armchairs with her feet curled under her and I put myself at the table. The space between us was taut with emotions that came suddenly to the surface in both of us: my guilt over Bruce's death and Sandy's hostility to me as the cause of it. As I began to speak I felt like a man making a confession. I sat stiff and tensed up and hardly recognized my own voice, it was so stiff with formality.

But as the story progressed, as the Channel crossing led to the meetings in London with the police and Harry Seddall, to the expedition to the Isle of Wight and my identification of the two bodies, and to the bizarre dinner in Heneage's club, I found I was listening, not to how my voice sounded, but to what I was saying. It was the first time I had given the full, unedited version to anyone, and I had dreaded the moment when I would have to make my account to Sandy, but as I went on, my interest in what I was saying became paramount. It was as if I was hearing it all myself for the first time. I had gone over and over it in my mind, but always these attempts to make sense of the incongruous series of events had tripped over my own exasperation and failure to make sense of them. Now I was not trying to make sense of them; I was simply listening, taking it all in.

I found myself walking up and down, gesticulating, like an actor in a difficult play trying to woo the understanding of the audience; trying to compel the audience to keep its intelligence alert.

And the space between us, which had been an arid gulf when I started, had become the theatre. Sandy was absorbed, concentrating her whole self on what I was telling her. She was an audience not just hearing and looking, but listening and watching with the intensity that is meat and drink to the actor – and the playwright. I lost that grip on her when I came to Bruce's death. I made as little of it as I could, but I could not gloss over it without insulting what it meant to her, and to me; and as well as that, I found I was talking to her then not as the storyteller to an audience, but as myself to Sandy.

So she stopped watching me as she had been. She got up and stood looking out of the window into the dark, her arms wrapped round her with her hands hugging her shoulders. I wanted to go to her but I knew it would not be welcome.

She sensed me dithering behind her. 'Don't stop *there*!' she whispered. 'For God's sake go on!'

Somehow the telling started again. I told her about my dealings with the Toronto police, about meeting Tozzetti after the funeral and all that followed. While I was talking Sandy came away from the window and sat down again. There were unshed tears in her eyes and her face was pinched in, but by some extraordinary strength of will beyond my imagining she forced her emotion to give place to the effort of concentrating all her mind on what she was hearing, and gradually the pinched look disappeared and that look of keenly focused intelligence came back.

When I finished, she said simply: 'That's some story, all right. Look, somebody's going to have to go out to the woodpile and bring in some wood. How about if you do that and I get us a meal, okay?'

'Fine,' I said.

She walked over to me where I sat on the edge of the table and took my face lightly between her hands, and looked at me out of her bright blue eyes. 'Thanks for telling me,' she said. 'I guess it wasn't easy for you.' Then she slapped me lightly on one cheek. 'Try not to bring too much snow into the house,' she said, and went off to rummage in the fridge-freezer.

After that she was reticent and non-committal until the meal was over, until as she sat sipping on her coffee she said suddenly: 'It's money, of course.'

'What is?' I said. I had gone back to thinking of this wild frozen waste we were in, and what life must have been like for the people who built the cabin in the first place.

'All this killing,' Sandy said, 'all these Tozzettis and Seddalls and Vosters. Money's the cause of it all.'

'If it's that,' I said, 'where do Heneage and Seddall come in?'

Sandy laughed. 'You mean its realpolitik? Secret and exciting government business? Well, it's not. I just know it's not. I can smell the money in this; I smelled it while you were telling me about it.'

'Well, that's very nice,' I said, 'but why should we rely on what your nose tells you? I mean, Sandy, this is pretty important to us. We can't just go on . . .' I stopped short.

'Woman's instinct, that's what you were going to say. I'm not talking woman's instinct. I'm talking historian's instinct, researcher's instinct. Money is my subject, remember?'

I did remember. 'Yes,' I said, 'yes, I do remember. You're doing a course on medieval banking.'

'Courses on medieval banking I have done,' she said crisply. 'I'm writing a goddam book on medieval banking. While you were talking I began thinking, I've been here before.'

'You mean you recognized something in what I told you?'

'Nothing marvellous. I just recognized that somewhere in this there is a scheme to make money.'

'What do you mean, do you mean it's just a plain honest-to-God piece of crime we're caught up in?'

'Yes, but you don't like that. You're too romantic. You want it to be cloak-and-dagger, CIA and MI6, trusty men going in and out of the back door of Downing Street.'

'Come on, Sandy!' I said laughing. 'I don't *want* it to be that; it's been that from the first.'

'So what do you think it is?' Her blue eyes were mocking. She was in a dangerous mood. I fumbled for the right word and when I found it I felt a bit foolish.

'I think the word is "statecraft",' I said.

When I told her long afterwards that when she laughed outright she hooted, she fell upon me with fists flailing. But that is what she did, and she did it now. She hooted with laughter and rolled about a good deal in her chair.

'Statecraft!' she said, when she had calmed down enough to speak. 'Why, what a sweet old-fashioned word!' She sat up straight. 'Listen, you great lummox, stealing money and what you call statecraft have gone hand in hand for so many centuries they might just as well be married!'

'I think that's rubbish, Sandy.'

'Listen, sweetie,' she said, 'I haven't studied ancient Egypt, but the old Roman proconsuls did it; give a man a province to govern and he got rich. Mazarin did it, combined your statecraft with lining his own pockets. Talleyrand did it. These are the *best* I'm talking about. Find a statesman today to match them. Philip the Fourth of France did it in the fourteenth century; he destroyed the Knights Templar to get his claws on their bank.'

'The Knights Templar? Their bank?'

'They were the biggest bankers in the Middle Ages. They invented the checking account, did you know that?'

'Good God? No, I didn't know that.'

'Come closer to our time: the Nazis did it. People in power do it, you know, and not just baddies like the Nazis. They do it all the time. So don't put me down when I say this is just about making money – a lot of money – just because you have men from your government involved in it.'

'Men in government service,' I said, 'not men in government.'

She tossed her head impatiently. 'Anyway, Sandy, it will be a strange thing if I ever manage to put you down. I thought it was rather going the other way.'

'I guess that's true,' she said, pleased with herself. 'Poor Anthony, I sure put it to you, didn't I?'

'That you did,' I said, but abstractedly, for my mind was moving on. 'That means it could be Seddall, doesn't it? It could be Harry Seddall.'

'What do you know about him?'

'Not much I haven't told you.' I recalled my encounters with him. 'He doesn't get on with his colleagues; not his colleagues in the police Special Branch, or with his boss. He's a loner, a non-conformer, and Kenna thought he was half in love with the seamy side of life, that he was becoming like the people it was his job to work against. I don't think Kenna trusts him.' I remembered Harry asking me, after that dinner in the club, if I wanted a woman. 'And he's lonely,' I said. I remembered something else. 'He despises authority. He has no time for his superiors – he doesn't acknowledge having superiors, so I should say he has no time for the men who are nominally his superiors.' I paused. 'I like him,' I said.

'Let's not bother about that,' Sandy said, surprising me with the harshness in her voice. 'You might have liked Talleyrand, or you might have liked whoever was governor of Bithynia in 56 BC. If your Mr Seddall is getting people killed, liking him has nothing to do with it. And to me,' she went on, 'he sounds like the guy to have set this all up. He knows the underworld, you said.'

'He certainly knows *an* underworld,' I said. I went on slowly. 'He knows the kind of underworld we've come across in Voster and Lehar, men who have a surface life and another one under the surface.' I looked back over what I had said. 'I think that's what Harry believes in: an innocent surface with the dirt below it. I think that's what he brings to his contempt for authority, the idea that under their civilized exteriors his masters, as he calls them, are no better than the people – Kenna called them scum – he's sent out to deal with.'

'Maybe he's right,' Sandy said, surprising me again, 'but whether he's right or wrong makes no difference. If that's what he feels it makes him even more likely to be the man we're after.'

'After?'

'Yeah,' she drawled. 'After!' Her eyes were colder than the night outside. 'That's what we're about, isn't it? We're going after the son of a bitch that had Bruce killed, aren't we?'

I looked at her. Yes, that was what we were about. It was what Tozzetti had meant when he talked about the Irish and the Sicilians and the vendetta. It was what I had felt in the police station that evening in Toronto, when I had stood staring out into the emptiness and thought that 'they', whoever 'they' were, had killed my friend.

'Yes, Sandy,' I said. 'That's what we're about.'

'Because if you're not, Anthony, I'll do it myself.'

'No,' I said. 'That's what we're about.'

'Even if the man we're after is Harry Seddall – and he's the odds-on favourite right now.'

And I heard myself say: 'Even if it's Harry.'

As soon as I had spoken I found myself listening with something like unbelief to the words I had said. I sat staring at her.

Sandy broke the spell. She got up. 'I could do with a drink,' she said, and poured Scotch into two glasses. 'There's something under the bed we might want to take with us when we leave here. Why don't you get it out?'

'What is it?'

'Go and see,' she said.

She had stuffed the small suitcase we had bought at North Bay in there, and beside it was an old leather guncase, big enough to hold two guns. I brought it over to the floor in front of the stove and undid the straps.

There was only one weapon inside, wrapped about with light canvas. As I took the wrapping off my hands became covered with grease and under the grease was a rifle, far from new. As I inspected it, I smiled: it was part of White Denver's image of himself, an old-fashioned 7mm Mannlicher. Even under the grease its aristocratic lines showed.

Sandy knelt beside me. 'Well, it's pretty,' she said.

'You know about guns?'

'I can shoot. I was hoping for a couple of shotguns, but I should have known. I guess your friend shoots deer in the hunting season; that is when he's not away in England.'

'And this is the hunting season?'

'Yeah.'

'It's a light weapon for shooting deer.'

'A lot you know. I could drop a deer with that at half a mile.'

'Could you, by God?'

'You bet. Let's drink whisky and clean up this old blunder-buss, and start working out a battle plan.'

That brought me up short. It was all every well dedicating ourselves to putting the skids under our assorted foes – once we knew which *were* our foes – but Sandy was right. When it came to thinking what we would do to come to grips with them, my mind was a blank. We still had no idea what was behind the killings, or what it was that had brought these strangely different groups together. I said so to Sandy.

'Sure we do,' she said, putting layers of newspaper on the floor from the kindling box. 'They've kidnapped Monteith and his family and they're going to extort ransom.'

'It feels more sophisticated than that to me.'

'So it's more sophisticated, so it's sophisticated ransom, that's all.'

'You make it sound very simple.'

'Here,' and she gave me more whisky. 'Crime is always simple, because it has simple objectives. Slice it where you like and it's still sausage.'

'Are you getting drunk?'

'I certainly hope so.'

'This is a firearm we're dealing with.'

'So long as it's not loaded.' Which it wasn't. 'Hey – there are no cartridges with the damn thing.'

'Look under the bed again.'

And she found a box with fifty shells in it under the bed. So I cleaned the Mannlicher while Sandy sat cross-legged and watched me. When it was done she put it to her shoulder and aimed down the room. 'It really is pretty,' she said. 'My Daddy would have liked this one.'

She gave it back to me. 'Load it,' she said.

'No, Sandy,' I said. 'I'm not having a loaded gun in the house.'

'This ain't a house, it's a log cabin. Anything could come through that door. Grizzlies and moose could be bearing down on us right now.'

I laughed. 'I may be a tenderfoot, but I know the great grizzly bear lives out West, not around here.'

'Load it anyway, or I'll do it. And that would be dangerous, with me getting looped.' She threw back her head and emptied her glass.

Safest to humour her, I thought. I loaded the rifle and laid it against the wall with the safety on, along the top of its case.

'I won't touch it,' she said. 'And I'm not really drunk. I just have a feeling, is all.'

'What feeling?'

She shivered, though with the stove burning merrily the room was warm. 'Take the whisky away, will you? I don't want to drink any more.' I took the bottle from the floor beside her, and the two glasses, and put them away. 'Thanks,' she said. She smiled, and I realized that her face was suddenly very tired. 'Just a feeling,' she said. 'I don't know what it's about.'

'I know one thing,' I said. 'You're tired out. You get ready for bed and I'll clean up this mess.'

By the time I had cleared away all the greasy rags and newspapers and the kit for cleaning the Mannlicher, Sandy was sitting up in bed. I built up the stove and laid out my sleeping bag, then I went over to kiss her good night.

'That's a big old moon,' she said.

'Do you want to look at it,' I said, 'or shall I close the shutters?'

'I guess it might keep me awake.'

169

So I closed the shutters, put out the lights and got into the sleeping bag.

There was no wind now, and no sound except for the stove and the occasional creak as the wooden cabin settled itself for the night.

'We never got around to making the battle plan,' Sandy said sleepily.

'Neither we did,' I said. 'We'll start on it tomorrow.'

Chapter 18

I woke to a hand gripping my shoulder and Sandy's voice in my ear. 'There's someone coming!'

'Well, why not?' I said, still half awake. 'Maybe it's hunters. You said it was the hunting season.'

'Come *on*, Anthony, hurry! Hunters wouldn't be out this early. The sun's not up yet.'

I disentangled myself from the sleeping bag clumsily and got into my clothes, stumbling about in the dark. 'Well, who is it?' I said, hopping around on one foot trying to pull on a woollen sock.

'I don't *know*,' Sandy said. 'I heard a snowmobile a little way off and then it stopped.'

'Is that all? Why don't you open one of the shutters and have a look? Here, I'll do it.' I was in a bad mood.

I opened the shutters and a dismal grey light crept into the cabin. The first thing I noticed was that Sandy was hefting the rifle. 'What the hell are you doing with that?' I demanded.

She ignored me. 'What do you see?' she asked.

I looked out of the window. 'Nothing. It's frosted up.'

'Then we'll have to open the door.' She stood back from the door with the rifle pointing to the floor.

'Put that thing down,' I said. 'or I won't open it.'

She glared at me. 'Sandy,' I said, 'suppose it is somebody we know, somebody we *think* is the enemy, just which of them would you be ready to shoot right now and no questions asked?'

She thought about it. 'Okay,' she said, and leaned the rifle against the wall, with the safety catch on.

I opened the door a crack and peered out. There were three men at the foot of the slope facing the cabin. I could not see clearly in the half light, but I could make out that one of the three wore city clothes and that the other two were dressed for the weather and the place, and carrying skis and humping packs on their backs.

They began to walk towards us. I recognized the man in the topcoat and hat. He had a scarf wound round his head to keep his ears from freezing. 'It's Collet,' I said. 'Tozzetti's security man – he's from a respectable firm.'

'How do you *know* that?'

'Until we know different we can't start shooting them, that's for sure,' I said.

They were forty feet away now, and still coming.

'Oh, God!' Sandy said in exasperation. 'At least hide the rifle. Fast!'

So I hid the rifle, and some instinct made me put the safety catch off.

'Make coffee,' I said quickly. 'Go on, be making coffee.' and I opened the door with a nice smile. Collet was a yard away with his companions behind him. No one made any startling moves. 'Early callers,' I said cheerily.

'Yeah,' Collet said, watching me with a curious kind of interest that I could not interpret; his look was almost friendly, but at the same time alert and careful. 'Yeah,' he said again. 'Mr Tozzetti only found out where you were last evening.'

'You're quite a surprise,' I said, 'and not entirely welcome, you know. We came up here to get away from all you people. How did Tozzetti track us down?'

'He has means,' Collet said. 'The lady's inside?'

'The lady's making coffee,' I said.

Collet looked a little disappointed. I could not make that out either. I thought perhaps I should try.

'Don't you like women?' I said.

Collet went on watching me and said nothing. One of the men behind him spoke, and despite the hood of the parka over his

172

head I recognized the short bald man on his team. 'He likes women,' the bald man said, 'but sometimes they get in the way.'

Collet's face expressed mild irritation. 'Shut up,' he said, and then to me, 'How about some of that coffee?'

I stepped aside and Collet came into the cabin while the others propped their skis against the outside wall of the cabin and unshipped their backpacks. 'Good day, Mrs Baldwin,' Collet said. 'I guess this is something of an intrusion.'

'I won't say it isn't,' Sandy said.

'Why *are* you here?' I said.

'Mr Tozzetti thinks this is not a safe place for you.'

'What does he think?' Sandy said smartly. 'We'll go skating and fall through the ice?'

Another odd expression crossed Collet's face. This one seemed to say she had almost hit the mark, but not quite. 'Something like that,' he said, and the tone of voice said the same thing as his face.

I thought suddenly: they've come here to kill us. To kill me, but Sandy is here so she has to be killed too.

'They brought skis,' I said to Sandy, 'and one of them has a tent.'

She was incredulous. 'A tent! You're not going winter-camping? Look at you!' She waved a hand at Collet's top coat and pin-stripe suit. 'You'll freeze to death!'

Collet pulled a pistol out of his pocket. 'I'll shoot the girl first,' he said. 'Don't move. We have no intention of freezing to death.'

His henchmen took their cue and came into the cabin. The bald one sat himself on the bed with a pistol resting on his thigh and the other, the tall ugly blond lad, leaned against the wall behind me. I held my hands away from my body to show I was docile, and went over to Sandy. I put an arm round her.

'I told you,' she said, 'I told you, you damn fool! But you wouldn't listen.'

'What did you tell him?' Collet rapped out.

'She said she did not believe you were security men,' I said quickly.

'She can speak for herself,' Collet said. 'Who did you think we were?'

Sandy stepped out of my arm. 'It's okay, Anthony,' she said. 'Anthony, this is them. This is the kind of hood that killed Bruce.'

'You don't know that,' Collet said.

'I believe it,' Sandy said. 'That's good enough for me. And I know who you are. You're hoods from Montreal.'

'And just how do you know that?' Collet asked her.

'Why, that's easy,' Sandy drawled. 'People I can tell apart. Scum all looks alike to me.'

The young blond boy came off the wall in a hurry, but Collet simply turned his face a couple of inches towards him and he stopped where he was. 'I mean, how do you know Montreal?'

'I know the accent,' Sandy said. 'I worked there.'

'Then it's a good thing you were here after all,' Collet said, and stood up. 'You two go outside and put your skis on,' he said to his men.

The bald man spoke. 'We haven't had coffee.'

Sandy knocked the coffee pot off the stove. Coffee and grounds spattered the floor, me, Sandy and Collet's nice top coat. He didn't move a muscle, except in his face. 'There's your answer,' he said to the bald man. 'No coffee. Get going.'

They went outside, and began putting their skis on again.

'They're going skiing?' I asked.

'You four are going skiing,' Collet said, and stood up. 'I don't ski.'

'Why are we going skiing?' Sandy demanded. Her voice was as nervous as I felt.

'You don't need to know that,' Collet said flatly.

'I want to know,' she said earnestly. 'Tell me.'

Collet sighed, but ever so slightly. It was the most emotion I was to see him show. 'You're going to go skiing, and you'll go too far, and you're going to camp out.'

'Camp out? Up here? Do you know how cold it is at night?' Sandy understood what he meant at the same moment that I did, and Collet confirmed it. I expect my face went as pale as hers, even before he told us.

'I know how cold it gets,' he said. 'And you won't have any down-filled sleeping bag with you, either. If the first night doesn't get you, the second will.'

He moved to one side of the door and said to me: 'Get those skis off the wall and outside.' To Sandy he said: 'Come here.'

The skis were stacked against the wall beside the spot where the blond boy had been leaning. Sandy had not moved. I went to get the skis and they began to fall over as Collet said again to Sandy: 'Come over here!'

They fell over because I put a lot of concentration into ignoring them. I took the rifle I had hidden there into both hands and turned it on Collet. When it went off he fell down and said: 'Jesus!' He looked at the blood on his chest with no expression at all, and died.

The pistol had jerked from his hand and slid over the polished planking to Sandy's feet. She picked it up and looked at it. She looked at Collet.

I had another cartridge levered into the chamber when the blond kid threw himself into the cabin at floor level and then got stuck there, trapped by the skis he was wearing. He lost his pistol too. It slid over beside Collet. The boy looked at the corpse and then at me with fright on him. I thought he seemed reassured for a moment, reading in my face that I was not going to kill him too.

Then Sandy shot him in the back with Collet's Smith & Wesson. He bled a lot more than Collet, because it turned out the bullet had smashed his collar bone and gone through him into the maplewood he was lying on.

He made a lot more noise than Collet had too, which was annoying, because I wanted to talk to the man outside, before he tried to run for it or make another of these death-or-glory charges through the door. The adrenalin was pumping in me and it had gone to my head: I had an idea. It was an idea that needed me to have the bald man in one piece.

I moved to one side of the door and reached out quickly to grab the kid's pistol in case he was feeling braver than he sounded, then jumped to a window and looked out.

The bald man was not waiting for a bulletin from the front. He was skiing as fast as he could go among the scattered pine trees off to the left, where the slope that rose in front of the cabin shallowed into a little hump. If he got over that we would be into a stern chase, and if he reached the snowmobile we could lose him.

'Can your really drop a deer at half a mile?' I asked Sandy.

'Yup,' she said.

I grabbed her arm, we negotiated the obstacle of the moaning boy and his crossed skis, and outside I gave her the rifle. Before I let go of it I said: 'We need him unhurt. Let him see you could hit him.'

She gave herself an extra second to take this in, then nodded, lifted the Mannlicher to her shoulder, and fired three times. I saw a puff of snow knocked off a tree to his left, and one off to his right, and her third shot threw a shower of it off the end of a branch right in his path.

He sheered to a stop, found his balance, and held his arms wide to signal that he was out of business.

'Right,' I said, 'keep the rifle and watch the boy. He may have something up his sleeve yet. A game like this isn't won till all the pieces are back in the box. And, Sandy – I've got the glimmering of an idea. I'll want Baldy scared stiff and demoralized so don't be surprised at how I treat him, and if you see an opening, follow my lead.'

She gave me an up-from-under look that wondered if I was going to torture the man, but she said, 'You got it,' and I left her with the rifle on the crook of her arm, facing the casualty in the doorway.

To the bald man I yelled. 'You have a pistol. I want to see it thrown into the snow.'

He let go of one of his ski sticks so that it hung by the loop, and put the free hand to his body. It came away again with something held in it. He waggled the pistol about to let me see and then tossed it in an arc into the snow.

I sighted the boy's pistol on the bald man with both hands and called to him to turn round and come back. He skied slowly towards me, and when he came near I told him to place himself about fifteen feet away opposite the door of the cabin.

I moved over beside the cabin door, keeping the pistol on him, and said to Sandy: 'We're going to have a reaction in a minute and we want to get this wrapped up first. I'd like you to sit on the bed and keep the rifle on the boy. I may be five minutes, no more.'

I kept half an eye on her while she negotiated her way over the wounded boy, who had stopped yelling now, and was moaning and sobbing. I hoped he would not bleed to death before I was ready to attend to him.

'What's your name?' I said to the bald man.

He stared at me. I dropped my aim to his left knee. 'Palousse,' he said rapidly, 'Charles Palousse.' He pronounced his first name like a Frenchman.

'Good,' I said. 'Take your skis off, Charles, boots and all.'

'Out here? In all this snow?'

I put a bullet into one of his skis and he fell down.

'Are you okay?' Sandy called from the cabin.

'Fine,' I yelled back. 'I may shoot some more. Don't worry.' To Charles Palousse I said: 'Get up.'

He managed to get back on his feet, and without any more encouragement from me he got out of his boots and off his skis. 'My feet are freezing,' he said.

'Take your clothes off,' I said. 'Everything.'

'Aw –' he began.

'I won't shoot at your skis next time. You've got one dead and one dying. What makes you think you're special? Strip, Charles. Strip now and strip fast.'

He stripped.

'The wristwatch,' I said. 'Take it off.'

He looked thunderstruck, but took off the watch and threw it wildly into the snow.

'Sandy,' I called out. 'I'm sending a naked man in there. Make him sit in one of the chairs at the stove, and when he's set I'll come in.'

'You got it,' Sandy said.

'Inside, Charles,' I said.

He walked unhappily through the snow, a pale body with a bald head but a hairy pelt on his front. As he came close to the door I went off to one side. At the door he stopped.

'There's a lady — ' he began.

'You want to play hot buttocks?' I asked him, and lined the pistol on his shivering backside.

He looked down at the boy in the doorway for the first time. 'Jesus!' he said, and stepped over him carefully and went out of my line of vision.

'Sit there,' I heard Sandy say. Then, 'He's set,' she told me.

So I went in over the body of the wounded boy and sat myself at the table facing the door. 'Weapons check,' I said. 'You have the rifle, I have the boy's pistol. Where's Collet's?'

'Here,' Sandy said. 'I stuck it in my belt.'

'Jesus!' Charles said again. 'That was you?'

'Yeah,' Sandy said. 'And it was me that shot the kid in the back.'

He stared at her, shocked and shivering and covered in goose-bumps. 'You g-gotta be — '

'Shut up!' I said. 'This isn't a party.'

'It's just that I'm very angry,' Sandy said, in a terrible inflex-ible gentle voice. 'And now I want you to see if there's any life in that stove, and put some wood on it, and if you try to set the cabin on fire or anything witty like that, I'll shoot your backbone out through your front.'

While we watched him work at the stove I said to Sandy: 'We have to patch up the boy. I'm worried there may be a man out there still. They may have left one with their car.'

'Do we need the boy?' Sandy asked.

The naked man looked over his shoulder at her in horror.

'What are you thinking?' I asked Sandy.

178

'Well, if we don't need the boy you could go down and check out their car and I can just sit here and keep an eye on things till you get back. If we wait that long the boy will die, likely.'

'How many sets of car keys do you think they'd have?' I asked her, after thinking for a few moments.

'Yes,' she said. 'That's good. I'd say two.'

'That's what I think.'

'How many sets of car keys?' Sandy asked Charles, who was still squatting by the stove, watching us with a strange look in his eyes.

'Two sets,' he said. 'Collet has –' he swallowed – 'Collet had a spare set and the kid was driving. He mighta left them in the car.'

'Find out,' I said.

The small man closed his eyes tightly then opened them again and got up and went over to Collet; to Collet's corpse. I saw Sandy catch her lip in her teeth, and her expression change. I got up casually and said: 'I could do with a little Scotch, I think.' I put some in two glasses and gave one to her. She put it down, two swallows, and gave a shake as it hit her. She nodded at me, to say she was all right for a while longer.

The small man had found Collet's car keys and went over to the boy. He tried to lift the boy's hip to get at his pocket and there was a scream.

'Wait,' I said. I got the first-aid kit from the bathroom and found some morphine and a hypodermic. 'Charles,' I said, 'can you do this?'

'I can do it,' he said.

He managed to get at the vein in the boy's good arm without any more screams from the patient. Soon after the boy stopped moaning and he got the other set of car keys from a pocket.

'Is there a man at the car?' I asked, as I took the keys from him.

'You wouldn't believe it if I told you,' he said. 'But no, we left the car to look after itself. You were gonna be a pushover.'

'You get the skis off him while he's still under,' I said, 'and we'll get him inside and work on that shoulder. Sandy, can you keep an eye on the ridge, just in case?'

'That I can do,' she said, and sat herself at the foot of the bed leaning against the wall, where she could see out. The sun was up, and seemed to have as much south as east in it, but it was not blinding her yet. I realized that a well trained man, if he had heard the shooting, might wait till the sun was right behind him before he came up to the ridge. We had a lot of work to do before then, and I thought it would help to have something to eat.

However, first things first. I watched Charles while he shivered and cursed outside the doorway, struggling to get the skis and boots off the injured boy. When he had done it at last I helped him get the boy inside, and closed the door. Warmth would help, but I wondered if we were too late tending the boy. He had been in the cold a long time since he was shot. When we moved him, to lay him on my sleeping bag, with a couple of sheets over it, the blood, which had stopped, started again, but sluggishly. I wondered what that meant, but not for long.

'Can you cook bacon and eggs?' I asked Charles.

'Sure.'

I went over the kitchen corner and took all the sharp knives away, and a pair of scissors. I found some string and made him tie his ankles together so that he was hobbled, with about two feet of movement, one leg from the other.

'Can you give him a robe, or something?' Sandy asked.

So I cut the pockets off my dressing gown, new as of two days ago, making it impossible for him to hide anything he might come across, and he put it on.

'God, you're a careful man.' Sandy said.

'He kills for a living,' I said. 'So yes, I'm careful.'

He glared at me. His eyes seemed to grow smaller. But he said nothing to me. 'Thanks, lady,' he said to Sandy.

'For letting you cover yourself? Don't thank me, I was sick of looking at you.'

He went to pieces then, and started blubbering and shouting at the same time. 'You – you bitch! Bernie Collet lyin' there dead and Robbie that you shot in the back when he was down awready, who are you to treat a man that way?' He tried to walk at her but forgot the hobble on his ankles and fell down, staying there propped up on his hands and knees, snivelling like a child. But he went on yelling at her. 'Who are you to take away a man's . . . a man's pride and make him walk around bare-assed and freezin' in the fuckin' snow, tie your ankles cook the fuckin' breakfast see to the fuckin' stove.' The temper went out of him all at once and he sat up, kneeling. 'You're the coldest-hearted woman I ever seen,' he said quietly, 'and if I live to see you die piece by piece and screaming, I'll smile to watch you.'

Sandy was as pale as death and her mouth trembled when she answered him. 'You piece of shit,' she said. 'You and . . . and these killed my husband, who was nothing to you. You screwed that up and killed my man instead of him.' She pointed at me but kept her eyes on the man on the floor. 'So to tidy up the mess you made you came up here to kill two more of us. Don't you *remember*? You were going to freeze us to death out in the snow, don't you *remember*?' She laid down the rifle on the bed and went over to him, and sat on the floor within easy reach, if he had wanted to lash out at her, with her legs crossed in front of her. 'You think there are rules for this kind of thing? Do you think we should know the rules you play by? If we knew them, do you think we'd follow them? He shot Collet and then there were two of you, and I shot your friend Robbie because I was scared shitless, I didn't know he'd lost his gun but I'd have shot him just the same, because I was scared shitless and he was six feet of killer, man, and you were outside somewhere, anywhere, how the fuck did I know you weren't about to shoot through the window or come in the door? You can't start killing people, mister, and expect them to play by rules and think of your pride.'

She did a strange thing, then. She reached out and touched his cheek, and took her hand back and looked at it, and then began wiping it on the rug beside her, not knowing she was doing that, while she finished saying her piece. 'Lover,' she said, 'we're still scared shitless of you, and I hate you and despise you, and either one of us will kill you or worse if you look like being dangerous again in any little way. You killed my man, mister, and I don't have any pride in me at all since you did that. So don't you fuss me about your pride. You just go and cook us all a nice breakfast. You want breakfast, don't you? Sure you do. You cook breakfast, and I'll see to Robbie.'

Something changed in him as I watched. I could not tell whether she had broken his spirit, or whether he was storing his rage inside him until his time came to get even with her. Whatever it was, his face emptied of expression. He looked pretty sick. He had taken his eyes off her; they were turned on the floor between them. Finally, he rose carefully to his feet. He gave a strange kind of sigh, like a man who has been listening to himself too long, and wakes up to find the world is different from how he had told it to himself.

He said to me: 'Can we put Bernie outside?'

'Let's do that thing,' I said, affecting as much nonchalance as I could manage, trying to appear indifferent to what had passed between him and Sandy; as if I had not been shaken by the fury of contempt she had unleashed on him; as if I was not at the same time appalled and confused by hearing her naked hurt spoken in that room to one of the men who had caused it; as if, in fact, I was not ashamed to find myself sharing some of his own reaction to her: that she had broken some obscurely complicated set of rules that regulated his kind of warfare.

So we dragged – or rather I dragged, because I was not going to take that hobble off him until I was good and ready – the corpse of Collet outside and laid it on the snow. As I stood watching the man I had killed, the small waxed face that had held so much controlled intelligence, such tough self-confidence, and thought how odd it was that I had fired the shot that defeated him, a blanket fell over him like a shroud. Baldy had hobbled to perform this ritual of personal piety to his fallen commander.

He stood in the doorway and I thought for a moment he was going to speak to me, but he just stood there, nothing moving in his face, wearing nothing but the robe and the string round his ankles, shivering in the cold, and I could read nothing in his face, neither sorrow for Collet nor humiliation for himself, no hatred, no threat, no strength or weakness: he had gone a long way into himself, and whatever was happening there was hidden deep.

He went back inside and the door closed. I knew Sandy was attending to the wounded Robbie, but I knew too that Baldy had no moves to make against us for a long while; that he would cook breakfast and do whatever else we wanted him to do until the time came when he began the return journey from wherever he had hidden himself. The trick could be to recognize the early signs that meant he was coming out of his hibernation.

I went round the end of the cabin to the woodpile and took some armfuls of the corded wood to stack by the door, and when that was done stood at the back of the cabin looking out over the frozen lake.

The sun was up now, casting a long light over the snow and ice and making pale shadows of the trees. The place was hard on the spirit, as if it had been made a million years ago and the harshness of it shrank that million years to yesterday: as if it had been made yesterday a long time ago, and might end tomorrow.

I wished I had not killed Collet, though I knew too that I was lucky my shot had hit him at all; no one positioned as I was could have shot to wound him only. But I was starting to feel the weight of his death on me. The reaction I had spoken of to Sandy was setting in. I let it ride for a while, then went back round the cabin and opened the door.

Robbie was lying with his head on a pillow on the floor, his eyes open but still dulled with morphine, and a good-looking bandage swathed his ribs and injured shoulder. Sandy and Baldy made a companionable picture, she washing her hands at the sink and Baldy serving bacon and eggs and home-fried potatoes onto three plates.

I dumped some wood beside the stove, and the three of us sat round the table and ate our breakfast.

Chapter 19

———◆———

Baldy was wearing his clothes again and his ankles were untied. If he felt uncomfortable at all it was only because I was pressed up close to him in the phone booth with my ear on top of his, and because of the muzzle of the .38 Smith & Wesson I was holding right inside his zipper jacket, hand and all, gently nudging his stomach. My ear was there to let me share in both ends of his phone call as a silent participant, and the pistol was there to keep him in mind of what he had to do.

The earpiece stopped purring and said: 'Yeah.'

'This is Charlie,' Baldy said.

I scanned his face to see if he was showing any signs of getting back into the fight, but I got as much news from that as I would have learned from the Man in the Moon about what was going on behind him in space. I thought that maybe it was going to work, but I nuzzled the pistol against his sweater in a pointed way to help things along.

There had been a pause. 'Is Bernie there?'

'Not any more,' Baldy said.

'Where did he go?'

'Swimming,' Baldy said. 'He went swimming.'

'It must be pretty cold for that. Dangerous, even.'

'Yeah,' Baldy said. 'Dangerous. It could have killed me.'

There was more pause, then: 'Did anyone else go swimming?'

Baldy said: 'Uh-huh. A woman and a friend of hers.'

The voice in the phone lost some of the tension it had shown at the news of Bernie going swimming. For a moment I relaxed –

Baldy was committed, now that he had given out that Sandy and I had also taken part in the swimming party – and then I nudged him with the pistol again. There was no knowing what was going on in his head, or what he might do.

What the phone said next was: 'You didn't go swimming, huh?'

'Nope.'

'Robbie?'

'Well, you could say Robbie only went paddling. I have a problem with Robbie.'

After another pause the voice gave a little sigh. 'I've been thinking that Robbie should see a doctor. What do you think?'

'Yeah, that's what I think. I think he should see a doctor pretty soon.'

'Yeah.' Pause. 'Do you think a house call, or should he go to hospital?'

I held my breath. I almost poked the pistol at Baldy's stomach again but stopped myself. I had a feeling Baldy would follow the script better if I left him to it.

This time there was a pause from Baldy. The phone waited and I waited.

Meanwhile, out in the car park Sandy waited in the rear seat of the Volvo station wagon with Robbie beside her. Robbie was not coming along as well as had been expected after his first encouraging response to Sandy's fairly skilled treatment. The ride down the track in the snowmobile had taken it out of him and we had driven fifty miles since then. But he had a pistol pointing at his liver too.

'This should be a house-call, I think,' Baldy said.

'Okay,' the phone said. 'Bring the poor kid home.' Then it said: 'You musta done good, Charlie, by the sounds of that swimming party. Ah – was the water deep?'

'As deep as hell,' Charlie said bitterly. I looked at him quickly. It was the first flicker of emotion I had seen in him since he had retreated inside himself, but nothing showed on his face.

I had my ear back to the phone in time to hear it say: 'Now,

now, Charlie, stay cool, that's the boy. You bring Robbie back home.'

The man at the other end hung up on us and Baldy stood there with the handset clutched in his fist, staring at it. His look now was as bitter as his voice had been, so perhaps he was getting ready to be difficult. But it seemed to me he was hating everybody, the other end of the phone as well as the home team, so I thought we had perhaps one advantage – that he had no sides left – until I saw that this would make him completely unpredictable. He could be a man playing his game utterly at random, with no thought of the end result so long as he could make mayhem when he had the chance.

I said nothing, took the pistol out of his jacket and hid it in my own. Then I stepped away from the phone booth, a good few paces, and waited. Let him come on his own; don't drive him. He came on his own.

His fingers eased their grip on the phone and he put it back on its cradle. He came away from the booth like a man on his own and looked blankly round the shopping mall, still almost empty at this time of day, until he seemed to notice me. There was a difference in him now – I had no doubt of it. His eyes hardly touched me before he turned and went the way he was supposed to go, out of the mall to the car park and over to the car. He made for the driving seat.

'I'll drive,' I said.

He changed course without hesitation and opened the passenger door and sat down. I got into the driving seat and drove out of town. No one spoke a word until we were back on the road and making time over the highway.

'How'd it go?' Sandy asked as we passed the sixty mark, and added almost at once: 'There's a fifty mile-an-hour limit here. We don't want any trouble with the police.'

I eased my foot up a little. 'Went like silk,' I said. 'Baldy was a good, good boy.' I said it to provoke him; to see if he was ready to make a statement.

He was. Sandy disapproved of it, but she knew what it

signified as well as what it meant. 'Baldy's himself again,' she said.

We came to a clear space beside the road. I turned off and stopped the car, got out, opened the tailgate, found a hunting knife and the sinister remains of the coil of rope we had found in the snowmobile. It had been meant to tie us up while we froze to death, according to Collet's plan for us. Now some of it was holding him to the snowmobile under the ice of the lake.

When I opened the car door and Baldy saw the rope he thought of going into action there and then, but Sandy hit him so hard on the side of the head that the other side bounced off the door pillar. Then she yanked his head back with a hand on his forehead and stuck the gun into his mouth which was still open from the shock.

'I'll hate you till you're dead,' she said, 'and I'd as soon get it over with.'

Both of us believed her, just as we had believed her back at the cabin, and he held still and let me lash him to the seat. I tied the rope round his middle as tight as a southern belle's corset, and then I lashed his wrists to the rope at the sides of the seat. I took his shoes off and tied his ankles together. It seemed safe enough, and I did not want him to get cramp. Pins and needles I could put up with, but I wanted him ready to move fairly quickly when I was ready for him to move.

We set off again.

'He dialled that area code?' Sandy asked me.

'He did. And that number. I think that means he gave us the right address.'

'So far so good,' Sandy said.

Baldy came up with a coarse laugh.

'What's so funny?' Sandy asked him.

'The last guy I heard of who said that,' Baldy said, 'was falling through the sky halfway down the Empire State Building.'

'Just think of it this way,' Sandy said pleasantly. 'You're the awning, and if the sidewalk looks too hard we'll land on you first.'

It was a long drive. Baldy found a way of going to sleep, or giving a good imitation of it. Robbie had the worst of it, though Sandy fed him painkillers from the first-aid kit at intervals.

At last she leaned over the space between the front seats and said: 'I think Robbie has to go.'

Baldy was not as far recovered from his first horror at her callousness towards cold-blooded murderers as he had thought. He stared at her in amazement.

'Show me the way,' I said to Sandy, 'and tell me when we get there.'

We were coming down into North Bay and the street lights were on, but the city was asleep, except for the small percentage of night workers and night owls. Sandy guided me through the streets. When we were half a mile from our destination we made Robbie drink hot soup from a Thermos, moved Baldy's seat right forward to give us room, and eased the unfortunate Robbie into his own sleeping bag. Then we drove on again. When we were twenty yards from the Nurses' Home I stopped the car and untied Baldy. I gave him five minutes to ease himself and stretch his muscles, and told him to get out of the car and carry the kid down the street and up the steps of the Nurses' Home.

'What's that place?' he said. 'Why the drama? You gonna shoot him, shoot him here.'

'Nobody's going to shoot anybody,' I said, 'if you do what you're asked to do.'

'But if you don't do what you're asked to do,' Sandy said, 'I'll have this good rifle resting on the back of the seat and a clear shot out of the open window. We don't have as much to lose as you do, and I have plenty to gain. Even in this light I could kneecap you from here, and if I have enough self-control to leave your other knee alone, they'll let me off with a talking to when they know what it's all about. But you'll be a long time in hospital and then a long time in the hoosegow.'

'Hoosegow!' Baldy said, and opened the back door to take the kid out of the car. He lifted Robbie in his arms despite the boy's weight, and held him cradled there.

'Are we there?' Robbie said mildly.

'We're there kid,' Baldy said. 'Put my sleeping bag on his chest,' he said. Sandy reached the other rolled-up bag out of the back and laid it on the boy's chest.

We watched the pair of them go down the street, the small man carrying the big one as easily, so it seemed, as if it were the other way round. At the steps he stopped, gathering his forces for the short climb up. In my wing mirror I saw a couple wrapped up in parkas, oblivious to or even enjoying the cold, come slowly down the street on the other side, holding each other clumsily through layers of clothing, like a ponderous four-legged creature unknown to zoologists. Then a car came towards us and slowed when it saw them coming down the sidewalk.

'Oh dear no!' Sandy said.

I had no breath to say anything. The car came towards Baldy, the couple in the wing mirror grew larger, and Baldy climbed the steps as if he had the whole city to himself.

First he laid the boy down, then he untied the other sleeping bag and shook it loose, and lifted the boy up again and laid him on top of it. Then he came back down the steps and walked quite fast back to the Volvo, keeping pace, or so it seemed, with the car.

As Baldy got back into his seat the car passed us on one side and the couple on the other, and went their separate ways. I put the Volvo into gear and took the first turning I came to. Sandy began navigating.

'There,' Baldy said suddenly. 'You can phone from there.'

As I slowed the car, Sandy said: 'How did you know we were going to phone?'

'Because you're soft in the gut, baby,' Baldy said. 'That's why you'll hit the pavement with a smack.'

Sandy made the phone call.

When she got back in the car she said: 'We should have dumped the rest of their camping gear. If we're stopped it will tie us in with the sleeping bags.'

Baldy got a laugh out of that one too. 'If they stop the car, sugar-tit,' he said merrily, 'they'll think you're Bonnie and Clyde. You got enough weapons in here to hold up every bank in Montreal.

She had no answer to that one, and we drove out of the city. After a while Sandy took the wheel. Baldy slept, lashed in to his seat, and I kept yawning and dropping off.

'Go to sleep,' Sandy said. 'I'll be fine.'

I went to sleep.

When she woke me we were travelling in the grey light of dawn through a landscape of trees and bare granite. 'What's up?' I said.

'There's a car following us,' Sandy said.

Chapter 20

I came awake in a hurry, then calmed down again. I looked behind me, and there at a respectable distance, appearing now and then round a bend behind us, was a car.

'It's just a car.' I said.

'Well, maybe,' she said, 'but we're awful close to where we're headed. It's early for people to be on the road.'

I looked back again. It was a green Buick coupé, or what they call a coupé nowadays, which just meant it had a black granulated plastic roof. There were four men in it. I told Sandy this. 'They're probably making an early start for a train, going to work,' I added comfortably.

'No one goes this way for a train to work,' she said.

'Then perhaps they're just driving to work,' I said.

'What kinda car is it?' Baldy asked suddenly. He had been trying to turn his head far enough to see it, but the rope wouldn't let him.

'It's a green Buick with a black top,' I said.

'Ha!' he said. 'You got trouble.'

'What kind of trouble?' Sandy snapped at him.

'That's Palumbo's car, sweetheart.'

'Who's Palumbo?' I asked. I looked back again. The green car was still keeping a nice distance on the winding road; an intelligent driver knowing there was no point in trying to overtake until the road hit a straight. It looked innocent enough to me. Why should I trust Baldy?

'Palumbo is plenty tough,' Baldy said.

'What would you do if you were me?' I asked him.

191

'You got a rifle. I'd shoot him off the road.'

I thought about this. If it was Palumbo's car, where did Baldy stand? After that phone call he had made, he would stand very badly indeed: he had reported us dead, mission accomplished, himself on the way back with his wounded. If they caught us, and Baldy, they would know he had lied to them and led us down to the Ottawa River country.

That he had led us to the place where they were holding the Monteiths.

If it was Palumbo's car, it would be a very good thing for Baldy if I shot it off the road. On the other hand, it would do Baldy no harm at all if I shot a car with four innocent strangers in it off the road, while it would get us into a lot of trouble sooner or later. He also knew enough about Sandy and me by now to know that it would cause a lot of trouble between us – perhaps knock the stuffing out of us and prevent us going on – if we discovered we had killed or injured four law-abiding Canadians for no reason at all.

I said all these things out loud. I could tell nothing from Baldy's reaction. He was restless in his bonds and grinned nervously off and on, at intervals that bore no relation to this or that point of what I was saying.

Sandy was biting her lip. She was strained and tired from the long night drive she had made, but it was not that which began to affect her driving. I could feel it through the different motion of the car. Half her attention was on the fact of that following car, and she was either slowing more than she needed on the corners or taking them too wide and too fast, braking a lot at the wrong place on the road.

'What do you think?' she said.

'How far to go?' I asked Baldy, our unreliable guide.

'About five miles,' he said.

'Is the road like this all the way, or is there a straight stretch somewhere ahead?'

'Yeah,' he said, 'there's a straight quite soon.'

'All right,' I said to Sandy. 'I think we have to find out. When you get the chance, let them pass.'

'Is that wise?' she asked.

'How the hell do I know?' I said.

She bit her lip some more and Baldy laughed.

I checked that the Mannlicher had its full load of five in the magazine, stuffed one pistol down the side of the rear seat and holstered the other down the back. We had plenty of fire power if we had to bring it down on the target.

We swung round a bend in the road and there before us was a mile-long straight. 'Oh, God!' Sandy said. 'Here it is.'

'You're doing fine,' I said. 'Let them pass if they're going to.'

They came up behind and pulled out and went past, then they slowed down and two faces peered out of the rear window. Sandy braked and the Volvo wavered on the snow. Then the car in front speeded up and shot off down the road, dwindled in size and vanished at the far end of the straight.

'Ambush,' Baldy said tonelessly. 'That's Palumbo's car.'

'Go slow,' I said to Sandy. 'Look for a place to get off the road.'

'What kind of *place*?' Sandy demanded.

'Any kind of – there! Other side of the road, try that!'

The car slewed and skidded towards the patch of snow, a break in the trees that hedged the road, and rode up onto it with a bump from the front wheels as if the shock had gone right through the tires to the rims. Sandy did some swearing, steering and brake-pumping while the car bottomed out with a nasty grinding sound like metal on solid rock.

'Damn!' I said. 'We need the car in working order.'

'Well, I sure am sad about that,' Sandy drawled. 'You should of wrote and told me.'

'Okay,' I said. 'Sorry I said that. It's a tough car, probably took no damage.' I turned my attention to Baldy. 'They'll kill you, Baldy, won't they?'

He stopped chewing his lip. 'Yeah, they'd kill me. I fooled them good. I don't know how I come to do it.'

'You went to pieces, that's how,' I said. 'If I give you the car, what'll you do?'

'I'll drive it outa here like it's never been drove before,' he said. 'Is this some kinda joke?'

'No joke. We go into the woods, you take off in the car. Right?'

'Right,' he said. 'Just cut me loose and do it fast.'

'Sandy?' I said.

'Maybe,' she said. 'Maybe. Yes.'

She opened her door and got out. On the other side of the road the ground fell into the forest, and we threw snowshoes, skis, backpacks and everything we could lay our hands on in a hurry that might be useful down among the trees. First of all, though, I had cut Baldy's arms loose to let him move about and get the use of them again. When we were set I cut the ropes from his body and he scrambled stiffly across into the driver's seat.

'A gun?' he said.

'Get going,' I said.

I followed Sandy into the trees and we found cover among the debris of fallen timber that floored the forest and waited, looking up at the road. Baldy took the car off the rock. He did it well, engaging reverse only when it was needed and letting the car coast when it was not scraping the crankcase, or whatever it was scraping, against the granite. He made the road, got the rear end pointing the way we had been going and set off back down the way we had come, took his speed up and went out of sight like a bat out of hell.

'We left marks on the snow,' Sandy said.

'They won't look for that,' I said. 'There's enough to show we took the car off and turned her round.'

'I almost hope he makes it,' she said.

'You *do* hope he makes it,' I said. 'The further he makes it the better for us.'

'Yes, well,' she said, looking at the litter, spread over a suprisingly wide area, that was the equipment of our impromptu expedition. 'Why don't we get all this stuff together while you tell me what we do next.' Suddenly she yawned. 'Apart from

194

falling asleep,' she added.

'We ought to get moving, once their car's gone past.'

'I can still move, but how do you know their car will go past?'

'I don't. I hope it will. If they were waiting for us down the road and we don't turn up, they should come back looking for the car.'

I was thinking about something else. 'I'm beginning to think I should have left Baldy one of the handguns,' I said.

'So that they can shoot each other up?'

'Yes. I've got one besides the rifle, and you've got one.'

'No. I haven't. You had them both, Anthony.'

I thought back, and remembered how I had stowed the two pistols, one down the side of the rear seat – the one I had brought with me – and one down the back of it, which I had forgotten about.

'So Baldy's got himself a gun,' Sandy said when I had explained to her.

'If he finds it.'

'He'll find it. He'd smell it at fifty paces.'

There was the sound of a car, distant and coming closer. We went down again into cover and watched the road. The green Buick came tearing along, braked as it drew level so that it snaked all over the place, then changed its mind and went pelting on.

'Thank God for that,' I said.

'We should get out of here, all the same,' Sandy said, 'and go wherever we're going.'

She was right, and we gathered together everything we had tossed down from the roadside.

'Let's move into the forest a way,' I said, 'and we can bury what we don't want in the snow.'

'Good thought,' Sandy said.

We loaded up and set off into the trees. It was slow going at first, with the floor of the forest a mass of dead wood under snow, but when we had climbed about a hundred feet and the ground levelled off, the walking became easier. The snow was not so deep as it had been up at the lake, and the air was a good deal less cold, although we were near the Quebec border now.

The forest opened out and became a mixture of birch and pine, and we soon found a patch of thick brush to hide the skis in, with the rest of the superfluous weight we were carrying.

We did, however, take the tent that Baldy and his friends had thoughtfully provided for us to freeze to death in, and we took our sleeping bags, because although we were within a few miles of the place where Baldy had told us the kidnapped Monteiths were being held, Sandy had been driving all night and was out on her feet. She, at least, would have to rest, and it would do me no harm either.

There was a chance that Palumbo and his companions in the green Buick would have second thoughts about the place where we had left the road, or that they would catch Baldy and he would give us away. But I thought both of these possibilities were unlikely ones, and, besides, there was not much we could do about it. We were to some extent in a trap. We could not, just the two of us, simply march up to the kidnappers' headquarters in order to avoid being attacked in our rear, and though Sandy was game, she could not go much further. We had little choice but to hole up for some hours, leaving our tracks clearly marked behind us in the snow.

At this point the weather took a hand. Fresh snow began to fall. Soon it was falling thickly enough to hide our trail, so we went on, feeling a little more confident, but looking, all the same, for a place where the tent would be as inconspicuous as possible. We found it at last: a kind of knoll which would hide our camp from one side, with the other side protected to some extent by a dense growth of birch.

We cleared the snow away with snowshoes, which we had brought along not so much because we expected to use them, as because they weighed so little. As soon as the tent was up I made Sandy get into her sleeping bag while I heated up some soup on the gas cylinder stove. When she had drunk the soup she fell asleep almost at once. I wrapped myself up in the other bag and sat in the entrance to the tent, which I zipped up to about two feet from the top, and looked out at the falling snow.

I had some thinking to do.

Luck and the euphoria of our initial success had brought us this far, but the euphoria had now worn off, and it would be pushing our luck to walk into the lion's den, which was staffed, we knew for certain, by Gabriella's hot-heads from Italy, by Palumbo and his fellow gangsters in the green Buick, and for all we knew by Voster and his own henchmen.

There was also the fact that I had not been quite straight with Sandy. I had been putting off the question of what we would do when we got here; partly because I had not fully believed, until that green car started tailing us, that Baldy was not leading us on a false trail; and partly because luck and improvisation had served us once and might bring us through again.

But I think the chief reason I had postponed making a definite plan of action was that my mind was divided. If we did, in fact, locate the house where the Monteiths were being held, the obvious move was to get our news to the police. Even if Sandy was still hell-bent on pursuing her private war, there was little she could do about that once they came on the scene.

What held me back from that, though, was that I differed from Sandy in her near certainty that Harry Seddall would prove to be the man at the back of it all. Since the late lamented Collet and his men had shown themselves in their true guise, Tozzetti seemed to me to fill the bill rather better than Harry. And although, to Sandy's objective ear, and even to mine as I told her about him, Harry came across as the likeliest candidate for Mr Big, and though I knew he was capable of setting up just such a complex operation if he had a mind to, yet I found in myself a strong revulsion against believing it. I disliked a great deal about Harry Seddall, and a great deal about what he represented, but my instinct had told me there was something in the essential Seddall that I valued; I did not want that instinct to be betrayed. I would hang on to it until I knew for certain that it had been.

All of which meant that, logically, I had to regard Harry as being on the side of the angels until and unless I saw him fall from grace. And Harry, for whatever reasons, had not wanted the police brought into this. He was playing his own game, and however secretive and offhand he had been with me, he had entrusted me with the secret of his presence in Canada. To that extent he had made me his ally, and here that question of betrayal came back on the scene: I would find it hard to betray him until I knew for certain that I had cause.

There was still one course of action to be followed before any decision had to be taken. We had to find the house Baldy had described to us: a big, isolated house called Cameron House after the family who had built it for their holiday place. It was one of four or five houses each standing in acres of its own ground and built, like most Canadian holiday houses, on the shores of a lake. Cameron House was at the west end of the lake, on a high bluff.

Taking into account the distance we had walked from the road, it was not more than two or three miles north of where we were right now, and perhaps a good bit less. The thought made me restless.

Sandy slept soundly; she had hours of sleep in her yet. The snow was still falling but it was thick enough already for me to lose myself if I wasn't careful. I left a note for Sandy, just in case she woke, to say I would be back inside the hour.

I took the Mannlicher, checked it over, and eased myself out of the tent. We had come from the road in roughly a westerly direction, and, reckoning from the information Baldy had given us, if I struck south I would be heading for the lake. This was a pretty rough way of navigating, but the distances involved were so small that it seemed to me I had a good chance of finding the lake.

The depth of the snow varied. Some of the time it was shallow enough for me to kick it aside and here and there I had to lift my feet high, but it was not hard work and I made good progress. I had slung a pair of snowshoes on my back in case the going became difficult, though I had never used them and was not sure how much use they would be to me. As it was, I used first one and then the other as markers, at what I estimated to be the quarter-mile and half-mile points from the tent, to reinforce the sightings I tried to photograph on my memory by looking back every now and then the way I had come.

The ground began to slope downwards before me and became suddenly steep and bare of trees. I slipped, and when I had recovered my footing and looked up I saw, about half a mile away, a house standing opposite me at about the same level as myself. At first it was just a shape and then as it became gradually clearer I realized that the snow was thinning. As I looked across at the house the snow stopped falling and the sun began to come through.

Then everything began to happen at once. Just before I turned to get back into the shelter of the trees I saw a man climbing diagonally across the slope below me, and beyond him the sun gleamed on the black water of a lake. I went back up the slope as fast as I could. I reached the top and put myself behind a tree. It was not big enough to hide me but I was less conspicuous than I had been standing against the bare snow. When I looked out and down the slope again, the climbing man was looking up; I wondered if he had seen me or if he was just working out a route for himself.

He threw a glance over his shoulder and changed course, coming up at a sharper angle: coming straight towards me. I started crawling backwards and as I did so he lifted his head and I saw who it was.

'Harry,' I called out. 'This is Anthony Moore, and I've got a gun.'

'Thank God for that.' His voice was a hoarse gasp. He put on a spurt and I came up onto my knees. 'Get down, you idiot,' he croaked. 'Get back from there.'

He threw himself over the crest and lay panting there for a moment, then dragged himself on towards the trees, came up to a crouch and ran forwards past me until he was about twenty feet into the forest. 'You stay there,' he said. 'Keep your eyes peeled, but keep down.'

I could hear the rasp of his breathing as he recovered from the effort he had made to climb the hill. I looked across the lake at the house. It was big, brick-built, with a porch round the ground floor and a gallery above it that ran all along the front. Something moved in the corner of my eye and I looked down.

'Two men,' I told Harry. He got up and moved off to one side through the trees.

They were following his tracks in the snow, and they were carrying rifles. They stopped for a moment when they saw his trail turn up the face of the hill, and then came on again.

Harry was beside me. 'Have you got another weapon?' he asked me.

'Nothing but a knife.'

'Give.' He held his hand out and shook it impatiently.

I took the hunting knife from its sheath and gave it to him. 'Keep low,' he said, 'and follow.' He circled back again to where he had rested in the forest and set off into the trees, so that his footprints in the snow picked up where he had stopped originally. He was wearing a parka with a hood, but otherwise he was ill-dressed for the snow, with sopping city shoes on his feet and the pinstripe of a suit clinging wetly to his legs.

There was little cover for me to lie low in, but I worked backwards a few feet until I was partly sheltered by a snow-laden windfall. If they looked down they would see me, and if they stopped to rest as Harry had done there was a good chance of that. I kept the rifle clear of snow but it was nowhere near a firing position, and I was about to put that right when I heard their voices, so I stayed as I was and hoped for the best.

They came noisily to the top of the hill, puffing but still talking, and they sounded in much better shape than Harry. They were talking Italian, and as I peered up through the snow-covered debris of my hiding place I saw them come into view. They were very young, and I realized they must be colleagues of Gabriella; they had a callow look and were excited, so they could be no part of the professional team that had been led by Collet. They were wearing duck-billed caps and parkas, with plaid shirts showing at the neck, which made them hunters out after deer. But their quarry was Seddall, and they set off in his wake without looking to left or right. The rifles they carried to complete their disguise were not, I presumed, what your modern Red Brigade urban terrorist was used to in the way of sophisticated weaponry, but they were heavier than the Mannlicher and would make nasty holes in Harry Seddall if they were properly handled. And all Harry had was a knife.

I came out of my lair and followed them. I made, it seemed to me, a bad job of it. Twigs cracked under my feet, and my feet showed no woodsman's instinct for the secure ground just as my eyes showed none for telling me the depth of the snow. I lurched into snow-filled holes and tripped over fallen timber just below the surface with impartial clumsiness, when I should have been scudding noiselessly in pursuit of my enemies, flitting like a shadow from tree to tree like a fleet Iroquois.

Luckily the lads of the Red Brigade were equally unskilled, and since there were two of them I let myself believe that they would be making twice as much noise as I was. Fortified by this hopeful view of things I kept as close to them as I dared, moving on a course parallel to theirs and a little behind. I had them always in sight and Harry some of the time.

I began to wonder what I ought to do, and to think that perhaps if I saw a chance for a clear shot at one of them I should take it. But, though they were obviously intent on running down Harry and were armed, neither of them, so far as I knew, had yet tried to shoot him, and this left me with a scruple about gunning them down in cold blood.

For what it was worth, Tozzetti's account of them had given me an impression that they were, as the Red Brigades go, a pretty half-baked group and, except possibly for their leader, untried. I felt a strong lack of inclination to cause the death of a politically infatuated student who was not yet a full-blooded anarchist willing to kill for the revolution, or whatever it was they killed for.

So in the end I stayed after them and hung close.

When it did happen, because of where it happened I was taken by surprise. Harry came into my view starting up a bank of snow which I then saw was the start of a marked rise in the ground. And immediately after that was the hillock where we had pitched the tent, and where Sandy lay sleeping.

I threw whatever caution I had been using to the winds and angled through the trees to bring myself out behind Harry and his pursuers. In the glimpses I had of him he was making heavy weather of getting up the side of the hill, floundering about in the snow. The Italians speeded up as if they thought they had him. He stopped floundering and it looked as if he would be over the top in a few minutes, and one of the Italian's lifted his rifle and shouted something. Harry floundered again and got going again and the rifle exploded.

I stopped cold.

Harry fell onto the snow as if he had been thrown there. He landed face down and one of his feet kicked spasmodically; his body jerked and he came up onto his side and fell over on his back. After that he lay still.

The Italians looked at each other and hurried forward. I followed them, cold and clever with rage, as light footed now as any native of these woods, gaining on them until when they reached the foot of the slope I was in close pistol-shot range of them. I screened my body from their peripheral vision behind a silver birch, though if they looked straight at it they would see me at once, and put the Mannlicher to my shoulder.

Harry's blood had spread from his forehead to the snow. His left knee was drawn up and his left arm was flung out beside him, the right leg out with the foot turned grotesquely pigeon-toed, the right arm hooked into the snow as if he had been scrabbling for a hold on life.

He was still breathing, in short shallow gasps with long seconds between them, and the fact that he was still alive appeared to disconcert the Italians. The one who had fired the shot was urging something on the other one, who shook his head when he answered. The first one stood over Harry and held his rifle loosely with one hand and gestured with the other. The second one backed off and slowly raised his rifle.

Harry came up off the snow on his left leg and his right hand flashed into the stomach of the youth standing over him. It was a hell of a blow and I heard the thud of it clearly before the Italian screamed. He dropped the rifle and stared at Harry's hand still stuck fast to him, with blood pouring over it, then he fell slowly down onto Harry while Harry's arm bent gradually under his weight. The boy arched up again and I saw the bloody knife come clear of him. The screaming stopped, but he went on dying, and the noises he made were as bad.

The other Italian was as firmly rooted to the spot as any of the forest trees. Harry rolled the dying youth off him and the other one began firing his rifle at nothing in particular. He was holding it loosely at waist height and each time it fired his right arm jumped until I thought he would dislocate his shoulder. He sent three shots into the forest before I came up behind him and slammed the Mannlicher against the side of his head. He dropped to his knees and made a sound between a sigh and an exclamation of surprise, and when I hit him again he fell over sideways.

'Out to the wide,' Harry said. He took a handful of snow and wiped some of the blood off his face, and sat up and looked about him. 'A considerable carnage,' he said, and pointed to the boy I had hit on the head. 'I don't know whether you saved his life or mine, but thanks for the backup.' He looked at the arm he was pointing with, covered with gore to the elbow, still holding the knife. He just looked, and gave no other reaction. 'And thanks for the knife.' He was still looking at the arm that had driven the knife home. 'I've never done that one before.'

It was not only his arm – he was covered with blood, both the life's blood of the corpse now lying beside him on the snow and the blood from his own wound that was drying on his face, for the snow he had wiped it with had done little more than clear his eyes.

'I thought you were done for,' I said. 'That bullet must have come within a hair's breadth of killing you. I don't see why it 'didn't knock you out; you fell as if you'd been kicked by a mule.'

'It didn't touch me,' he said. 'I was play-acting. I slashed my forehead with the knife when I fell. To make it look good.' And almost apologetically, as if I might despise such histrionics, he added: 'Well, a scalp wound makes a lot of blood.'

'You mean he missed you altogether?'

'Either he missed, or he was putting a shot over my head to make me stop. I thought the little berk was never going to shoot.'

I was staring at him. I watched that lurking contemptuous smile grow onto his face. 'What d'you think?' he asked me. 'That he wouldn't have fired again to kill me if I'd gone on up the slope?'

It took a little while for the implications of this to sink in. 'You were pretending to be stuck in the snow? You were trying to bring him to the the point of shooting at you? I mean – you made him do it?'

'I didn't make him do it. I set up a situation, but he fired the gun.'

There was another side to it. 'You took a hell of a risk.'

'Yeah.' The drawl, and the lop-sided smile. 'But not so much. He only had to shoot once, and he'd be doing it in a hurry. Only a kid, and likely no marksman. They don't go in for rifle shooting. I had to do *something*.'

I looked at the 'kid', a boy in a man's game, but that did not seem true either. There were soldiers his age, and good ones. He had been young and he had been dangerous; and he had been out-manoeuvred by an old hand. Why should that bother me as much as it did?

'You're right,' I said. 'It was you or him.'

'Well, maybe,' Harry said, 'but only maybe. Perhaps he didn't even know himself what he meant to do. And now he'll never find out.'

He came to his feet. 'This is bleeding still.' He put a hand to his brow. 'Have you got a first-aid kit? Where's the car?'

'No car, we're on foot, but there's a first-aid kit in the tent.'

'No car?' Harry looked back through the trees. 'That *is* good news. Who's we? You and 2 Para, I hope.'

'Me and Sandy Baldwin. She thinks you're the master villain of the piece.'

'I could be, at that. How far's the tent?'

'Just over the top, thirty yards.'

He looked back into the forest again. 'And she didn't hear the shot, or the noise that laddie made when I gutted him?'

Snow or no snow, I went up the slope like a scalded cat. There was the tent, and there, crawling out of it, standing and stretching herself awake, was Sandy.

'Hi!' she said. 'Boy, did I ever sleep! And did I ever have nightmares!'

She looked past me and her eyes widened. 'Is this a nightmare, too?'

I turned to introduce her to Harry Seddall: Harry, covered with blood from head to thighs, wearing the rueful sardonic smile that mocked himself and everyone else, the gash on his brow bleeding steadily.

'Hi!' she said, and put out a hand.

'Hello!' he said. 'I'm Harry Seddall, the villain of the piece.'

Her hand dropped and her eyes lost their warmth while she measured him against the prototype she had invented. She studied him for a long time, but I seemed to be the only one who grew fidgetty. Harry bore her scrutiny and looked back at her the way he looked at everything and everyone – as if she were a record-player, or Genghis Khan closing in for the kill, or a tier cake at a wedding.

Sandy made a decision, and when she spoke to me the injustice of it almost took my breath away. 'Well, you sure gave me a bum steer,' is what she said. 'He's on our side, right?'

'Right,' I managed to say.

She put out her hand again to Harry. 'So, Hi!' she said. He took it in his left hand, the right was covered with drying blood.

'We can't stand here gossiping all day,' he said. 'People are going to come looking for these people.'

Chapter 21

———◆———

I left Sandy to patch up the cut on Harry's forehead and went down to see how my victim was coming along after his two thumps on the head. He was standing up when he saw me, tried to run and fell down.

'Take it easy,' I said, and went to help him up again. He was weak and shaky and scared, but he let me take his arm across my shoulder and get him up the slope to the tent. A convulsion went through him when he saw Harry, whom he had last seen killing his friend with a knife. Sandy had cleaned the blood from his face and stuck plaster over the cut, but the rest of him made a gruesome sight.

'You want fresh clothes,' I said to Harry. 'There's a pair of jeans in my pack and a shirt, and you can take the parka off our friend here and maybe that sweater as well.'

'The boy will freeze to death,' Sandy said.

'No, he won't,' I said. 'He can swop with Harry or he can dress himself in his buddy's clothes.'

Harry grinned. 'There's a hard streak in you, Anthony. I'm glad it's showing. We're going to need it.'

He threw his parka on the snow and stood on it, took off his shoes and said: 'We've got to get on the move. Can I have those jeans? How did you two get here?'

While he changed, swearing and shivering in the cold, we told him our side of the story. He stored it away, saying little except for the odd irrelevant facetious comment, as when I told him we had sent Baldy off in the car.

'Your friend Denver will love you for that,' he said. 'It's time you were getting back to the real world.'

'I thought *you* thought this *was* the real world.'

'Did I say that? Whistling to keep my courage up. I'm never in the real world. Here take this shoe and compare it with Sunny Jim's feet for size. I'd like his boots if they'll fit me.'

Sandy had been heating up soup on the little stove. She gave the first batch to Harry and me and heated a second for herself and our reluctant guest.

'Options,' Harry said. The boots were the right size, he was all kitted up, he had burnt his tongue on some hot soup and he was raring to go. 'First, what to do with our prisoner. Second, what to do with ourselves. Him first. We can kill him, tie him up, take him with us, or let him go.'

The subject of this brisk passage was now planted in his socks on the parka, taking in soup as fast as he could and shuddering with the cold. He made no reaction to any of Harry's proposals, so either Harry spoke too fast for him to grasp what was being said, or he had no English.

'We don't kill him,' Sandy said.

'Right. I don't want him with us, either,' Harry said, 'and I don't want him to follow us.'

'Where are we going?' I asked with interest.

Harry frowned. 'That's next on the agenda, and we'll discuss it in his absence, if you don't mind.'

'They're going to come looking for him and –' I nodded to the crest of the hillock, in the direction where the body lay. 'If we tie him up and leave him in the tent, they're sure to find him.'

'God, he could die there if they don't,' Sandy said.

'Rubbish,' said Harry. 'He'll last out forty-eight hours or so, and we'll have this wrapped up by then. We can leave him as cosy as a baby in his cot in there, can't we, sonny?' He leered at the chilly youth, who had just swallowed the last of his soup. His body must have been exchanging heat at a rate of knots.

'Good,' Harry said. 'That's what we'll do, so let's do it. Tie him up and make him all cosy and tuck him away for the night. I'd do it myself, but he'll die of fright if I touch him. I think we should move out in ten minutes.'

We were five minutes late by his watch. We left a confused and alarmed human being trussed up not too tightly, so that his circulation would keep going, and wrapped up in a sleeping bag. We carried rations and the invaluable camping stove in our packs, and we carried three rifles, one pistol, and a clean knife. Sandy took the Mannlicher; Harry and I took the other rifles, which were heavy gauge Rigbys. I had the pistol and he had the knife. For a forty-eight-hour tour we were a well found expedition.

'We want to be in touch with the enemy,' Harry said, 'but I see no point in lying out in the snow unless we have to. Let's think about that. I wonder what the weather's going to do.'

'There's a storm coming up,' Sandy said, 'from the south and east. It should be here by morning. I heard it on the car radio.'

'What kind of storm?'

'Snow,' Sandy said. 'Can we stop for a minute?'

We were following what we had reckoned to be a direct line to the road, purely as a first move, since we had as yet concerted no plan. But whatever we decided to do must rest on the fact that most of the daylight hours were behind us, and when dark came we would be able to make little progress in any direction through that forest.

'I'd like to keep moving,' Harry said. 'What's up?'

'I have an idea,' Sandy said. So we came to a standstill, to listen to her. 'According to Baldy,' she said, 'there are three or four big houses round the lake. Some of them could be holiday houses, rich people's summer houses. They could be empty.'

'That's not bad,' Harry said. 'We could lie snug overnight and with luck have a sight of the enemy's movements tomorrow.'

'Not if the storm lasts,' Sandy said.

'You can't win 'em all. I think it's a good idea. We need to lie up and we need a base for whatever we do tomorrow. Let's do it.' Harry thought for a moment. 'If we use the road we'll cover ground, but there is quite a risk, so we'll go in a loose file and keep our eyes and ears open. You may have to jump for it at any moment, so as you go keep looking for cover by the roadside. And if one jumps, we all jump. They'll be on the alert since I escaped.'

'Escaped?' I said. 'You mean they made you prisoner? How did you get away?'

'Tozzetti's house guests roped me in. We've no time for this now. We can talk when we've gone to earth. Let's go.'

'Tozzetti? You mean . . . ?'

But Harry was already off again into the trees. Sandy grinned at me and went after him and I brought up the rear. I saw his point. It would be dusk within the hour and dark not long after. The sooner we were on the road the better.

As we came out of the forest the last of the sunset bloomed in the low clouds in front of us, but overhead the sky was pale, as if the winter landscape had chilled the colour out of it. We set out along the road. To our left the land stretched into the distance, a sea of long still waves of snow-spread rock glittering in the last of the day's light, but on our right the trees came darkly to the road's edge. We went along by the trees. Harry had spaced us about thirty feet apart, himself still in the lead and myself last, with Sandy between.

Harry set a brisk pace and we rounded the head of the lake in the early dusk. There was ice here, to some way from the shore, and beyond that the water ran black until it was lost in the falling darkness. I wondered if Baldy had got clean away, or if Palumbo had gone after him and caught him; and if so, whether Baldy had found the pistol and given a good account of himself. And I wondered how many of what Harry called the enemy – as if we were dealing with units of an opposing army at war – were ensconced in the house they had made their headquarters.

Ahead of me Sandy slowed down and I saw Harry had come to a stop at a bend in the road. We came up beside him and he said: 'Take a look.'

Past the bend the road dropped down a long hill and then climbed again, turning from the lake, and beyond that everything merged into the gloom. Night was closing in around us.

But up to the right, where the road curved away from it, was the bulk of a large house, and I could see enough of it to recognize the house I had seen across the lake.

'Wait here,' Harry said, 'and I'll see if we're going to have any problem getting past.' He gave me his rifle. 'Can't use this, all hell would break loose,' he said and added, as if he were quoting some general in the Crimea: 'Cold steel, gentlemen, if you please.' Then he went off down the hill. We watched in silence till he was out of sight.

'You all right?' I asked Sandy.

'Sure,' she said. 'I'm okay. What do you think he's going to do tomorrow? Some sort of showdown?'

'I don't know,' I said. 'I wouldn't put it past him to believe the three of us could make a commando attack on the house. Kick the doors in and shoot at everything that moves, and keep going till the bleeding slows to a trickle.'

Sandy shivered. 'If I didn't know I was cold as well as scared,' she said, 'I'd be asking myself what was giving me the shakes. I'd rather watch that kind of action at the movies. The good guys always win.' Her face tilted up to mine. 'I guess he's on our side,' she said, 'but he's not quite my idea of one of the good guys.'

'Not mine, either,' I said. 'But I think he does a lot of winning. He takes risks with himself too, which would mean he'd take risks with other people.'

'You mean me?'

'Yes.'

'Uh-huh. This is my fight.'

'You've done your share,' I said. 'For that matter, maybe I have too.'

'You're cheating,' she said. 'You only mean half of that.'

'Oh, yeah?'

'Yeah. Hold me and rub my back. I'm freezing.'

I held her and rubbed her back vigorously, and over her shoulder I saw Harry coming back up the hill.

'How was the cold steel?' I asked him.

'Not needed,' he said, and took the rifle I had laid against a tree.

'I don't like that,' he said. 'It could have fallen and gone off.'

'The safety's on,' I said. 'Surely?'

'Is it shit,' Harry said. 'No matter. We can get by. I spotted two men in the grounds, moving around but nothing clever. We'll keep closer together this time; it's getting too dark for an extended file. Make it six feet between us.'

We followed him down the hill and started up the other side. Harry stopped and when we reached him he pointed and said: 'Gate.' It was a tall metal gate. 'Wire,' he said, and gestured with both hands. I saw fence posts and dimly made out something like pigwire between them, and saw that the wire also spanned the gate.

He took us up to the gate and watched and listened for a long time. He held my shoulder. 'Quick and quiet,' he said into my ear, 'and keep on up the hill. Go.' He let go of my shoulder and I took long strides as quick and quiet as I could past the gate and kept going. The fence left the road almost at once as the hill turned leftward away from the house on its flat promontory over the lake. Soon Harry came loping past me so I fell back to put Sandy in between us as before, and we came to the top of the hill and started our search for a night's lodging.

We did not have far to look. We had been walking for another ten minutes, with the stars growing brighter at every step, when I walked into Sandy. Harry had stopped. 'Now here's something,' he said.

To the right of the road the bulk of a house made a dark patch against the sky. We opened a simple wooden barred gate and went slowly up to the house. No light showed and no dog barked. The snow was deep and unbroken. When we got there I went to a window and ran my hand down it. Snow was frozen to the glass. We moved round the house to the back. It was the same with all the windows: there had been no heat in that house for a while. We completed the circuit of the building and came back to the front.

'This seems to be the one,' Harry said. 'There's a door at the back I liked the look of. You two wait here. I'll go in and give the

211

place a quick once-over. If it looks good I'll come and knock on a window and you come round the back and I'll let you in.'

Ten minutes later we were in the big kitchen. It was as cold as an ice-house, but before we could turn on the power we had to go round the whole house in the dark making as sure as we could that table and floor lamps were not connected and that wall switches were off. It was a big place and an irritating job, which meant falling over furniture and fumbling blindly over walls and along skirting boards.

'Gee, you're a fussy man,' Sandy said when we met again at last in the kitchen. Sandy had come into the room from a door to a back passage where she had found the main power switch, but Harry was not ready for it to be turned on yet.

'That's why I'm alive,' Harry said.

His next demand was that we black-out the kitchen windows, so, still working in the dark, we took thick lined curtains from the living room. Searching for tools to nail them to the walls, Harry cut himself for the second time that day – on a set of kitchen knives – and took a vengeful relish in using them to skewer the curtains into the pine panelling. Then he went outside when the lights were on and came back to report that the rest of the house showed dark and a proper job on the curtains would make all secure.

An hour after that we had a room with the chill already off and the thermostat for the electric heating on full, and we had a meal on the table. Sandy had raided the cupboards for likely-looking tins, and reported that we could live here for weeks if we had to.

'Great God!' Harry said. 'We're not some gangsters holed up after a bank robbery. We are the forces of law and . . . well, we're the forces of order about to smite the evildoer. It'll all be over tomorrow.'

'To me,' Sandy said wryly, 'it seems more like we're a bunch of vigilantes.'

Harry frowned. 'Analogy,' he said, pretending to a singular shortness of memory, 'is a spurious form of argument. Besides, vigilantes always outnumbered their victims ten to one. In this case, we are the outnumbered.'

'What are we going to do about that?' I asked pointedly.

'I don't know yet,' he said. 'Probably something obvious. That'll fox 'em.' He stood up. 'You people sit still. Seddall will make the coffee.'

He cleared the supper dishes from the table and began washing them while the kettle came to the boil. We made a pleasantly domestic scene in that big, expensively modernized old room, two of us taking our ease at the table and Harry doing the washing-up. The sense of comfort was emphasized for me by the thought of the impending storm. I began to see our situation as a scene from a play, and the idea was strengthened by the knowledge that we had broken into the house: the refuge did not belong to us, was uncertain and temporary.

And then suddenly the stage kitchen vanished and I was back in the real one. I noticed – in the meaningless way that these things happen – that Sandy was wearing much the same outfit of jeans and sweater she had worn when I first met her. But that had been in her own kitchen; and the other man there had been Bruce, not Harry.

The thought must have shown on my face, and some intuition revealed the sense of it to Sandy. Tears sprang to her eyes and her mouth shook. She got up and went round the table and said to Harry that she would make the coffee.

'Absolutely not,' he said, and then looked at her. He turned his attention back to the sink. 'You make the coffee,' he said.

Sandy made the coffee and Harry finished washing the dishes, and we sat at the table again and listened to the wind rising outside.

'Story time,' Harry said. 'How much does Sandy know about all this?'

'Everything I know,' I said.

'You told her about me, and Heneage, and what he told you about our little outfit?'

'Yes.'

He raised his eyebrows. 'So much for security,' he said.

213

'I pay taxes,' I said. 'I'm not an employee of your little outfit. I'm a client.'

'Goodness, what a way to look at things!' He swallowed some coffee, and spilled some cigarette ash. 'Never mind, it saves me some of the explaining.'

He told the story to Sandy, rather than to me, as if he recognized that she had a special right to hear it. This was plainly the case, but that sign of sensitivity seemed incongruous, coming as it did from the Harry Seddall I knew.

'The man who died in the cabin on that Channel steamer,' he told her, 'who was called Marco Reggi, was killed because he knew something which he was going to tell us; me and my boss John Heneage in London. We paid him money to tell us things.'

'Your function is to be aware of large movements of sterling before they happen, right?' Sandy asked.

'Right,' Harry said. 'Any movement of money like that out of England to another country is a clear signal of some commercial intention, and people often want to keep such an intention secret. That's business. But killing to protect this kind of secrecy is not common.'

He poured more coffee all round and lit one of his Gauloises, breathing out a long sigh of blue smoke. 'I went to see Marco's mother,' he said.

'His mother!' I exclaimed.

'Why not? Everyone has a mother, and a mother needs to know if her son has died. She lives in Lerici on the Italian coast.' He was watching me quizzically, as if he guessed that I found it hard to reconcile my idea of him with this touch of humanity. 'And I knew Marco quite well. I didn't think he'd go out on a limb without leaving a message somewhere on the tree. So I told her my name and broke the news about Marco, and after a while she asked me to go for a walk so that she could be alone for a little. When I went back again she gave me an envelope Marco had sent her. Inside it was another envelope with just 'Harry' written on it.'

'Did you tell her how he died?' I asked.

'I told her he had drowned, falling overboard from a small ship in a big gale. That is a thing that does happen. It happens to fishermen off that coast, and I think she believed it. She wouldn't take money from me for the information Marco had left me, but I got Heneage to send it, saying Marco had earned it before he died.'

We waited to hear what Marco's message had been, but Harry was scowling at his cigarette. 'I must be growing old,' he said, and got up and walked out of the room into the darkened house. When he came back he said: 'With a summer cottage like this, you wouldn't cut the phone off when you were away from it, would you, Sandy?'

'Why, no. There'd be no point in that.'

'What do you mean?' I asked him. 'Do you mean they've cut the wire outside? They know we're here?'

'No. I think they've been cutting phone wires all round about; they probably thought of it after I ran out on them.' He stood looking crossly at the floor. 'It gives them a breathing space. Maybe that's what your friend Palumbo was doing out driving. And Baldy – they'll be worrying like hell about him putting in a call to the police, if he did get clear.'

'Spilling the beans?' Sandy said.

'Yeah, that the Monteith family is being held by kidnappers up on Lake Whatsitsname.'

'I don't think he will,' Sandy said. 'Wouldn't it be bad for what's left of his career?'

Harry smiled reluctantly. 'Well, it would that,' he said, 'and it's true he has nothing against them, unless they caught him and did him some damage and were stupid enough to let him go; and they're not that stupid. But they'll worry about me getting to a phone, and I was thinking of it. There's a big bunch in that house. I was thinking I might have to bring in the Mounties. It would be bad for me but maybe good for the Monteiths.'

'What are you saying?' I asked.

'I'm saying they'll move the Monteiths as soon as they can fix up another place to take them. They may even have a place to fall back on. Either way, they'll move them before morning.'

'Why?'

'Because if there's a big snow they might not be able to get out – certainly not until the roads are cleared.'

'That's right,' Sandy said. 'I doubt if this neck of the woods will be top of their priorities when they order out the ploughs.' She looked at Harry. 'What do you mean it would be bad for you to call in the RCMP?'

'Ah,' Harry said. 'I'll come to that later. Back in a minute.' When he came back this time he said: 'Sky's still clear, but that's quite a wind. They'll be worried about whiteout when the snow comes.' He chewed his upper lip. 'I'll have to make my move tonight.'

'You?' said Sandy. 'Don't you mean us?'

'Sweetie,' he said. 'I hardly think I do mean "us". This is do-or-die stuff we're into. You two have done your share already.'

'Well,' Sandy said, 'my folks have done their share of dying too.' She lifted her face to let him see what she felt. 'I want something back for that.'

'You might not like it after,' he said, 'if we pull it off. And if we don't, your husband wouldn't have wanted you to die just because he has.'

'No, damn you, he wouldn't,' she said, 'but he's not here, is he? The grief is for him but it's my grief.' There were no tears in her eyes but they were in her face. 'Anyway, you said "if *we* pull it off".'

'A slip of the tongue, you know. But equally, nervous as they must be, you're in danger right now, living in the house next door to them. Let's see what we come up with.'

'Okay,' Sandy said. 'Okay. So finish the story, huh?'

'I'll keep it short,' Harry said. 'What Marco had got wind of was an impending movement of sterling equivalent to one billion – meaning one thousand million – Canadian dollars, from Arab accounts in London to Toronto.'

'That's about 550 million in sterling,' Sandy said.

Harry looked a little suprised. 'Yes,' he said, 'it is. When the

216

Arabs plan to move that amount of money we like to find out why, if we can, especially if someone is willing to kill people to stop us finding out about it.'

'It doesn't seem as if Arabs are doing any of this killing,' I said.

'No,' Harry said. 'It doesn't.'

'You know what this money is for, don't you?' Sandy asked him.

'I do, yes. Are you going to tell me?'

'I would make a strong guess that it's to buy the office blocks Monteith is selling, all the way from Montreal across to Vancouver. That's the price he's rumoured to be asking.'

Harry said: 'You put two and two together pretty quickly.' He was appreciating her alertness, but for him, it was impossible to do that without bringing an ironic flavour to it.

Sandy lifted her chin and vertical lines appeared above her nose. 'Why the sarcasm?'

Instantly contrite, Harry in his attempt to show himself sincere was almost comically unctuous. 'Believe me, there was no sarcasm,' he said. He opened his hands deprecatingly like the stock Levantine in a film. The whole effect was wretchedly unsuccessful. 'I'm just surprised you take such an interest in high finance.' Then, reverting to the Harry I was accustomed to, he looked inquisitive and even suspicious. 'You were very quick to make the connection between the billion dollars and the apartment sale.'

'Not so very,' Sandy said. 'Anthony told me about Monteith at the cabin, and I read the financial press, now and then. Medieval banking is my area of study and I like to keep an eye on modern practice. It refreshes the perspectives.'

I doubt if Harry ever looked at anyone with respect, but he regarded her now with lots of interest. 'Fugger's Bank at Augsburg, and all that?'

'No, no,' Sandy said testily. 'People always say that. That's well after my period. By medieval I mean the Middle Ages.'

'Well, could you bring the medieval perspective to bear on this – why does one kidnap the Monteiths because he is selling a

217

billion dollars' worth of apartment buildings to what is presumably a consortium of Arab businessmen?'

'I've said it to Anthony already,' she answered. 'For profit, for money, for a rake-off.'

'You have the banker's mind, all right,' Harry said, not very winningly. 'How does the kidnapper get his rake-off? Other than by demanding Monteith's profit – or even the whole billion – in exchange for letting him go. It would seem clumsily timed to me. The deal isn't through yet, they'd be better to wait till it was, surely. Even a straight ransom would be hard to get, and from the scale of this operation they're thinking of a great deal of money. Wherever Monteith keeps his money, the banks and whoever else looks after it would smell a horde of rats if he started drawing it out at long distance. They would hardly cash bearer cheques for huge sums without wanting to know a little more about what was going on. So where's the rake-off?'

'Yeah. Let me think about that one,' Sandy said. 'I could use some coffee.' She shoved back her chair, put her feet up on the table, and began chewing on the knuckle of her thumb.

'Make the coffee, will you?' Harry said to me. 'I'm going scouting. Shan't be long.' He went through into the front of the house.

I tiptoed around getting the coffee. 'Don't do that,' Sandy said irritably. 'I'm trying to think. Act normal.'

It seemed to me I was very much the bystander at what was going on in this kitchen. It was like being a playwright at rehearsal, where the action is all with the actors and the director. Except that in this case I had not written the play. So I did my best to act my bit part properly, though I am not much of an actor.

Harry was carrying a radio when he returned. 'We'll get an update on the weather,' he said. 'I've been up on the roof, you can see the house from there. I don't see any activity; not that I *would* see much, but the house feels normal – lights in the window and I made out three cars. I think three's all they had. So we're still in time. Boy, it's cold out there! Is that fresh coffee?'

I poured him some. 'How's the financial genius coming along?'

Sandy peered at him out of her thoughts. 'Don't be so damned ebullient,' she said. 'Drink your coffee.' She glanced at the watch on her wrist. 'News time coming up if you want to hear about the weather.' She want back inside her head. The coffee was dreadful, but she was drinking it without any sign of discomfort.

Harry turned the radio on, and music came out of it. Sandy reached out and tuned it to another station without leaving her intellectual nirvana, and we heard the CBC News. Oil-rich Alberta was still mortified at the amount it paid into the federal coffers in Ottawa. Montreal was still Canada's bank robbery capital and the Toronto Maple Leafs were not playing as well as they should. The snowstorm that had come up from the States and was affecting western Ontario was apparently now moving north-west, so eastern Ontario and Quebec were likely to escape it. That meant we would escape it, since the lake was in eastern Ontario, some thirty miles from the Ottawa River and the Quebec border.

'Well, that's something,' Harry said, 'perhaps that gives us – ' The radio interrupted him. 'Mr John Monteith,' it said, 'whose absence from Toronto this week has caused speculation in business circles in view of the sale, thought to be imminent, of a large number of Monteith-owned office buildings across Canada, this morning issued a statement to say that the deal would be finalized this week. The statement, issued by his Toronto office, said he would be in the city in two days' time to finalize the agreement, the last details of which had now been negotiated by Mr Monteith personally at a secret conference. Monteith did not say where the negotiations took place or with whom he was negotiating.'

With that the News ended and I switched the radio off with a not entirely steady hand. We sat staring at the silent and, considering the size of the impact it had made, rather small item of modern technology as if it had been the cave where the oracles were uttered at Delphi.

Harry lit a cigarette, although there was one smoking in the ashtray, lit only a minute before. 'What the hell does that mean?' he demanded.

'Search me,' I said.

'Bingo!' This came in a kind of exultant whisper from Sandy, who came slowly to her feet as if she was emerging from a trance, and said: 'I'm gonna think out loud. Don't speak, just don't speak. That's the answer all right. That is the answer.' She picked up the spare cigarette from the ashtray and walked up and down the kitchen telling us what the answer was.

'Monteith is selling to the Arabs for one thousand million dollars. It's been calculated as far as you can calculate a thing like that that he will clear between three and four hundred million personally. So, it's simple. The kidnappers tell Monteith to have the Arab buyers pay the ransom – say it's a hundred or two hundred million dollars – direct into bank accounts held by the kidnappers.'

She stood with her hands on her hips, cigarette in her mouth, and looked at us triumphantly. She took the cigarette from her lips and explained some more. 'The kidnappers' share goes to Nassau or Switzerland – one of those close-as-an-oyster banks; the buyer gets his original deal with Monteith; Monteith gets maybe half his original expected original profit, but he gets his wife and daughter back; and no one else knows anything about it.'

Harry looked half-asleep, slouched back on his chair with its front legs in the air, and his eyelids almost hiding his eyes. This meant he was functioning on all eight cylinders at high revs, but all he said was: 'Dear God, right under my very own nose!'

For my part I was stunned into silence for a while by the amounts of money involved, not so much in the business deal, but in the amount Sandy thought the kidnappers could get out of it.

I found my voice. 'How can they *do* that?' I asked her. 'How can they hope to get away with it?'

Sandy was patient. 'What's to stop them?'

'Monteith for one. He can stop the cheque, can't he, just as I can stop a cheque? Or, since he's acting under duress, the deal won't be legal, he can get the money back once he's free.'

'The money will be paid out again into other accounts quicker than you can blink, but the *first* payments will be cleared pronto and there will be no way of stopping anything after the money has moved on. And they can hide its trace any number of ways; turn it into gold and back into money on any one morning on any gold market. It's easier than stealing a stereo off the counter – try hiding *that* under your coat. It's neat, it's very neat. And in the end that's why they killed Bruce.'

Saying that she lost her composure, and slipped out of the kitchen through the door beside her into the back corridor.

'God above! We'll have to move fast,' Harry said.

His eight cylinders had left me far behind. I had no notion whether we should move fast, slow, or not at all, and I said so.

'It's like this,' he said. 'They think if I can get to a phone, I'll call the police, probably the RCMP. And that statement from Monteith, probably phoned to his office at their dictation, tells the RCMP that any sign or whisper of activity from them means that Mrs Monteith and the daughter get killed. It's a bid to create a stalemate until the money has passed, and as Sandy pointed out, that means until the money has passed out of sight.'

'What does that get them?' I asked. 'They won't be safe in that house forever.'

'No,' Harry said, 'they won't. But perhaps that's okay with the big man behind it all, so long as he's not in that house, and you wouldn't think he would be, would you, if he didn't *have* to be? He'd be doing it all from outside. He could run it all from a telephone anywhere he liked. They needn't even know where he was; he could call in now and then for them to report. And now the last stages are set up, probably, to a fixed timetable, he gets them to cut the phone wires, because all he can do now is wait and see how it turns out. He's planned everything to the last-minute detail, and when the countdown starts, he just watches while the rocket starts moving out onto its appointed course.'

Which means while the money starts moving to where he's arranged for it to move.' He grinned at me; the same self-mocking grin he would show whether he had just heard he was about to be shot at dawn or whether he was watching his own horse win the Derby. 'So,' he said, 'I think the countdown has started. Don't you?'

I thought I saw a flaw in all this. 'But the kidnappers – whoever is in that house – they're not going to sit there and risk their necks just so that he can get rich.' I had another thought. 'Is Tozzetti in that house? That would mean it's not Tozzetti.'

He grinned again, but mocking me this time, not himself. 'Tozzetti's not in the house, but anyway it's not Tozzetti. It wasn't Tozzetti who had Collet's boys put the arm on me and bring me up here, it was Collet himself. Tozzetti is simply acting under threat; the threat to his beautiful niece. Tozzetti was chosen to put through the change in the property deal – it's his line of business too, remember – because he had the niece, an impressionable girl at university back in Italy. That's why this Red Brigade is such a poor imitation: it was set up just so that it would have her in it. Then they were conned into coming over here to make money for the Cause, something like that.'

I was almost stammering in my haste to tell him his whole construction was a fallacy. 'Damn it, Harry, how could anyone get hold of all these facts. Only the KGB or the CIA could put a thing like this together, and it would take a year's planning even *with* their computer systems.'

There was a heavier sarcasm than usual in Harry's voice. 'You're selling your own country short, Anthony. We have computers and one or two capable men even in London.' His drawl was becoming so relaxed you might have thought he'd swallowed a tranquillizer a little while before and it was beginning to take effect. 'I could have set up a thing like this myself, couldn't I, John?'

'You mean Anthony,' I said stupidly, but another voice overrode mine.

'Yes, Harry, I do believe you might have,' the voice said

behind me, 'but I have always held that if a thing's worth doing, then one should do it oneself.' And John Heneage came in the door holding, as elegantly and surely as if he held a Queen Anne coffee pot, a machine pistol which looked strikingly uncouth in his long white hands. 'Mr Moore,' he said, 'please don't get up. Harry, you've been a very naughty boy. I thought I sent you to Japan, or somewhere far away.' His eyes flickered. 'Where's the girl? I heard her in here, not two minutes ago.'

Then all the lights went out, and somewhere in the house one of the big Rigbys crashed three times.

Chapter 22

I threw the radio at where I thought Heneage was; I went to the floor and skated my chair across at where his legs were supposed to be; hot liquid hit me in the face; a burst from the machine pistol battered the air; there was a thud, a scrambling noise, somebody fell and something clattered towards me and hurt my hand, and I grabbed it.

'I've got his gun,' I shouted, but the sound came out like a crow cawing.

'Lights!' Harry yelled.

No lights came on, but the Rigby crashed again.

'Anthony, you bastard, get the lights on,' Harry yelled again.

I took the gun with me, hoping like hell I wouldn't shoot myself on the way, and bounced off hard edges and solid walls towards the door, round the corner where the power switch was, fumbled, panted and cursed and found it. Light from the kitchen doorway glowed into the hall.

I ran to the other door, made out Sandy faintly illuminated at the far end of the long hall and on the kitchen floor Harry sitting all over Heneage. I slammed the door shut and ran up the hall to Sandy. She was standing with the rifle to her shoulder and as I reached her she fired again out into the night.

'What are you shooting at?' I gasped. I wondered when I'd get my voice back.

'There's a guy out there, behind that bush with nothing but clear snow behind him.'

I peered out. The moon was up. Whoever he was, he could no more run away across the snow under that big rifle than fly.

'I've got the machine pistol,' I said. 'I'll get out the back and flush him out. Don't shoot *me*.'

'Can you work that thing?'

'Let's see,' I said. I fiddled with it a bit and fired a burst into the night. The pistol jumped all over the place in my hands.

'See you,' I said. 'Be careful.'

I went down the hall again and out of the back door. I made long, plunging strides through the snow under the starry moonlit sky. I was all euphoria and adrenalin. I bore a charmed life. I thought I heard a plopping sound and something tugged at my sleeve as I cleared the front of the house. The Rigby fired twice. I drew level with the bush and fired the machine pistol. A man rolled out and lay flat on the snow with his arms stretched out wide.

'Don't shoot! Don't shoot!' he shrieked.

I strode over to him. 'Where are you hit?' I demanded.

'Nowhere,' he said. 'I am unhurt.'

'Get up,' I said. 'Hands behind your head,' I remembered.

He got up and clasped his hands behind his head. He was vaguely familiar, a small man.

'I'm bringing him in,' I called to Sandy.

'Come ahead,' she called back.

I strode powerfully towards the house but the little man made heavy weather of it. 'Get a move on,' I said irritably, and he did his best to run through the snow with his hands holding his neck. We went into the house.

'I'll take him straight on in,' I said. 'Can you hang on here a little longer?'

'Yeah,' she said, 'but not too long, huh?' She punched me on the arm.

In the kitchen the tableau had changed. Heneage was in a chair with a glass of liquor in his hand, and Harry was swinging his legs on the kitchen table with the Smith & Wesson resting on his thigh.

'Well, well,' he said. 'We *are* pulling our chestnuts out of the fire. You,' he said to the small man. 'Sit there.'

He sat. I looked at him and he looked at me, and we recognized each other. He smiled shakily.

It was the man who had thrown my play overboard from the Channel steamer. The same rage I had felt then burned up inside me but almost instantly it dwindled away again. Perspectives had changed: things had happened since then that made the loss of the play less important than it had been at the time.

I looked from him to Heneage. Heneage was growing old while I watched, as if a block of ice inside him was feeding a chill into his veins.

'Things are moving too fast,' Harry said. 'They'll be here in a minute to see what all the shooting was about. Sandy on the door?' I nodded. 'There was a clothes-line in the cupboard where we found the hammer. I want to tie these two up.'

'I concede the game, Harry,' Heneage said. 'No matter how you play them, your spades are good,' Harry ignored him.

We cut the clothes-line into lengths with the hunting knife and trussed them callously; wrists and legs bound as tight as if we were tying the legs of dead chickens. Then we tied them by their throats to the legs of the heavy old table. It would discourage movement, Harry said.

Harry picked up the machine pistol. 'Can you hit things with this?'

'No,' I said. 'All I can do is fire it. Give me the thirty-eight.'

We took the Mannlicher too – we had a box of ammunition for that – and joined Sandy at the front door where we had left the two Rigbys.

'See anything?' Harry asked her.

'No.'

'They'll be coming,' Harry said.

'I know,' she said.

'Thanks for throwing the power off,' he said. 'Brilliant and fast – fast thinking. Guess where Heneage has been directing his game from – another of these damn great houses. He said there were just the two of them there, and I believe him. He's given up.'

He went away and came back almost immediately. 'I've bolted the back door,' he said. 'At least if anyone comes in the back you'll hear them coming, if you're lucky.'

'You're talking to me,' Sandy said.

'Yes. I want you at the door, is that okay?'

'That's okay. That's good. How be I take the Mannlicher? This thing hurts my shoulder.'

'Fine, fine. Anthony, will you take the left side of the house, and think of moving forward at them when you get the chance. Try not to move past that big pine, at first at any rate. I'll be moving around in that quarter there –' he waved his hand around ' – and we don't want to shoot each other. Anthony, don't start shooting until you feel sure you'll hit one of them. Sandy, hold yourself in reserve until you think it's time, unless you *need* to shoot. That's a good moon. Let's go.'

We did not have long to wait. I had time to adjust my vision to the night; to the shadows cast by the moon; and to distinguish separately trees and bushes that had at first seemed to be one dark conglomerate mass. I kept my head moving, to the front, behind and to the side, standing close to a small maple with the Rigby propped against a branch and the revolver in the pocket of my parka, my hands warm inside sheepskin mitts until I should need them. The first euphoria had gone, but I felt efficient and fairly hopeful. Harry's crisp leadership inspired confidence – the big question was how many men would be sent to investigate our little gun battle.

When they did come they took us by surprise, but not the kind of surprise any of us had feared.

The headlamps of a car shone on the road and then turned in towards the house. I took the rifle into the crook of my arm and shook off the right-hand mitt. The car stopped a good way off and the light blinded me briefly until I turned my head away, trying to see what was happening out of the side of my eye. There was the sound of a car door being shut, and then a man came into view in the beam of the headlamp.

He walked slowly forward, with the car following slowly

227

behind, so that he was always in the beam of the lights. I had a nasty feeling that this was Monteith being forced to walk in front of the car and I tried furiously to think what we should do, but my mind froze.

I hoped Harry would come up with something.

The car turned as it approached, following the line of the drive, until it was sideways on to me. The interior lights were on, showing the driver. Apart from him the car appeared to be empty. Just about level with me it stopped and the walking man stopped too, and turned to face the house. I moved forwards cautiously, until I could make out the man standing in the full glare of the headlamps.

It was Voster. Voster in his beaver-fur coat and brown Homburg, and a state of complete self-possession. He stood patiently in the bright light, moving a little this way and that, no doubt to give us the best chance of recognizing him.

I moved back to my position beside the maple tree, and watched and waited. There was nothing to be gained by making an immediate response to Voster's arrival – his strange but oddly characteristic arrival. Either he wanted a parley, or he wanted us to think he did.

At length Harry's voice whispered my name and he came up behind me. 'I wonder what this means,' he said close to my ear. 'There's nothing doing round the house, but it's very likely a trick all the same. How do you feel about going to talk to him? You'll have to get the other guy out of the car, you want them standing together in the lights, where Sandy can cover them.'

'Right,' I said, and went forward again. I placed myself off to one side of the car, level with its rear end. I knew the driver now, and remembered his name.

'Martin,' I said. His head jerked round. Voster's head moved too, and he blinked into the headlamps.

'Ah,' he said. 'Mr Moore.'

'Shut up,' I said, 'and just stay where you are. Martin, out of the car please, and go and stand beside Voster.'

Martin sat still with his head cocked sideways. He was

listening too hard, trying to place me by the sound of my voice. Probably it was just habit. They had not come up here in this way, putting themselves at such a disadvantage, to try anything now. But I had known Martin for a dangerous man the first time I met him, and I was tense and nervy.

'Goddamn it, man,' I said. 'Do it *now*, or I'll shoot your goddamned head off.'

Martin opened the door and climbed out, dressed like a chauffeur as he had been before. He was night-blind from looking down the beams of the headlamps.

'No,' I said. 'Don't turn this way. Over beside Voster. You'll have a gun – drop it in the snow.'

He went on standing there.

What the hell, I thought, and slammed a shot from the Rigby into the coachwork of the limousine. He reached into his jacket and drew out a pistol and threw it down, and went over to stand beside Voster.

I made sure the car was empty, turned off the ignition and took the keys, and then shepherded them into the house. Sandy, just a figure in the gloom, stood to one side to let us enter, and Harry came in a moment after.

'We need a bit of light,' he said. 'We'll talk here. Let's open the kitchen door, that should be enough to keep an eye on them without exposing us to any second front that might be on the way.'

'Mr Seddall,' Voster said urbanely, 'I am so glad to meet you at last. One has heard a great deal of Mr Harry Seddall.'

'Stuff it, Voster,' Harry said. 'Civilized conversation gives me a pain and I've no time for it right now, even if I did like it.' He grabbed Voster by the arm and went down the hall with him. Some light came in to us as he opened the kitchen door. They were gone for a few minutes and I heard some talk, presumably uncivilized, going on in the kitchen.

By some unspoken consent Sandy and I said nothing to each other, but kept our rifles pointed at Martin, until the others came back.

When they came they brought Heneage with them; at least, Voster brought him while Harry followed. Heneage still had his hands tied and could hardly walk, so Voster had both arms round his body and was having a hard time keeping him upright and moving him along at the same time. Finally he dumped him on a kind of blanket chest against the wall.

'I need to feel more secure,' Harry said thoughtfully. He went purposefully to the front door, handed the machine pistol to Sandy, took up the second of the big Rigby rifles that was propped there and came back into the hall. When he had passed Martin he turned round and hit him a pile-driving blow on the head with the butt end of the rifle. The big man fell like a steer in a slaughterhouse.

'Holy cats!' Sandy said, and then, rather obscurely: 'Well, I suppose so.'

'That's better,' Harry said, and took the machine pistol back from her. 'Anthony, why don't you keep an eye out and spell Sandy at the door. Maybe you'd like some coffee, Sandy, you've been there a long time.'

'We could all do with some,' she said. 'How many?'

'Three, please,' Harry said, sounding shocked. 'We're not giving aid and comfort to the enemy. We want them to feel nervous and discouraged, don't we, Voster?'

But Voster was paying very little attention to what was happening around him. Even the cold-blooded and brutally violent blow with which Harry had felled Martin had drawn no more response from him than a spasmodic, astonished jump of the arms.

His whole interest was for Heneage.

Heneage was in a very bad way. While Martin seemed as likely as not to die from the physical trauma of his injury, Heneage looked likely to die from trauma of another kind. Harry had said earlier that Heneage had simply given up, and though from my stance at the door I could not make out his face in the faint glimmer of light which shone into the hall, his whole posture had fallen in and the man himself had shrunk, as if he was ready to

230

turn his face to the wall.

Voster, who had been stooping over him, stood up with a sigh. 'So that was Mr Pertinax,' he said.

'Yeah,' Harry said. 'That was Mr Pertinax.'

'Pertinax?' I said.

'Pertinax was his *nom de guerre*,' Harry said. 'That's what he called himself when he embarked on his dream plan. It's the name he used when he phoned them their instructions, the name that validated his messages on the telex or through the mail. None of them ever *saw* him. He used the Military Intelligence computers in Mayfair for central casting, and when he had his cast, he directed the show from outside the theatre.'

Heneage lifted his head. 'The metaphor is inexact, Harry,' he said.

'That's what I mean about civilized conversation, Voster,' Harry said. 'That's why it gets up my nose.' To Heneage he said roughly: 'What did you come in here for, waving that fancy machine pistol?'

'I came to kill you,' Heneage said. 'Isn't that obvious?'

There was a brief silence. 'When you go into a room to kill people,' Harry said at last, 'you go in and start killing. You don't go in and start being elegant with your voice. You used to know that.'

'It's twenty years since I knew that,' Heneage said. 'Ah, Harry, when I knew you had come so close, I felt my nerve grow frail. You are so like the Mounties, Harry; you always get your man. When I knew you were *here*, I sensed the touch of fate on my skin, the fall of the shroud.'

'That's just a long way to say good-bye, John,' Harry said. 'It doesn't mean anything any more.'

'It does to me, Mr Heneage,' Sandy said, entering the scene with a tray of coffee mugs. She spoke with a chill in her voice that struck against Heneage's beautifully modulated and elegiac speech like the clash of civilizations. 'It means that Harry is the only human being in all this that you knew as a real person. The rest of us that you killed or wanted to kill were just ciphers to you. When he turned up, real, that's what your fear was. That's what you couldn't handle.'

Heneage straightened his back against the wall, as if to get as far from her as possible, and turned his head to one side.

'You see,' Sandy said simply.

'Coffee,' Harry said. 'Good!'

She brought coffee to me at my place by the door, and my hand touched her arm. It was trembling. She moved quickly away, shaking her head, and squatted in the corner beside me, clasping her coffee mug in both hands.

She looked up at Harry. 'I'm sick of this,' she said. 'Let's get it over with.'

'Yes, yes!' Voster said eagerly. He had been standing with his head leaned far back on his neck, watching Heneage. Now he shrugged his shoulders and let out a sigh. 'What's done is done,' he said. 'We must think of the future.'

'You think you have one?' I knew at once, from the ambiguity lurking in Harry's sarcasm, that Voster's unconscious effrontery had struck the right chord with him.

Voster knew it too. 'When two people can be useful to one another,' he said, 'they should let it happen, Mr Seddall.' He sighed deeply, for effect this time. 'I have made a big mistake. I allowed myself to be misled. I have been working,' he added mournfully, 'on a contingency basis.'

'Come off it,' Harry said flatly.

'Well, a small deposit and my expenses I have received, but for the rest . . .' He looked again at Heneage for a moment, but only a very small moment. Heneage was a failure: a brilliant and ambitious schemer who had lost his nerve in the crisis. To me the most striking aspect of this was that he had let a superstitious fear of Harry Seddall drain the courage out of him. To Voster, it was that Heneage had become yesterday's man, and was, therefore, no longer tomorrow's paymaster.

Despite my fascination with these thoughts, I kept my eyes resolutely to the front and concentrated on studying the terrain. Nothing moved on the snow under the moon. The headlamps of the limousine still lit up the patch of ground before the house.

'You know what I want,' Harry said. 'I want the Monteiths out of there.'

'Good!' Voster said. 'It would be the best ending to a badly bungled affair.'

'Let me get this straight,' Sandy said. 'Are you two going into partnership together?'

'I think maybe we are,' Harry said.

'Well, my God!' Sandy said. 'Talk about amoral. I mean my *God*, that's all.'

'My dear young lady,' Voster said. 'You are too cynical. A criminal conspiracy is no different from an ad hoc consortium in business. If a member of the consortium fails in what he has promised, it is quite open to the others to protect their own best interests.'

'Don't call me your dear young lady, you degenerate middle-aged shitheel,' Sandy said nastily. 'And as for *you* calling *me* cynical, you know where you can put that.'

'This is not useful,' Harry cut in. 'Let's get down to it. Who's in the house now, Voster?'

'First of all, Mrs Monteith and her daughter.'

'Not Mr Monteith?' I exclaimed.

'Watch your front,' Harry said. 'I told you the countdown had started. Monteith's on his way to Toronto, right?'

'You are quite right, Mr Seddall. Your friend Franz Lehar, Mr Moore, is driving him to Toronto. And one other.'

'Who's the other?' Harry asked him.

'One of these young Italians who think they are the Red Brigade. One of the two they sent after you Mr Seddall. When Mr Palumbo came back from his wild-goose chase – '

'So Baldy got away,' Sandy said.

'Yes, he got away,' Voster went on. 'When Mr Palumbo came back and heard that you too had escaped, Mr Seddall, he was very angry. When he heard that the two young men had gone after you and not returned, he was still angry but he laughed, also. He sent two of his own men to find, as he put it, the bodies.'

Behind me there was a silence. I wondered what it meant until Voster spoke again. 'I am not used to such killings. I am not used to killings at all, and what you did to that boy, Mr Seddall . . . Well, no doubt it had to be done, from your point of view.'

'From mine and from the point of view of the ladies Monteith as well, Voster,' Harry said, all cold and curt. 'And listen to this – Heneage may have been the composer and those Italian kids and Palumbo's mob may be the players, but you had a hand in the orchestration, so stop pretending to be one of the beautiful people and remember that you came here to double-cross the rest of the band. You're doing it very nicely too, so keep going. Lehar has gone off with Monteith and the kid. Who's minding the store?'

'Very well, Mr Seddall. But you leave a man with not much of his self-respect.'

'A man makes his own, Voster. No one gives it him or takes it from him. And stop kidding. You love yourself enough for both of us. Who is left there, over in that house?'

'Palumbo,' Voster answered promptly, suddenly all business-like. 'Three of his men. Two of the Italian boys. They were upset by the death of their friend, but Palumbo made them stay. The other one who was there when you . . . when their friend died, was too demoralized. So they have sent him off to Toronto to fly back to the bosom of his family.'

'And Tozzetti?'

'At his home in Toronto, where also is his niece. Tozzetti had prepared all the papers for Monteith to sign, you understand, and set up all the little companies that Canadian law requires for such a big financial deal: I do not sufficiently understand these things. They put pressure on Tozzetti through his niece, you realize? First they got her involved in this so-called Red Brigade who would come across to raise funds for committing those profitless acts of terrorism they perpetrate in Italy, then they threatened her life, and now Tozzetti is deeply involved out of fear for his niece, for the reputation of his family in Italy – you know these Italians and their family bond: quite extraordinary! – involved with

234

blackmail, since he has done so much of the work necessary to the successful outcome of this rash conspiracy.'

I did not have to turn away from my post to know that Voster was sighing once again. He verbalized it. 'Aaaah!' he said, on a lingering melancholy fall. 'And look,' he said, 'at poor Martin!'

'That guy is pure horseshit,' Sandy said.

'Isn't he though,' Seddall said. 'Martin's breathing, Voster. He may not be a well man, but he's no weight on my conscience and he's the least of your troubles.' There was a pause, then Harry spoke again.

'John,' he said. 'I'm going to need you. What have you got left that I can use? A little stamina? A little remnant of the guts you used to have? Any of the old actor still in there?'

After a long moment Heneage answered him. 'Why, Harry? What can you give me that I should help you now?'

'Oh,' Harry drawled, 'just the fitness of the thing. Your life's no good to you now, and anyway you can't have it. But just for the fitness of the thing, don't you think?'

The stark words came out in a curiously intimate tone. The language was uttered in the cadence of a friendship that was ended, but which no one else had ever entered. To me it was like being present at a tragedy performed in a foreign tongue, where you can sense the feeling of events, but where only the protagonists experience the whole meaning of what is taking place.

'That was why I came to kill you, Harry, for the fitness of it.' There was a touch of vigour in Heneage's voice now. 'To kill you or to be killed.' There was, also, something like contentment in the way he spoke, as if he had feared that there was to be nothing but silence between them.

'To make an end,' Harry said. 'A pledge to be honoured: would you say that, John?'

'I think that's close,' Heneage said. 'It's close enough for me, since I think you're short of time. What do you want of me?'

Harry said: 'I want you to go over to that house and be Mr Pertinax, and tell them it's time to let the ladies go.'

'I wonder if I could do that,' Heneage said, like a doctor trying to assess the extent of his own illness. 'Perhaps I could. Who goes with me?'

'Voster, for one.'

'I?' Voster's reaction was at once indignant and full of fear. 'I have told you all I know, and now you want this?'

'Get used to it,' Harry said. 'It's going to happen. Sandy, can I ask you to get some of that brandy from the kitchen? Hold out your wrists, John, I'll cut that rope. Stand up and move about a little.'

Harry came over and joined me at the door. 'All quiet?'

'Yes,' I said. 'I know, Harry; you want to send me in too.'

'Well,' he said, 'it could go wrong, you see. And I've been working it out. I don't think anyone over there knows who you are, but I may be wrong. There was that picture of you in the paper, and Collet and two of his men are out of the way, but there was another one at Tozzetti's house who'd know you on sight. I don't think the picture counts, I really don't, but if the fourth man is with Palumbo in that house, then you'd be a dead pigeon.'

'Who am I? What part am I playing?'

'They don't know Heneage, you see. He is just Mr Pertinax, the faceless man who set it up at long distance. So you would be with Pertinax, that's all; his aide, his bodyguard, his valet, for all they know. He's the boss and the boss always has his own man with him.'

'And what's the plan?'

He smiled in the light of the moon and the diffused glow from the car's lights, Harry Seddall's cheerful sarcastic smile. 'Yeah. Well, there is no plan. They have four men and two boys, and we have you and me. They may listen to Heneage and they may not. He looks like death, but for all they know that's how he always looks.'

'And?' I said.

'And that poor bugger tied to the kitchen table had a silenced pistol. We might get hold of that and see what's left in it. *If* they still have two on patrol outside the house, I can maybe account for them with the silencer and the knife. Sandy we'll leave here; I think I may have hit Martin too hard but we'll tie him up to be on the safe side.'

'You don't think the Monteiths. . . ?'

'I think they're all getting pretty nervous over there. *I* think at any moment they might cut their throats and head for the tall timber.'

'So far,' I said, 'so bad. We get in and the talking starts. You do your commando stuff outside. Then what?'

'Then I come inside and take my cue from what I hear. The best I can think of is this. Whether the room you're doing all this talking in has the door open or shut, if I think it's time to come in shooting I'll knock loud twice, and when I come in have the Smith & Wesson in your hand and fall to the floor. Two reasons: one, a gun lifts when it fires and you'll be safer from *them*, and two, I'll be shooting at anything standing on its feet.'

'Christ, Harry!' I said. 'How do you think it sounds?'

'It sounds rotten,' he said. 'So let's go and do it now.'

'The fourth man,' I said. 'Voster should know.'

We turned to ask Voster, and saw him leading Heneage slowly up and down the shadowy hallway, as solicitous as a nurse with a patient on his first day out of bed after a serious operation. They stopped beside Sandy, who had been watching this performance, and each of them held out a glass for a refill.

'How many is that?' Harry asked.

'That's their second,' Sandy said.

'Two's enough,' he said. 'Two should be about right. Damn it, I'll have one myself.' He took a swig from the bottle and passed it to me. I had a swallow and gave the bottle back to Sandy.

'Voster,' I said. 'Among Palumbo's men, is there a tall thin joker with a yellow face – yellow as if he had jaundice? This is important. Have a good, clear think about it.'

Voster thought about it. Slowly, one after the other, he held up three fingers of the hand that was busy holding his brandy.

'No,' he said. 'There is no tall thin joker with a yellow face.'

'There you are,' Harry told me cheerfully. 'The omens are propitious. You're clear to go.'

'I was afraid of that,' I said.

Chapter 23

———— ◆ ————

To say I was afraid was putting it low. I was scared stiff. Two of the three of us going up against Palumbo and his friends were scared stiff, but in my case it took me literally: I walked into that house on rusty joints, and when I turned my head it moved taut and careful on my neck as if testing for broken vertebrae. The effect on Voster was different. He went small and flabby with fear. He smelled of it, and his face was smeared with a constant lard of sweat. When he got out of the car he stumbled, and going up onto the porch of the house he put both feet on each step like a child climbing the stairs.

Had it not been for Heneage the balloon would have gone up long before it did, and we would have lost the whole shooting-match. When it was over, and before he died, Heneage quoted the Duke of Wellington's line after Waterloo: 'By God! I don't think it would have done if I had not been there.'

It would not have done at all.

Palumbo was as nervous as a chief of the Sioux Nation who has seen too many treaties broken by the white man, and too many ponies come riderless home with blood on their hides.

Voster had driven us in his limousine the few hundred yards to the house, while I sat in the back with Heneage. When we got there Heneage told Voster: 'Right up to the door. It might help Harry.'

There were two men on watch, a youngster with a shotgun whom I took to be one of the imported Italians, and an older man. They knew the car but when Voster had climbed out and I emerged from the back – shutting the door again to keep my awesome master warm – they looked at me and peered in at Heneage.

The older man put a gun in his fist and began to ask questions. 'Okay, what's going on? Who are these guys? What was all the shooting about?'

'Be quite, you fool!' Voster said, holding himself steady on the wing of the car. 'That is Mr Pertinax himself. The Big Man. The Boss. Go and tell Palumbo he is here.'

The man waved a hand at his sidekick who ran into the house. Heneage lowered the window at his side and said to me: 'The pistol: tell him to put it away.'

The man stared at him.

I picked up my cue; we were being goddamned limeys to the life. 'You heard Mr Pertinax,' I said. 'Tuck the firearm away, there's a good chap.'

He stared some more, put the automatic in a shoulder holster, and went on staring.

The young man came out again. 'They're to go in the house,' he said.

'Take a look, Jonathan,' Heneage said to me, using the new name I had been given for the part I was playing. He spoke the words as if we had been through this scene a hundred times before. Then he closed the window and sat there in the car, snug and comfortably isolated, with the heater still running off the engine to keep him in the style to which he was accustomed. He was Mr Pertinax, all right.

I stood there for a moment in the cold, wondering what the hell he meant by telling me to take a look. Then I said, 'Stay here,' to Voster, and went up the stairs into the house. The man with the gun in his armpit came with me.

We walked together not speaking into a big room off the hall. The heating was up high. Three men were standing there grouped together, and one of them took a step forward. He had thick shoulders that muscled up high to a short neck, so that they almost met his head. His move towards me was aggressive and I nearly gave ground as if a bull had come at me. Instead I walked past him.

'My name's Palumbo,' he said to my back. 'I don't get this. Where did Mr Pertinax spring from?'

I ignored him and walked on, walked stiffly round the room, looking at whatever I could think of to look at. I thought of Seddall bursting into the room shooting off a whole magazine with one burst of that machine pistol, and focused on a handsome wing chair between the two tall curtained windows.

'The room is warm enough,' I said. 'Mr Pertinax will sit there.'

My perambulation about the room had brought me back face to face with Palumbo. My own features felt as rigid as plaster of Paris but *his* face, which looked to be high-blooded and choleric at the best of times, was perplexed by an excess of activity. It was trying to accommodate a complicated mixture of uncertain belief, instinctive mistrust, and the frustrated desire to go off at half-cock.

Suddenly I knew it was all going to work. I was acting up a storm, my brain was improvising words and actions for me. In just two minutes Heneage would dominate the stage and Harry was out there in the bushes waiting his moment to do what he was trained to do.

But then Palumbo grabbed my arm with fingers that felt like steel pincers, and his free hand began working restlessly, as if it was not sure whether it was going to punch me in the face or pull out a gun and shoot my head off.

'Just where do you think you're going?' he demanded.

'I am going out to the car to bring in Mr Pertinax,' I said coldly, and for the life of me could not have spoken another word.

His grip loosened, but he still held onto me.

'Take it easy, Palumbo,' a voice behind me said. I never knew which of them had said it, but I could have kissed him at that moment, and none of them was pretty.

I prised Palumbo's fingers off my arm and with a back like a ramrod stalked out of the room, out of the hall, out of the house. I thought it would be a good idea to get into the driving seat of the limousine and go away from there. I opened the door for Heneage and he stepped out of the car.

He entered the house like a Renaissance prince come to receive an accounting from an insignificant and unsuccessful vassal. The effect was helped by the fact that Palumbo, full of suspicion, had dogged my footsteps to the door and his boys had followed him, so that it looked as if he was standing there to receive his lord and master with his retainers around him.

Heneage passed them all as if they were invisible, I came in his wake while Voster crabbed up the steps behind me, and the rest of them trooped after us back into the big room. I ushered Heneage to the chair I had picked out for him and he gave me the slightest nod of approval. He sat down, eased the skirts of his elegant topcoat so as not to rumple the fine cloth, hitched up the creases of his Savile Row trousers at the knees, and shot the cuffs of his Maddox Street shirt to show the prescribed centimetre of cream-coloured silk.

His face was pale, his mouth thin and bloodless, and his eyes had almost lost their colour, as if they had been chipped from the heart of an iceberg. He was in his fifties and he looked almost ancient, but this would serve him well with that audience of Montreal thugs who lived in a world where a man who survives to grow old in the highest echelons of crime must deserve respect.

Palumbo stood six feet from him and the rest drifted into places about the room. Voster had collapsed onto a couch and gave an unseasonal representation of a man about to succumb to a fit of asthma. There was no harm in that: they would think he was terrified of Mr Pertinax. I stood like an equerry, a pace behind and to one side of the wing chair.

Heneage lifted his chin to regard Palumbo, and Palumbo studied him intently. Palumbo was keyed up to a high pitch of alertness, shifting his weight from one foot to the other in a slight swaying motion like a tennis player about to receive a serve. He looked extremely dangerous.

'What's it all about, Mr Pertinax? What was that shooting?'

Heneage looked at him for five full seconds before favouring him with a reply. 'A little local difficulty, he said. 'It has been handled.' Then he added: 'You appear to be under some stress, Mr Palumbo.' He made a half turn of the head towards me and back again and flipped a hand impatiently.

'Mr Pertinax has not come here to answer questions,' I told Palumbo. 'He has an agenda for this meeting.'

I realized that I had used the kind of language Heneage probably played with every day in Whitehall, and his white head dipped for a moment in acknowledgment. 'Mr Palumbo,' he said. 'I read a story once about a ship that came across a whale's carcass floating on the ocean, with a myriad of seabirds flying around it and fighting each other to feed off its rotting flesh. If I had been on that ship, Mr Palumbo, I would not have watched these disgusting birds squabbling to maintain their useless lives. I would have crossed to the other side of the deck.' He paused. 'I wonder if I could ask you to move a little further off, Mr Palumbo.'

Even Voster stopped trying to breathe. I thought that if ever a man had overplayed his hand it was Heneage just then.

Palumbo's eyes expanded till the blood showed and his mouth opened to reveal a faceful of bad teeth. He looked wildly from side to side at his men, as if one of them might tell him he had not really heard what he had just heard, and power surged up into those massive shoulders. He was a fighting bull now, ready to charge.

Heneage judged the moment like a matador distracting the enraged animal before him at the last possible second. He brought out what was, apparently, a magic name, as the bull-fighter will flick his cloak to one side of the bull's eye.

'Mr Carini,' he said, and watched while the energy that had been about to annihilate him began to ebb away. 'Mr Carini,' he repeated, 'is displeased with you, and I am displeased with Mr Carini. I am displeased because I have already paid him one million US dollars on this contract, and he is displeased because he stands to lose another ten million dollars which will be due to him unless the job is fouled up. And the job is being fouled up, and it is being fouled up here. That is why you and I are talking now. That is why I have come.'

Voster had repressurized too fast and was fighting for oxygen again, but no one else was paying him any attention. Palumbo was staring at Heneage but listening to the name Carini echoing in his ears, and everyone else was looking at Palumbo. He became conscious of this.

He glared about him, looking for ways to reassert himself. 'Gimme a drink,' he said to no-one in particular. 'You two,' he said to the pair who had met us when we drove up. 'Back outside and keep your eyes peeled, if it's not too much trouble.'

That was a relief. I knew by now, having seen him in action, that Heneage would have contrived for them to be sent back on watch if he had to, but it came better from Palumbo. I did not think they would last long. There had been plenty of time for Harry to get himself set.

I began to look for the right place to fall when the shooting started, and it seemed to be behind the chair Heneage was sitting in. This brought it home to me that one of the reasons why Heneage was giving the performance of his life was that he knew it was his last. Harry had told him this, and he had accepted it as a final judgment. The cold nerve he had shown when he played his bluff against Palumbo was the nerve of a doomed man.

There was nothing I could do about that, but I made an absurd gesture. When one of his lackeys brought Palumbo the drink he had asked for, I said: 'What's in that glass?'

'Brandy,' the man said.

I took it from his hand and sniffed its contents. It was good enough cognac. 'Mr Pertinax will have this one,' I said. 'Get another for Palumbo.'

I gave the glass to Heneage who said with a caustic tint of something like humour in his voice: 'Thank you, Jonathan.' Then I went back to the position I had chosen, the place that would give me the best chance of life.

The man poured another drink and brought it to Palumbo,

who drank it at a gulp. Heneage sipped at his glass and gave a little sigh. 'This is quite drinkable,' he said.

As a playwright I recognized that line. It was in character, all right, but it was the line you put in when you have not worked out what comes next to move the action along. I knew Heneage had to fill in time to let Harry have his chance at the two guards outside, and I wondered what he would come up with.

What he came up with appalled me. 'Jonathan, go and make sure Mrs Monteith and her daughter are in good shape, will you?' he said, and turned his head to regard me with a nasty glint of malevolent humour in his eye.

I stared at him, completely thrown.

If he was going to double-cross us now, then to get me out of the room was the best way to go about it. Everything had happened so fast there had been no time for me to come to terms with the *volte-face* he had made in agreeing to play a crucial part in this scheme to destroy his own conspiracy. I knew that he and Harry spoke a language that they alone understood. And I knew, or up to this moment had thought I knew, that something had broken in Heneage; that in the history of the mysterious affinity between him and Harry some final battle had been fought, some last surrender of the will been made.

I had even begun to believe that Heneage had come at us in the house next door expecting to be beaten; wanting despite himself to be beaten. Harry had come so close, and Harry always won. Heneage simply wanted to get it over and done with: that was what I had begun to believe.

Now what I believed or did not believe had no meaning. I did not trust Heneage, but there was nothing I could do about it, except hope that Harry would not have let us in for this without being sure, from his knowledge of the man, that Heneage was safe.

I looked at the wicked joke in the eyes of that corrupt and devious man, and saw nothing to tell me whether they were the eyes of John Heneage or Mr Pertinax.

'Yes, sir,' I said.

I made for the door and the man who had poured the drinks

came with me. We climbed a wide staircase, went along a landing and climbed more stairs. They were narrow and steep and took us to the top of the house, where the servants used to sleep, I supposed. A man was lying back in an armchair up there, with his feet on a windowsill, and when he saw us he brought his feet off the sill and stretched and stood up slowly.

He was a fair-haired young man with blue eyes, but I knew that this was the leader of the group from Italy even before he spoke. He looked nervous and uncertain and alone, and far from home.

He looked at me. 'Who is this?'

'Somebody from high up. You don't get to know who he is. Open the door.'

The Italian went on looking at me, and I had a superstitious feeling that if he looked long enough he would see one of his friends pouring his life's blood all over Harry Seddall. 'Open it,' I said coldly.

He took a key from his pocket and unlocked the door beside him. I went in and my companion followed, shutting the door with the Italian on the other side.

The room was comfortable enough. It held a double bed and two easy chairs, a small table to eat at and two women. The girl was in one of the easy chairs reading a book and Mrs Monteith lay on the bed with her hands behind her head. The girl had red hair and the redhead's creamy skin, and the mother had red hair with grey in it, and skin that was not so creamy as it used to be. Their faces were marked with fear, and with the waiting.

Mrs Monteith turned her head towards us and said nothing. The girl said: 'What is it now?'

'Are you all right?' I asked them. It was the best I could think of to say, but the trouble was I meant it.

Mrs Monteith began to sit up and the girl got out of her chair. 'Have you come to help us?' the girl asked, and I knew there had been a wrong sound in my voice.

'No,' I said. 'I'm just here to make sure you are not ill-treated.'

Mrs Monteith lay back again but she was watching me with a line of doubt along her forehead.

The girl stayed on her feet. 'Ill-treated!' She laughed, or almost laughed. 'How can you ask if –'

'That's enough,' I said, and turned to go, to face the man who had come with me. I had sensed him react to the false note in my performance, and now I saw him notice how stiffly I moved when I made myself face him. He was wary but baffled, not bright enough to make sense of what he had just seen and heard. And there was another question in his eyes I failed to place.

'Let's go,' I said, and opened the door and marched to the stairs and went down through the house, leaving him to tell the turnkey to lock up again or follow straight after me, whichever he chose. As I descended the main staircase I heard him running down behind me. I heard a sound in the hall I couldn't account for, but I went straight into the big room and the other man passed me as I went up to Heneage.

Nothing seemed to have changed in the room. There was a live tension there but I might have brought that in with me. 'The ladies are all right,' I said to Heneage.

He nodded, that was all. He looked exhausted, and there was no joke in his face now, but there was no way for me to know whether he had betrayed us or not. I took my place at the side of his chair. Voster was respirating like a landed fish.

However, the thing was to end; the ending must come soon now.

The man who had taken me upstairs was in some distress. He wanted to say something to Palumbo but was not sure what he wanted to say. He was back at the serving table against the wall, about to pour himself a drink, when he swung round and looked at me. 'I knew it!' he said. 'I knew I seen him before someplace!'

Palumbo's eyes moved between me and the man who had spoken and he tensed like a cat that meets a dog walking round the corner.

'Where?' he barked. 'Where'd you see him?'

'Jesus Christ!' the man said, trying to put down bottle and glass and go for his gun at the same time. 'In the fucking car with Charlie.'

Then all hell broke loose.

Palumbo's hand flashed to his belt and came out with a revolver. I threw myself to the carpet and the machine pistol hammered at my eardrums as Harry came in the door. Bullets hit flesh and men cried out. Something tore up the carpet just in front of my face. A voice shrieked in despair and woe, its last living attempt to be heard above the noise.

The shooting stopped and there was no sound except that of a man choking. It was the man who had seen me in the car, and he was choking to death on the blood that poured from his mouth, his chest crushed and bloody. The side of Palumbo's head had been blown off and the rest of it was lying on Heneage's galoshes, but he had shot Heneage twice before he died and Heneage was going fast. The third man had taken a lot of bullets in the stomach and lost his throat as well, and I guessed he was the one who had shrieked against his death as the bullets rode up his body.

Voster had stopped breathing again, but only from fright. He was alive and unhurt.

There was a strange odour in the room.

Harry lay against the wall with a bloody leg twisted under him. 'Oh, shit!' he said. 'Get upstairs, Anthony, get upstairs.'

I had forgotten why we were here. The women, the Monteith women! I pulled myself together and made my legs go as fast as they could out of the door and up the stairs. I saw the top half of a man running towards me, towards the top of the staircase, and fired the revolver at him. He came on and became a whole man. I fired again and missed. I fired again and he fell down at me just as a tremendous blow sent me back falling through the air.

I knew I had died.

Then a voice said: 'Not you! Not you too!'

It was Sandy. I changed my mind about being dead.

'No,' I said. 'Not me too.' I had an intelligent thought. 'Don't be here,' I said. 'Be at the other house. This isn't safe.'

'Oh, shut up,' she said.

So I fainted.

Chapter 24

I was long, lonely weeks in hospital; first in a city called Pembroke and then in Ottawa, where they approved what the surgeons in Pembroke had done and perfected their repairs. The bullet which had knocked me downstairs had bounced around inside me instead of going straight through, irritating several organs and necessitating the removal of my spleen.

They said I would hardly miss it, since I was a playwright and not a drama critic, and I had to laugh at this one more often than I thought it was worth. They also said it was dangerous to wander in the Ontario woods in the hunting season without wearing brightly coloured clothes, because hunters tend to grow over-excited and take anything that moves for a deer. They said I was lucky to have got off so lightly, and with that I was able to agree wholeheartedly.

Sandy came to see me as soon as I was allowed visitors. She told me she had driven me to Pembroke, and that Harry told her to say it was a hunting accident. He would not come with her. Voster, he said, would take him where he wanted to go.

On the same day, although they refused to let him see me until I had rested for four hours after Sandy's visit, a man came to see me from the British High Commission in Ottawa. He closed the door politely behind the nurse who showed him in, put a finger to his lips, and walked round the private room I was in, inspecting everything with deep interest. Then he pulled a piece of paper out of his pocket and held it where I could read it comfortably. It was typed in capital letters and triple spaced. It looked like this:

1. H.M.GOVERNMENT IS MOST GRATEFUL FOR WHAT YOU HAVE DONE.
2. H.M.G. WILL MEET ALL YOUR HOSPITAL EXPENSES.
3. PLEASE SAY NOTHING TO ANYONE OF THE RECENT AFFAIR, NOR MENTION THE NAMES OF H S— OR J H—

'Fine,' I said weakly. He put the paper back carefully in his pocket and said he would come to see me again.

Sandy came to see me every day, but by the time I had been in hospital for ten days and was growing stronger, the feeling between us was strangely diffident and remote, and on that tenth day she told me she was checking out of her hotel and was going back to Stratford.

'I need to go there,' she said simply. 'It's where home is.'

She meant Bruce was still there, in their home; her home now.

'That's right,' I said. 'You should go.'

'It's too soon for the future,' she said, and kissed me lightly and left.

After that she wrote to me regularly once a week, and though her letters urged me to get well quickly and were signed 'much love', their weekly regularity gradually acquired a dutiful air.

The High Commissioner flew me back to London in January, first class and with a young diplomat to accompany me – although I was pretty fit by that time – and I settled back into my flat off Kensington Church Street.

There was a letter waiting for me among my mail from White Denver, thanking me for replacing the stolen Volvo, but really I was an ass; the insurance company had paid up and here was a cheque for the amount I had paid for the new car. He also thanked me for the use of my flat in London, and for leaving the cabin so neat and tidy.

I did not think it would be long before Harry Seddall appeared at my door to start explaining things like this, and I was right. He came on the third day, when I had recovered from my jet lag, and he came at six in the evening, when I had just risen from an afternoon nap, advised by my own doctor.

He looked smarter than usual, and he limped a little. 'They've moved me to Defence,' he said. 'Suits the limp. Besides, they've closed up Heneage's old shop. What about you, Anthony? I hear you've lost your spleen. I'm sorry about that.'

'Apparently one can manage quite well without it,' I said. 'Just don't make the joke.'

'What joke?'

I told him about the hospital sense of humour. 'Dear God,' he said thoughtfully, 'I see what you mean. It's a wonder you survived.'

I showed him White Denver's letter and he laughed. 'Yeah, we got him a new car. Baldy vanished without trace. Wise man.'

'This cheque,' I said. 'This is thousands of quid. I can't send it back or refuse to cash it; White would be offended and confused. He's got his new car from the insurance company. I'll have to pay it back to your people.'

'Can't do that,' he said cheerfully. 'That's government money accounted for. Get yourself a new Peugeot. Don't you think you've earned it, for goodness' sake? If you're worried about fraud on an insurance company, just think that the Mafia probably have shares in it.'

'That would help,' I said.

'By the way,' he said casually. 'The mob doesn't hate you, or me, or any of us. I paid Heneage's friend Carini in Montreal to clean up the mess. All the bodies are buried, and all the evidence destroyed. Not even the Monteiths know what happened. I hear Monteith himself has been going spare trying to find out who to thank.'

'What did you pay Mr Carini?' I asked.

'One million US dollars. We made a deal and they'll stick to it, they always do. We're not friends and we're not enemies. The slate's clean between us.'

'Great heavens above,' I said softly. 'A million. Yes, I think I will get a new Peugeot.'

'That's the boy,' he said. 'Do you want to know anything else?'

'No,' I said. 'Yes, I do though. How did Collet find us up at the cabin? I'd swear no one followed us.'

'Routine,' Harry said. 'The beat policeman reported that your house was occupied although you were away abroad. All reports on you went to your friend Kenna at the Yard, and were passed automatically to Heneage's office. It wouldn't take Heneage two hours to find out everything there was to know about White Denver.'

Then a silence fell, and I realized Harry was nervous about something. 'What is it?' I said.

He smiled sarcastically to himself to avoid becoming totally shamefaced. 'Will you tell me what Heneage did back there, when you and he went into that house?'

So I told him. The smile faded away as he listened. When I had finished he said: 'He did all right, don't you think?' He was anxious for me to agree with him, and I began to know what it was I liked about the man.

'He did all right,' I said.

'He knew it, too,' Harry said. 'I was sitting with my leg broken against the wall and he was sitting there dying, and all he said was: "By God! I don't think it would have done if I had not been there."'

'Wellington,' I said. 'After Waterloo.'

'Yeah,' Harry said absently. 'Well, mustn't tire you out. I'll call you, but if you want anything, call me at the Ministry. Colonel Seddall.'

'Did I know you were an Army man?'

'I didn't know. I'm not sure that I am, and neither are they. We never have been.' He grinned. 'It runs in the family – in this day and age. Still, I do my best not to . . .'

He left the sentence hanging. 'Well, so long,' he said.

We had dinner after that about once a month, usually at some little restaurant he had found where the food was good and where no one else from Whitehall would have been seen dead. Twice he brought a girl along and we made up a foursome, but for me the fourth should have been Sandy Baldwin. Sandy and I had exchanged a few careful postcards and short letters, but they were wide-spaced.

I grew completely fit again. I wrote a new play, which I thought was better than the one that had been lost at sea. I thought I would let the ocean keep that one. I finished the play in June and it was accepted for production by a West End management in the autumn. So I decided to head for the sun and picked up some travel brochures from an agency.

It was a while since I had heard from Harry, and when the phone rang I was not surprised it was him. 'Let's meet tomorrow,' he said. We arranged where and when, and then he said: 'I've sent a parcel round to you by messenger, it should be with you in about fifteen minutes. I think it will interest you.'

In a quarter of an hour the doorbell rang, and I went to collect the parcel.

It was wrapped in a gold dress, and wore gold lipstick and other gold things. It had eyes like the summer sky and its pale blonde hair shone like the stars.

'Hi!' it said. 'Aren't you going to unwrap me?'

I gripped her by the wrist as if she was in danger of falling over a precipice, and pulled her safely into the flat, and closed the door.

Michael Stewart
MASTER OF THE *NEW* THRILLER

Grace

Grace Holmwood has been seeing things. Bright lights, the figure of her brother, who died five years previously, and finally strange, beatific visions. The local priest, Father Gregory, is convinced that the hand of God is involved. But Dr Leonard Grigson knows that something far less holy is at work, and he is determined that the horrific truth should remain buried.

Grace, at seventeen, has only recently questioned her faith. Now she is caught in the crossfire between religion and science as the community around her, sceptical at first, comes to believe that she has been touched by the divine. When Grace becomes inexplicably pregnant, even Father Gregory is ready to believe that she has been blessed by a virgin birth. Leonard has his own disturbing theories – neither divine nor diabolical, but the all too human legacy of his shameful past. Grace miscarries and the terrifying visions return with nightmarish force . . .

'Stewart's style is effortless and his plot construction superb in this utterly convincing novel. Powerful, fast-paced and compulsively readable.'   *Oxford Times*

'Chilling . . . the shocking twists and turns will keep readers glued to the page.'   *Publishers Weekly*

'Astonishing . . . a brilliant mix of science and spirituality, the sacred and the profane.'   *She*

FONTANA PAPERBACKS

House of Cards
Michael Dobbs

The election has gone badly for the Government. After a less-than-glorious victory, the battle to replace the Prime Minister is on with a vengeance.

Francis Urquhart believes that finally his time has come. As Chief Whip he has his hands on every secret in politics, and he is willing to betray them all to grasp his place in 10 Downing Street.

With ultimate power in their sights, Cabinet colleagues turn into bitter rivals. Urquhart will stop at nothing to fulfil his burning ambition. Eventually only one woman stands in his way.

Mattie Storin, a tenacious young political correspondent, faces the biggest personal and professional challenge of her life when she stumbles upon a scandalous web of intrigue and financial corruption at the very highest levels in Parliament and Fleet Street. She is determined to reveal the truth, but she must risk everything to do so . . .

'Fast moving, revelatory and brilliant.'
Daily Express

'It has pace, a beguiling authenticity and a cast of Achilles heels.'
Julian Critchley, *Daily Telegraph*

'A rollicking plot . . . a hugely enjoyable read.'
Evening Standard

FONTANA PAPERBACKS

GERALD SEYMOUR

'The finest thriller writer in the world today.'
Jonathan Cox, DAILY TELEGRAPH

HARRY'S GAME
THE GLORY BOYS
KINGFISHER
RED FOX
THE CONTRACT
ARCHANGEL
IN HONOUR BOUND
FIELD OF BLOOD
A SONG IN THE MORNING
AT CLOSE QUARTERS
HOME RUN

'Not since Le Carré has the emergence of an international
suspense writer been as stunning as that of Gerald Seymour.'
LOS ANGELES TIMES

FONTANA PAPERBACKS/Collins Harvill

Fontana Paperbacks: Fiction

Fontana is a leading paperback publisher of fiction.
Below are some recent titles.

- ☐ ULTIMATE PRIZES Susan Howarth £3.99
- ☐ THE CLONING OF JOANNA MAY Fay Weldon £3.50
- ☐ HOME RUN Gerald Seymour £3.99
- ☐ HOT TYPE Kristy Daniels £3.99
- ☐ BLACK RAIN Masuji Ibuse £3.99
- ☐ HOSTAGE TOWER John Denis £2.99
- ☐ PHOTO FINISH Ngaio Marsh £2.99

You can buy Fontana paperbacks at your local bookshop or
newsagent. Or you can order them from Fontana Paperbacks,
Cash Sales Department, Box 29, Douglas, Isle of Man. Please
send a cheque, postal or money order (not currency) worth the
purchase price plus 22p per book for postage (maximum postage
required is £3.00 for orders within the UK).

NAME (Block letters)_____

ADDRESS_____

_____